welcome to conception ridge

chloe maine

before he was her headmaster

an age gap romance

my one night stand? he's sitting behind the headmaster's desk.

We met at a truck stop. The chemistry was immediate, and we both do something out of character: one night, no explanations. The next day, I arrive at my new private school. Now I'm the off-limits forbidden temptation Sebastian Craig can't forget, and we both try our best to behave. It works for a few weeks…until our secret cravings come tumbling out in the library after hours. How will we keep our private connection hidden until the end of the term? I want to be his sweet girl forever, but the age gap and responsibility of his job might be too much to overcome…

1
lily

THE BRIGHT LIGHTS of the truck stop are a relief. As soon as the trucker turns off his big rig, I toss him a twenty-dollar bill and holler a rushed thanks over my shoulder before jumping down to the concrete parking lot below.

Hitchhiking after my car broke down was a stupid choice, and I regretted my decision as soon as I got in his truck. We're closer to the city now, so I'll get a rideshare in the morning to take me to Edgewood Academy.

My home for the next three months.

My father's voice rings in my head. "One more term, Lily. Try not to get kicked out of this school."

I hate how it sounds like a taunt because I did nothing to deserve to be kicked out of the other schools. But despite his best efforts, I'm almost done.

One more term and I'll have enough credits to go to college. It doesn't matter that I'm technically an adult. To access the trust fund left for me by my grandfather, I have to get my high school diploma.

I would love to move across the country—or to another country—and lose myself in my studies.

I love school. You would think a girl like me would have

breezed through the three other private academies my father sent me to. But just like Edgewood Academy will probably be, those schools were repressive and rigid. The opposite of the type of environment I need to thrive.

Does my father listen?

Nope. He has his own agenda. A dangerous one I want nothing to do with.

Getting myself kicked out of my last school only got me a few months of freedom at a public school before my father found another academy to take me in. Take his money, more like it.

Everyone tells me I have a chip on my shoulder, but they don't understand what I know.

So to them, I seem like a bitter, rich girl who doesn't appreciate how good she has it.

Edgewood is my last chance to get it right. To be a good girl, a polite girl, a privileged girl who plays by the rules. I can do that. It's only three months.

I'll be free by Christmas.

The irony is, I actually am a good girl. I've never been drunk, never had sex, never done any of the drugs that other kids at private schools do. How could I when I know exactly where they come from? I'm just a mouthy brat with an authority problem.

I head into the store. There's a restaurant on the other side and signs for showers. If I play my cards right, I can find a place here to sleep for the night.

I'm lingering by the refrigerators of cold drinks, hoping to overhear someone ask the cashier about the showers. Like how much they are, or if anyone would notice if I bunked in one all night—when a tall, broad-shouldered man comes in from the gas station side. He pulls off a sleek black helmet and stops just inside the entrance, rolling his neck like he's just been on a long motorcycle ride on the highway.

He unzips his leather jacket as he stalks in my direction, and when his gaze collides with mine, I quickly look away. But from that moment of connection, heat zaps through me. My chin lifts again as if pulled by an invisible force, and I catch him looking at my legs as he stops a few feet from me.

I'm frozen to the spot, which is unfortunate because he clears his throat and points behind me. "Can I...?"

I turn and realize he wants a soda.

Not looking at my legs. Wondering how to get the awkward girl out of his way.

Stammering, I shift sideways, then pretend I'm looking at the orange juice in the next section.

"Thirsty?"

I jerk my head back to him.

He's really tall, and his hand, when it settles on the handle of the glass door, looks like it's twice the size of mine. He opens the door and gestures at the juice. "If you want one, I'll buy you a drink."

I laugh. "Is that how you usually pick up women? Buying drinks for them from the convenience store?"

"I rarely buy women drinks," he says seriously. His eyes lock on my mine, dark and intense. "But you look like you need something, and I like to help people."

I almost snap that I don't need anything.

But something stops me. I look at him again. He's beautiful in a wild animal kind of way. His hair is thick and standing up on end, and his eyebrows are dark, angry slashes over hooded eyes. But for all his fierce beast-mode aesthetic, he seems like a gentle giant. *He likes to help people.* That has to be a line, right?

I deliberately run my gaze down his body, from the leather jacket down to where his dark jeans hug both muscular thighs and a prominent bulge at his crotch.

I jerk my gaze up to his face, and one of those dark brows lifts in surprise, like he wasn't expecting me to check him out.

I wasn't expecting to, either.

We stand there together for a silent, extended beat, and then he nods at me and backs up. Clearly, I don't want him to buy me orange juice because if I did, I'd say something, right?

But I'm not sure what I want.

Then he frowns and stops, and a second later, I feel an unexpected warm heat behind me.

I spin around to find the trucker I caught a ride with leering over me. "Hey darlin', you ran away so quick. I was hoping we could get a bite to eat together."

I jerk backward and collide with Mr. Motorcycle's front. He smoothly moves me to the side, putting some space between our bodies, then steps in between me and the trucker before glancing back at me. "You okay?"

I nod.

He jerks his head at the other guy. "Do you want to have dinner with him?"

I shake my head.

A grin, bright and unexpected, appears as quickly as it disappears before he turns back to face the trucker. He schools his features into a more serious look as he pointedly addresses the other man. "We'll let you get your juice in peace, then."

And without a word of conflict, he somehow moves the trucker away from me, pointing the older man to the restaurant.

I can tell they're both older, but Mr. Motorcycle looks like an actor who would play a hot dad on TV, and the trucker looks like… well, my actual father, if he wasn't rich and was missing some teeth.

I shudder and grab the orange juice I was just pretending to want. I'm looking at chips at the end of the aisle when Mr. Motorcycle returns and grabs the soda he had initially been looking for.

I step back into view. "Thanks for intervening." My face heats. I know I don't need to explain more, but an explanation tumbles out anyway. "I caught a ride with him, and he clearly got the wrong idea."

"You were hitchhiking?"

"I'm done with that now. This is my destination."

He frowns and looks around. "This truck stop?"

"This city." I don't elaborate, not wanting him to know I'm here for school. I want him to think about me as a woman. Tonight is my last night of freedom before I need to behave for three months.

Tonight, though, I want to misbehave. And I want to do it with Mr. Motorcycle. "I start a new job tomorrow. It comes with lodging, so I'm just looking for a place to stay tonight. Thought about crashing here, but if you have a better idea...."

His frown deepens, like he didn't hear me just hit on him because he's apparently fixated on my choice of accommodation. "You were going to spend the night at a truck stop?"

I shift uncomfortably under the stern appraisal of my not-great idea. "It would be fine."

"Do you need money for a motel?"

A rush of heat colors my cheeks. It hadn't even occurred to me to get a motel room. "I have money. But that's a good idea. Thanks."

I spin on my heel, but I don't get far before his hand catches my elbow and turns me around again.

He's closer than he was before, almost right up against me, and I catch my first whiff of his scent. Warm, spicy, masculine. He smells nice, not like a bad guy at all. And definitely not like a man who would fool around with an eighteen-year-old girl desperate to break free from the confines of her life.

Which isn't a thing one can tell from a scent, but it's the entire package. The concern in his eyes, the stern furrow now etched between his eyebrows.

So much for the lasting appeal of my bare legs.

"Look...." He stops. "What's your name?"

"Lily." I infuse confidence I don't feel into my reply. "What's yours?"

He smiles. "Sebastian."

I don't know what I was expecting. Duke or Hank or Mr. Motorcycle. Not something as elegant as Sebastian.

"Look, Lily, I'm on my way back to work myself. I have a curfew of sorts." I get another smile at that, like there's an inside joke there I don't get. "I'd like to see you somewhere safe, though. There's a motel across the highway. Can I take you there?"

I shrug. "That depends. You wanna come to my room when we get there?"

The stern frown is back, and his gaze drops to my mouth. A stern frown isn't a *no*, though. I move in closer. Who is this woman saying this shit? Because it is *not* me. Virgin Lily would never. Has never.

But maybe tonight is the night Virgin Lily disappears. "Or maybe we could go back to your place."

He winces. "The thing is, I also have the kind of job where I live where I work, and we're not allowed to bring people back there."

I glance toward the showers. "Then we should make do right here."

"You want me to fuck you in the showers of a truck stop?" He blinks in disbelief. "Are you kidding me?"

"I've never done this before, I swear. I don't know why I'm suggesting this, but tomorrow will be the start of the longest three months of my life. I could use an escape tonight, you know?"

He mutters something under his breath, and I sway even closer. Close enough that he has to catch me in his arms, his hands going around me, then traveling down my back and settling low on my hips. Close to the hem of my jean skirt. His body is hard and hot, and just rubbing up against him is more exciting than I ever thought possible.

Of course, I'm nervous. And a little terrified. But there's something about him that soothes my fear in doing something this out of character.

The way he looks at me feels magical and intense. "You want an escape, Lily?"

I nod and square my shoulders. "But only if you're willing."

The corner of his mouth quirks. "That should go without saying, but I'm glad you checked. You're willing, I'm willing…."

"We're both adults," I breathe. It's true, even if I know that there's no way we are equals in this. Even if I'm risking everything here, and he does this all the time.

"All right," he mutters. Then he nods, his gaze dark. "Go head down that hallway. I'll rent a shower stall and meet you there."

I watch him stalk to the next aisle, my legs unable to move as he told me to. But when I realize he's stopped to grab a pack of condoms, motivation zaps through me, and I hustle out of sight.

Oh. My. God.

He's going to take that pack of condoms to the counter and rent time in a shower stall. Is that obvious? Are there cameras?

Of course, there wouldn't be cameras *in* the showers. That would be gross. And an invasion of privacy. But are there cameras recording us going in there together? Should I hide?

I'm still scanning the ceiling for security cameras when Sebastian appears, grabs my hand, and tugs me through a door he's unlocked.

As soon as the door clicks shut, his helmet and my backpack hit the ground. He presses me against the door, his mouth on mine.

His kiss is hot and demanding.

My first real kiss, and there's nothing sweet about it. It's all *Hello, I'm going to fuck you soon,* and *You better get wet or this might hurt.*

"I rarely do this, either," he grinds out between taking tastes of my lips. "I swear."

I hope he's telling the truth. I don't think he is, but he's very good at playing his role. The combination of nice guy/bad boy with the kind gaze and cruel kisses that I thought only existed in fairy tales of the filthiest order.

"Once in a lifetime truck stop adventure," I pant.

He hoists me up and presses me against the door, his body wedging between my thighs. My skirt rides up to my hips, and I can feel the heavy ridge of his erection rubbing against my panties. I feel all slippery and wet between my legs, which I know is the point. It will make what we do next easier, but I'm now painfully aware of it.

My focus is between my legs, how good and wild it feels, how much I want this, and how out of my depth I know I am. *Please don't think I suck at this*, I pray in my head.

I like the way his breath sounds just as ragged as mine. The way his hands grab me roughly, then pet me softly immediately after. Like maybe he isn't sure about how to do this, too. Not that he's not hella confident. He's not letting go of me and seems singularly focused on making me feel good.

Somehow he knows exactly where to rock his hips to make my brain short-circuit.

"There," I gasp. "Oh, Sebastian, yes."

"You like that?"

I rub my face into his neck. "I want more."

He tightens his hold on me and peels me off the door, carrying me across the small room to a wide counter with a sink at one end and a space for fucking at the other.

Convenient.

After he sets me down on the cold, solid counter, he kisses me again, then pulls the condoms from his back pocket.

I reach for his belt. I like the way he watches as I fumble with it, the little sounds he makes—restrained feral need, it sounds like—as I work my fingers around the button, then his fly. His jeans peel away as his cock springs forward, bulging in the softer cotton of his black boxer briefs.

Tracing the size of him, I make a desperate sound of my own.

We're just two animals in heat. Nothing more complicated than that. People do this all the time, and it feels good.

I have no doubt when he puts that thing inside me, it's going to feel amazing. After a little pinch of hurt, maybe. My thighs shake in fear and anticipation.

I want it all. I want to make some memories tonight to keep me focused on my goal: three months to true independence. Three months until I get to do this all the time, with anyone I want because I live far, far away from my family.

Glancing up at Sebastian, my heart squeezes in a weird and unexpected way. I can't imagine anyone else standing between my bare legs, looking at my panties as I rub my fingers over their briefs.

I can't imagine doing this with anyone else, and he's a stranger. It's kismet that we're doing this now. He's my perfect stranger, and this is going to be good. I know it in my bones.

And it's that wild, unfathomable connection making me so brazen.

"I want this inside me," I whisper as I lean back. I barely recognize myself as I tug my panties down my hips. I watch his eyes darken as I peel them away from my sticky, wet pussy. "Do you want that, too?"

"Fuck. Show me. Show me where you want me to put my monster cock." Then he catches my panties as they slide past my knees and carefully sets them aside. Mr. Monster Cock is a considerate sex buddy.

Feeling shy, I ease my legs apart, knowing I'm blushing but wanting to show him, anyway. I like the way my pussy looks. It's cute, especially when it's swollen and pink the way it is right now. Sometimes I look at it in the mirror as I try to get myself off, but it's awkward.

This is actually less awkward than that. There's something about the heat crackling between us, the raw animal desire rolling off Sebastian, that makes it totally natural to rock my legs up and give him a peek.

"I want to see you, too," I murmur.

He covers himself with one of his big hands, then eases his cock out of the top of his briefs. Like he's being careful not to scare me. With good reason. It is a monster cock.

No way is that fitting inside me is my first thought. But my second is, *Holy crap, that's going to be inside me.* And the second thought is so fucking delicious I want to die at the promise of it.

I will *feel* that. It will *change* me.

He rolls a condom on, then lays the heavy length on my belly. I shiver at the obvious promise/threat of just how much space he'll take up in my little body.

"We'll go slow," he says, reading my mind.

He rubs the head against my clit, back and forth, making me moan, and I lean back. He growls as I show him more of my pink slit as it spreads open for him.

"Gotta have a taste." He grunts and slides me back on the counter so he can brace his arms on either side of my hips. Then his head ducks, and his mouth slides over my pussy. His tongue is on my bare skin, and now I'm the one grunting because, oh my God, why didn't anyone tell me it felt this good?

All this time, I thought sex was something stupid people did instead of studying.

Now I know those people were fucking smart, and I'm the dummy for not doing this before. A grown man's tongue sliding through my folds? "More," I whine.

"You want my fingers?" He shifts his position to bring his fingers to where his cock had just been. And yes, yes, yes, I want that now.

"Please," I pant. "Yes, fingers. Put them in me."

He presses against my hole, where I've rubbed before, to no significant effect, and it pinches a little. "Fuck, you're tight, baby." He presses his face, wet from my pussy juice, into my thigh, kissing me there as he pulses one finger back and forth just inside me.

It feels so good and not enough at the same time. "More, Sebastian," I whisper, the sounds we're making bouncing off the cold tile walls. "Deeper."

"I can't get any deeper, sweetheart," he murmurs, rising to kiss me full on the mouth.

I taste myself on his lips, and I drag in a ragged breath. I smell myself, too. I'm all over his face.

"We gotta warm you up more. No way you'll take my cock. You always this tight? Your sweet little pussy is fucking perfect, though. I'll take all the time in the world to get you ready."

"Just do it." My heart is beating a mile a minute. "I think you just have to push it in, and then it'll be okay."

He stills his hand, his fingertip just inside my pussy, his thumb on my clit. "You think?"

My thighs shake as I try to tug him closer. I reach for his cock, still wrapped in the condom. His erection throbs against my fingers, but he doesn't let me bring it any closer to my aching hole.

He grips my chin with his free hand, making me look at him as he rolls his thumb slowly over my clit again. "Lily, are you a virgin?"

2
sebastian

HER SWEET FACE tightens as she thinks about lying to me. Then she rakes her teeth over her luscious lower lip, blinks slowly, and nods.

A reluctant admission from a wannabe sexpot.

The desperate, horny side of me wants to give in and take her virginity here in a truck stop bathroom, but the rest of me wins out. I cannot do that.

I drop my hand from her chin and wrap my fingers around hers so we're both holding my still-hard cock. Which is even fucking harder now because, Jesus Christ, she's gorgeous and so perfectly willing. There's something about the irony of her being just as needy right now as I am.

It's been too long since the last time I burned off some energy like this.

Correction. There has never been an opportunity like this.

Lily is a once-in-a-lifetime chance to make someone else's first time absolutely perfect, a gift I would cherish so fucking much for the rest of my life.

I want *that*, too.

But not here. Not in a truck stop washroom.

I think of the time. Could I get her to a hotel room and take the time to do it right before the clock strikes midnight?

Probably not.

And then she whispers two words that undo me. "Don't stop."

She wants this. She wants me, and I find I can't say no to her.

"I'm going to make you feel good." I groan against her skin. "I just can't take your virginity. It wouldn't be right. We'll have another chance."

"No, we won't." She rubs her fingertips over my mouth, and I part my lips for her, letting her touch my tongue. Her innocent exploration of my body makes me want to put her on the back of my bike and head for California. Never look back. My career can get fucked; all I want at this moment is this beautiful woman and all of her secrets.

Why is she still a virgin? She's stunningly sensual and clearly clever. Resourceful. Funny. Eager.

Take her. Take her now. Claim her before you lose her.

I will not lose her. "We will have another chance. Do you have days off at your new job?"

"Sundays."

I grin as I drop my head to her shoulder and kiss the bare skin there. She still has her top on. I should strip her down and worship her, but if I get her all the way naked, I'll fuck her. Her tiny tank top is a reminder that we're stealing moments here, and I need to give her more than this. "I have Sundays off, too. We can meet up. I'll take you out for brunch...."

"I want you to fuck me."

I laugh at the petulance in her voice. "And I'll do that, too. We can spend the next month getting to know each other on Sundays. Brunch, then sex, then... we can do the crossword puzzle together? Before we have to go back to real life. It'll be romantic."

"When I invited you to fuck me in this truck stop bathroom, I wasn't looking for romance."

I jerk her right to the edge of the counter and drop to my knees. I glare up at her. "And when I rubbed my dick against your virgin hole, I wasn't thinking about brunch, I fucking swear it. But life is more complicated than we ever expect it to be, so I want you to come on my face and then promise me you'll have brunch with me next weekend. Do we have a deal?"

She tangles her fingers in my hair, spreading her legs wide. Her perfect pink pussy is right there, and she tries to nudge me closer.

Which, of course, I want, but not before she agrees. I don't think I can do this if she isn't interested in getting to know each other more. I should have known I wasn't cut out for a random hook-up.

"Sebastian—"

"Lily." I almost bark it. I kiss the inside of her leg. "I know we don't know each other yet. But don't let the motorcycle gear give you the wrong impression of me. I've been alone for a long time. I think we met tonight for reasons that are beyond chance. Like it's—"

"Kismet," she whispers.

I nod. "I want you so much it hurts, sweet girl. Let me give it to you right."

A flash of something dark, maybe something scared, passes behind her eyes, then she nods. "I'll try."

That's all I can ask of her. I fall into her, desperate now for more of her taste. She jumps at the slide of my tongue against her skin, then lets out a long, slow sigh that makes my balls squeeze as her legs fall open.

My sweet girl likes my face between her thighs.

And I fucking love the sounds she makes as I discover where my tongue and teeth and lips elicit different responses.

I take my time. *A fucking virgin.* She's not shy, though. A virgin by choice, waiting for the right man.

Why me? Why now? I have dark thoughts about her new job and why she needed this tonight before she reports for duty tomorrow. Wish I was in a place to whisk her away to a cabin in the woods. Her only responsibility would be to come for me, over and over again.

I'd keep her naked and feed her grapes.

Brunch.

Fucking hell, I coerced her into a date. I pretended to withhold eating her out when, honestly, I'd let her ride my face no matter what.

One taste of her perfect honey and I'm ruined for life, so maybe that cabin dream needs to become a reality. I'll wake her up with her clit in my mouth and a sweet little suck to start the day. We can work side by side on a homestead…

I picture her in a flannel shirt and nothing else, riding me in front of a fireplace.

I'm a fucking cowboy in this fantasy, and she's my bride.

If there's ever been a sign I'm ready to leave my life behind, this moment has to be it. I lose myself in a woman I don't know, driving her to a release she barely understands but desperately needs.

I need it, too.

I need to give her this, to be what she needs tonight, because it's been too damn long since I've truly mattered to anyone. I've locked myself into a life I don't want anymore out of a misguided sense of making a difference.

When really I was just waiting for Lily to spread her legs and invite me to dive in.

Now her thighs are shaking on my shoulders, her sweet hips rocking against my face, and she's so close, begging my name. I pulse my entire mouth against her sex, sucking and licking and pushing her to the peak.

If this is Lily's first orgasm with another person, it's a fucking gift. She arches her entire body as if flying, arms going wide, then coming back to my head as she shudders back to earth.

She cries out as her cunt floods my tongue with a fresh burst of slick joy, then whines as I try to latch on to her clit again. Even my gentle licks at the pearls sliding down her pussy lips get a whimper of protest. "Oooh," she says with a shudder.

It's not a no. It's not telling me to stop, but I know she's sensitive now. I know she can't find the words to tell me she's had enough. That she needs a minute.

But I'm just enough of a horny fucking bastard to keep licking because I'm hungry for her taste, because I'm changed, and now she's inside me. I worry I won't stop until I've consumed every drop of her, but when she pulls on my hair, I let her drag me up her body.

And then she kisses me, her mouth soft and open, her tongue lapping at my face.

She's licking up the taste of herself off my skin, and I lose it. My hands dive into her hair, holding her tight as our faces smash together, the kiss turning into something else. Face fucking, I guess.

Hot. Mind-blowing.

So it's only when I feel her hand on my cock that I realize she's going to jerk me off.

I thrust my hips into her touch, her sweet little fingers almost too soft against my raging monster of a dick. Fuck, I'm close already.

And then I realize she's not just jerking me off. She's pulling off the condom I'm still wearing, sliding it down, and revealing the heavy, flared crown, wet at the tip. She's eager to get her little fingers on the drops of seed I've made for her, eager to smear it around my erection and use it to tug me closer.

I watch in disbelief as she strokes me off between her legs. She points my cock at her bare little mound, and the only soundtrack is our gasping breaths.

The tip grazes her bare skin, and deep inside, something

yanks tight. My balls squeeze, ready to spray, and I just need a few more strokes to get there.

"That's it, sweet girl," I murmur as she moves her hand up and down my shaft. "Make me come. What a gift. Yes, please."

"So polite," she whispers back. "So polite when I just want you to come on my thighs so I can rub it in."

I roar in response, falling in, closing the gap between us, and what started as a hand job turns into a grind, her sweet body a cradle for me to rut against. My cock slides against the sensitive skin she couldn't handle me licking a moment ago, and she gasps at the contact. It's a good thing I didn't fuck her tonight because I'm a beast just getting to touch the outside of her body, bare, with nothing between us.

She wants me to come on her body?

I'll mark her with my seed from her pussy to her belly, then feed her whatever's leftover.

My name is a prayer on her lips again as I hitch her hips into my hands, writhing with her. And then she clenches her thighs around me, and I realize she's coming again. My sweet little virgin, horny as hell, got a second orgasm for her efforts.

I spill my come between us in hot, sticky spurts, and she kisses me again as I slide my big hand between us and press it into her skin.

3
lily

I SPEND a restless night dreaming of Sebastian's mouth and fingers and cock and wonder how I'll continue the ruse of having a job when I'm really a student. I let myself fantasize about actually having a boyfriend—one who likes brunch and sex and *me, exactly as I am*—before I crawl out of the cheap motel bed at dawn and drag myself into the shower.

I slept with the scent of his come between my legs, and I can smell it now as the steam swirls around me.

I'm still a virgin by some bizarre technicality, but last night changed me. Sebastian gave me my first real sexual experience, and it was amazing.

Also, deeply dirty. Wrong. Delightfully wrong. And more than a little depraved.

The way he buried his face between my legs. An absolute stranger. The way he ate me out like a man on a mission, hungry and starved for the taste of a woman.

I shiver and cup my breasts, my nipples hard against my palms.

Next Sunday, I want his mouth on my chest. I want to sit in his lap, and when I tell him he should fuck me, he'll tell me he wants to take his time as he gobbles up a mouthful of my virgin tits.

I lose myself in the fantasy, spending more time than I should in the shower, so when I get out, I'm running late. I let my hair air dry because it doesn't matter what I look like and pull on my most ordinary clothes. Time to blend into the background for three months. It will kill my soul, but on the other side of this, I'll be free to do whatever I want with my trust fund.

As I pack, I reluctantly tuck the mini skirt and tank top I wore yesterday to the very bottom of my bag. When I get to Edgewood, they'll have a full uniform for me to wear, but it won't do to show up looking like the horny slut I realized last night that I truly am.

That's my secret.

Sebastian's and mine, I suppose. I'm not sure how I'll get away on Sunday, but I'll find an excuse. I can't wait to see him.

Before I call for a rideshare, I take out my phone and text Sebastian.

Heading out of cell range soon. I'll text you Saturday when I'm done with work for the week.

He replies immediately.

I start a new project at work today, so I'll be busy too. But I'm looking forward to the weekend.

Would it be wrong to tell him I miss him already? Maybe not wrong, but definitely desperate. Before I can give in to that instinct, I organize a ride and put my phone on airplane mode.

———

Edgewood Academy is on the edge of the city, surrounded by forest. The campus is set back from the road, down a long, winding lane, and it looks like literally every other private school I've had the misfortune of attending.

The driver pulls up in front of the main building.

"Do you work here?" he asks, giving me an appraising look in the mirror.

I shake my head. "I'm a student."

"Oh." His cheeks turn dark red. "Sorry, I didn't realize you weren't...."

"I'm eighteen," I tell him. "Almost nineteen. A full year older than the oldest students here."

"Let me know if you ever want to talk about it sometime," he replies, laughing.

I frown.

He stops laughing. "Sorry."

"It's fine. But no thanks." I take a deep breath. "I have a boyfriend."

It's sort of true. True in my heart.

I have a date, anyway. Brunch and fucking to look forward to. And I only want that with Sebastian.

I climb out of the car and hitch my backpack onto my shoulder. The forest is close enough I can inhale the lush, late summer scent of it. Pine and grass, and I imagine wildflowers, too. Maybe I'll be able to explore in there and hide from the school.

As I approach the front door, it swings open, and a girl younger than me and in a school uniform steps out. "Delilah Murphy?"

I nod. "That's me."

"I'm one of the office helpers today. I was told to bring you to the headmaster's office. I'm Stacey, by the way."

"Nice to meet you." I give her a polite smile. I'm not here to make friends; I'm here to finish my three credits, get straight As, and leave at Christmas. "Are you a senior?"

She nods. "I'm guessing you are, too?"

For the second time around, yeah. "Mmm."

"Do you know what classes you'll be taking yet? I have a full course load this term. I'm taking Latin, Calculus, Creative Writing, and the two-credit Independent Thesis."

A two-credit what? I like the sound of that. "Is that open to anyone?"

"You need to get permission from the headmaster."

"Any tips for winning him over? I only need three credits to graduate. I'd love to do a thesis and take one other course—creative writing sounds good—and be done."

"Mr. Craig is also the creative writing senior seminar instructor, actually. You don't have to win him over. Just tell him what you need, and he'll make it happen." She stops in front of the office door. It's a large, heavy oak slab surrounded by opaque glass sidelights and a soaring transom above it. The whole main hallway is like this—big, old, and impressive. It reminds me of my grandfather's company's headquarters.

The office my father has poisoned, made dangerous.

I hate it.

I'm definitely going to hate the headmaster on the other side of the door, no matter how much this bubbly sunshine girl seems to like him. I take a deep breath and thank Stacey for delivering me to the devil. Then I turn the handle and step inside.

4
sebastian

"HEADMASTER CRAIG, Delilah Murphy is here. The transfer student from New York."

"Send her in." I glance at the file on my desk. I've already familiarized myself with her records. An exceptional student with a real attitude problem is my general impression. I have concerns about the two private schools she previously attended, based on my knowledge of their administration. There's also something not right about her father. He made a significant donation to our scholarship fund to encourage this last-minute enrollment. His approach rubbed me the wrong way, even though we haven't met.

But that's not the fault of his daughter. There was something about her file that spoke to me. She's bounced around a lot but had good grades right until the moment they expelled her. Her transcript is missing credits she probably should have been granted, even if asked to leave a school.

It's a mess. And at Edgewood Academy, we put students first. So, combined with the opportunity to expand our scholarship program, I was happy to grant a last-minute acceptance to her.

Maybe making a difference for this student will knock me

out of the funk I've been in lately. I'm not sure what is wrong. Maybe I'm just getting tired of the same old, same old. I've been going out on my bike more often. Thinking about heading out West and starting over.

The six years I've spent here have been the longest I've stayed in one place my entire career. I was the youngest candidate for headmaster in Edgewood's history, but the board took a chance on me, and I've thrown myself into proving it was the right call. I set aside my personal life and devoted myself to this institution.

Maybe it's a midlife crisis. I tell the inner jackass in my head to shut the fuck up. But he's not wrong. I'll be forty-one next month. I thought I missed the clichéd meltdown because the big four-oh had been no big fucking deal to me.

Who the fuck knows what's wrong with me? I have a date on Sunday, a new term to look forward to, and a job to do right now. I shake off my malaise and stand, ready for my newest student.

But nothing could prepare me for who I see when the door swings open—or the sad, sullen look on Lily's face. She's not looking at me. She's staring at the carved wood desk I'm standing behind, so I have a second to deal with the "Holy Shit I Slept with a Student" klaxon sound in my head. It's followed immediately by an equally loud internal alarm at the look on her face because the Lily I met last night is not this woman.

Girl.

Woman.

Last night she'd worn a miniskirt, and that sweet fucking mouth was painted with bright red lipstick. Now she's wearing jeans and a plain T-shirt, and her face is bare of any makeup.

She looks like a girl. What the fuck was I thinking? I grab her file, hands shaking, and flip it open, relieved to see that she's definitely eighteen.

Great, I'm just a pervert, not a criminal.

I thought she was in her early twenties.

Very early.

Okay, I thought she was maybe twenty. I'd hoped she was twenty-one, but the depraved dirty man inside me also kind of hoped she was just twenty.

My beautiful, innocent Lily.

Delilah Murphy.

Fuck me.

Blonde waves float ethereally around her heart-shaped face as she lifts her head, confused because her new fucking headmaster hasn't said a goddamn word yet.

Her eyes go wide, her lips part, and she fumbles for the chair beside her. "Sebastian?"

The way she breathes my name makes my cock hard. Instantly.

But there's another reaction, a wilder, more dangerous one, right in the center of my chest. I need to make this okay for her. I circle around my desk and close the door behind her, then pull her into my arms.

This will be the last time I can hold her like this, so I fucking cherish it. I breathe in her scent and memorize the shape of her body against mine. I wrap her tightly against me and cradle her to my chest until she stops shaking.

Then I hold her a little longer because I fucking need her, and I don't want to let go.

It hurts when I step back and shove my hands in the pockets of my suit pants. "This doesn't need to be a problem."

She manages a watery laugh. "I don't see how it can't be. Fuck, I'm such a—"

"You did nothing wrong. You were—" Perfect. Sweet and sexy and fierce. She'd wanted an escape, she said. Before three months of hell at my school. I'm the hell-master in her nightmares. "You had to let off some steam before you focused on your schoolwork. Why don't we sit and talk about that?"

She glances at the hard wooden chair in front of my desk. "What we did?"

I groan. "No. Your schoolwork."

She's still staring at the chair. Where my students sit when I'm discussing their future.

She's my fucking student.

Shame tears the next statement out of my mouth. "I didn't know you were eighteen."

Her gaze jerks back to my face. And her shock is slowly replaced with something else. Suspicion for a second, then wariness. "Why didn't you ask?"

To anyone else, I'd lie. To Lily, I give her the whole damn truth. "In hindsight, I think it's pretty clear I didn't want to know."

Her cheeks burn as she absorbs that information. "Are you in the habit of not wanting to know how old your truck stop pickups are?"

"I told you last night." I exhale, and it sounds a lot like a growl. "That was the first time I'd ever done that. I didn't want to know how old you were because I wanted *you*, no matter what. But I wasn't really… thinking. I just needed you."

She shrugs. "I didn't know you were…." The tip of her tongue pokes into the corner of her mouth, and I want to laugh as she tries to speak more diplomatically. "Old enough to be a headmaster?"

She could have just said old. Because yeah, I fucking am. "I promise, yesterday was an exception to my usual life."

Her gaze drifts down to my suit, then back up again. "I should hope so."

I raise my eyebrows at the tone. The reaction is instinctive but completely ineffective against a girl—woman—who has bared everything for me and my ravenous mouth.

She shrugs. "What? You want me to pretend I'm something other than what you already know I am?"

"I don't know anything about you," I point out. "And vice versa."

A pink tinge spreads across her cheeks, even as her eyes

flash. "We know a few things. Maybe just enough to make terrible decisions."

Yeah. "There's that critical thinking ability I've read so much about," I say dryly. I move back around my desk and tap on her file. "I would like to know more about how you ended up here. You're obviously academically gifted. But you have a problem with authority."

Her eyes flare brightly. Stubborn Lily, I immediately nickname this version of her in my mind. We all have different versions of our true selves. I try not to assume that any one version I see of a student is their whole being.

I wait for her protest, but it doesn't come. So I lean back in my chair. "Isn't that true? You were expelled from two other schools. You had to finish last year, what should have been your last year, at a public school, and you weren't able to get enough credits to graduate with your class."

"I was sabotaged," she bites out.

"By who?"

She shakes her head. "It doesn't matter."

It does, but trust will take time, and what I did to her last night has fucked up the usual process of a headmaster winning over a new student. "Shall we talk about the three credits you need to graduate?"

She exhales, then sits primly across from me.

"I've heard you have an independent thesis project." Her back gets even straighter. "I want to do that. And take whatever class it is you don't teach, so no creative writing."

She knows a lot for having only been in the building ten minutes at most. "Would you take creative writing if I wasn't teaching it?"

"Would you not teach it so I can take it?"

"Absolutely." I would resign my whole damn position if it was what she needed to graduate.

She leans back in her chair. "You're not like other headmasters."

"I'll take that as a compliment."

"I meant it as one." She crosses her arms over her chest, and I force myself not to linger there, wondering what she would look like naked, her arms pressed against her slight breasts, nipples peeking out at me.

I never even got her tits in my mouth.

I should hope I'm not like other headmasters. I'm a fucking pervert. It's obviously a newly gained problem, and one I'm not sure how to handle. I close my eyes, which doesn't help, because then she's naked in my mind.

Clenching my fist against the edge of my desk, I force myself to pretend she's anyone else. Stacey, the office helper this morning. What would I say to her?

"If you do an independent thesis, what would your area of interest be?"

"What are my options?"

"Something that builds on your previous areas of interest. Do you prefer science or the arts?"

"Arts."

"Comparative literature, then?"

She smirks. "Can I compare Jane Austen to modern retellings?"

I won't raise to the bait of her smirk when the question is entirely appropriate. She needs to learn her experience here will be different from whatever trauma she had in the past. "Of course."

Her gaze narrows. "What about fan fiction?"

It's on the line for a senior thesis, but I know Mrs. Taylor will guide her appropriately. "It's a good direction." I encourage her. "Our English Lit teacher will be a great advisor. You can ask her about the wizard world fic she writes."

Lily's eyebrows hit the roof. "What now?"

I grin. "Welcome to Edgewood Academy. We do things differently here."

"How different?"

I take a deep breath. "Not differently enough that we can repeat last night." Unfortunately. "But we will do our best to foster your curiosity over the next three months and help you get to the next stage in your academic career."

"That's a good line."

"It's the truth."

Her chest rises and falls, matching my controlled inhale. "What would you say if I wanted to take creative writing? With you?"

I should say it is a bad idea. I should regretfully decline to teach the seminar this term because I am a bad man who made a big mistake. But there will be other students in the class, and another teacher can grade her final assignment. I sometimes ask for help when my workload gets to be too onerous.

Nobody will notice that I don't want to be the one to give Lily her final grade.

Nobody needs to know there's no way I could be unbiased about this gorgeous, clever young woman.

And nobody needs to know that I would give anything to spend the next three months watching her learn and grow in her craft.

"I would say…." My voice is a rough rumble, full of gravel and unexpectedly raw need. I swallow hard and try again. "If you want me to be your teacher, I will happily have you in my class."

5
lily

WHEN I LEAVE SEBASTIAN'S—HEADMASTER Craig's
—office, Stacey is waiting with my dorm key and a map. "I'll
take you to your room and give you a quick tour before my first
class."

"Is that the small group creative writing seminar?" I show
her the schedule he printed out for me. "I'm in it, too."

She gives me a wide, cheerful smile. "Awesome. He's really
nice, you know. Once you get past the stern stuff."

Stern? Was he stern?

I think once I'm alone with my filthy thoughts, I'll imagine
him even sterner. A little mean, even. "Good to know. What's
the worst you've ever seen him?"

Apparently, he assigns detention when people need to get
caught up on their homework and yells at people for bullying,
all of which places him firmly in the nice category to me. "He
doesn't smack rulers on desks or make embarrassing examples
out of people?"

"Headmaster Craig?" Stacey's eyes go wide, and she shudders. "No, never."

"What about any of the other teachers? Who are the perverts
to watch out for?"

Her eyes are genuine saucers now. "What schools did you go to before you came here?"

"Dangerous ones," I mutter. Schools where my father could exert undue influence and make my life a living nightmare so I'd stay under his thumb.

"I don't think Headmaster Craig would tolerate anything like that happening here."

Not here, maybe. Ten miles down the highway, though... "No, right. He seems really nice."

"He is."

"Good." I'm thinking Stacey might be a bit simple. No way is Edgewood this great. Not when their headmaster is a secret truck stop sex fiend.

She leads me across the quad to the dorm I'm staying in, a co-ed building. Every student has their own room; mine is on the first floor, near the back of the building and facing a forest.

"There are trails in there," Stacey offers, seeing my bright pink running shoes spill out from the top as I dump my bag on the bed. "If you run."

"I do."

"We're allowed free access to the property until ten at night, then we need to be in our rooms. Curfew lifts at six in the morning, so there's time for exercise before and after classes. Speaking of which...." She glances at the clock on the wall. "I better let you get changed into your uniform before the seminar begins." She gestures back at the quad. "McDonald Hall is directly across the quad, and our classroom is on the second floor."

After she leaves me alone in my room, I check out the uniform hanging in the closet, then unpack my bag. I have another suitcase in the trunk of my car, which will be delivered here once it's repaired.

I think back to last night. The freak-out I had when my car broke down and how I just abandoned it on the side of the road and grabbed a ride with the next trucker who stopped.

Stupid, really, but I can't regret it.

Being at my breaking point led me to Sebastian and that wild make out in the shower stall.

I glance at my phone, still in airplane mode. It's a defense mechanism I have, turning it off so my parents can't track where I am. But they know I'm here. They put me here instead of letting me return to the public school in the city.

My paranoia is hereditary. *Not paranoia. Trauma.* Caused by paranoid parents.

On the surface, my family is blessed. Third generation wealth and all. But the ugly truth is that my father doesn't know the first thing about business, not legitimate business anyway. As soon as I graduate high school, my parents lose access to the wildly generous allowance they get from my trust fund to "raise me."

They would rather spend it on private schools that will expel me for no good reason than just let me finish school and live my life.

Not that I'm one to judge fucked up decisions, I guess. I'm changing into a classic school girl outfit on my way to see the man who talked about fucking me last night.

And I like it.

I really should feel guilt, but... I don't.

I continue to tell myself that I'm fine as I head across the quad.

The charade feels doable until I get to the classroom. In Headmaster Craig's office, when it was just the two of us? That was fucked up, but it was *just the two of us.* We both know what happened last night. There are no lies between us, not about that, anyway.

Has he ever fucked another student?

He better not have. I will rip his heart from his chest with my bare hands.

Can I even ask him that question? Will I get a chance? Or was my only chance in his office, and now we have to start lying to each other in front of people for the next twelve weeks.

My hand shakes as I wrap my fingers around the doorknob and turn.

Inside, I find a small room with a whiteboard on one wall and an old-school blackboard on the other. Windows look out over the quad, my dorm, and the forest beyond.

Even though I'm not looking at him—deliberately *not* looking at him—I see Sebastian wave me into the circle of chairs. The small class is a mix of students, all wearing the same uniform I am, with some variation for personal style. A guy with long hair up in a bun smiles at me and taps the empty chair next to him. The person on the other side, who had been talking, pauses their thought until I sit.

"Sorry."

Stacey beams at me.

There are way too many smiles in this room.

And I still can't look at Sebastian, even as he says my name. "Everyone, this is Delilah Murphy. Is that your preferred name?"

I nod. No, it's not. I'm Lily, but he can't call me that in front of people.

He gestures to a basket of apples on a side table. "Help yourself to a snack. We were just going around the circle and talking about our goals for the term. We'll continue and come around to you at the end. As Raven continues, please familiarize yourself with the seminar outline, which was emailed to you a few minutes ago."

I dig out my tablet and check for the message from the school.

Heat rushes through me as I see his name in my inbox. It feels... dirty. Intimate.

I finally lift my gaze and find him looking at me, a soft, lingering assessment in his eyes. I get up and grab an apple. He watches me, a faint smile tugging at the corner of his mouth, as I chomp into it and sit back down.

Raven finishes her little spiel, and then it continues on with Clarabelle, Michael, Stacey, and Deacon. Finally, it's my turn.

"I'm Delilah," I say, my voice catching. "Actually, it's Lily." Another wave of heat comes over me, and I lock my gaze on Sebastian's face. "I don't know what I want to write yet, but I've heard good things about this class, so I'm glad to be here."

Everyone claps.

They're smiling and clapping. It's both bizarre and nice.

But I kind of fucked their headmaster, so I definitely don't belong here. I nervously return the smiles, anyway.

Michael clears his throat. "I was kicked out of another school before I landed here. You're in good company."

Raven nods. "You won't get into trouble here for keeping it real. Headmaster Craig is a pretty understanding guy."

Sebastian makes a rueful face. "Hey, I can be tough on you guys. Don't misrepresent."

Stacey laughs. "That's true." Her eyes sparkle, but it's completely innocent. "He's really more like our dad than our headmaster."

That doesn't help my secret, *your headmaster is hot* problem. Now I've got *your de facto dad is hot* issues as well. I slide a look at Sebastian, and his cheeks have gone dark up high, near his temple.

He's old enough to be Stacey's dad, too.

Old enough to be mine.

It should highlight the off-limits, completely forbidden nature of our new relationship. But my brain doesn't agree. When he instructs us to pull out our notebooks and do some free writing and word association exercises, I go in a filthy but innocent direction.

Kind / secrets / dad / nobody sees him but me / off-limits

Not so innocent. I flip the page and start over, being stricter with my brain this time.

Kind / stranger / surprising / singular moment / time slip / temporal warp / meet again / if only / maybe next time

My pen slows to a halt on the last point. I'm gripping it tightly, my fingers clenched with tension that echoes the ache in my chest. Maybe next time, what? Maybe next time I meet a hot stranger, it won't be a harbinger of *No, Lily, not for you.*

"Does anyone want to share their lists?" Sebastian asks.

I flip my notebook shut. Not me.

But I take part in the discussion that flows from other people's work, and the hour flies by. It's lunchtime before we know it, and everyone else is out of their seats before I even have my tablet away.

I'm the last student to the door, and I poise my hand on it when I hear Sebastian clear his throat. "Lily, do you have any questions?"

6
sebastian

SHE LETS the door swing closed, then comes back to the circle, sitting a few chairs away from me.

"We survived that," she says with a laugh.

"Did you look at the course outline? You have two graded projects. I'll have someone else mark your work."

"I don't mind—"

I mind, though. I put up my hand. "It's important to me."

She shrugs. "Okay."

"All the other students have had me in previous years, so if they're overly comfortable with me...."

She laughs. "Have any of them been as *overly comfortable* with you as I have?"

I shift in my chair. "Fuck no."

"Then it's fine. I'm not jealous of their familiarity with you." Another shrug. "It's nice."

"I wasn't thinking of jealousy," I mutter.

A small smile plays at her mouth. "They all think of you as their campus dad. Is that how I'm supposed to think of you, too?"

I stand up abruptly. "It's different."

"Exactly." She stands, too, and we're both moving to the door at the same time.

Which is how she ends up pressed against the inside of the door, me leaning over her. Somehow. She smells like apples and looks like sin. I like her as much without the lipstick as with it. Bare, her lips are a gorgeous shade of pale pink, vulnerable and soft.

"Sebastian," she whispers.

"You can't call me that."

"You get to call me Lily," she whispers. "What should I call you? Headmaster Craig?"

That sounds wrong, too. "No."

"Stacey's dad?" That drips too innocently off her lips. "Is that better than Sebastian? Do you want to be *Daddy*?"

A jolt of something forbidden punches the inside of my chest. It's a physical feeling that drives me right against her, our bodies hot and pressed together. "I'm not your dad."

"I know," she whispers, her breath fast and eyes wide. "I have a father. And he's a terrible man. Are you secretly terrible, too, *Daddy*?"

"Fuck no." I force myself to soften against her, to brush my fingertips against her cheek, then back up. This is important. "Lily, you need to believe me. I am nothing like your father."

"What do you know about him?"

Not enough. "I know you need to get away from your family."

Her brow furrows in surprise. "You do?"

"Yes. And I promise you're safe here."

"I'm never safe somewhere my father has paid a lot of money to lock me up."

"Is that what happened at the other schools?"

Her eyes glitter with the threat of tears as she searches my face. But she doesn't answer me. No, she won't give up her secrets that quickly.

"It's okay," I murmur.

She shrugs and changes the subject. "I wish things were different, though. Because I like you. I like Stacey's dad."

We're back to that. Sex is a safe topic for her. A new, exciting space that is all ours, where she knows she has safety and control. Her challenging gaze warns me I should end this conversation now, but I can't.

Her voice drops, husky and sweet. "I'm glad you're not a bad man. I like the hot guy on the motorcycle who cares that I'm a virgin."

Memories from last night slam into me. "I do care."

She nods. "I know. You knew I needed to get off and walked that fine line to make it good for me."

Lily might be an innocent girl in many ways, but she knows more about me than most people do. Nobody else has ever seen me so keenly.

"I wish I could take care of you again." The truth finally spills out of me like a forbidden firehose. "I see you, sweet girl. I see what you need. But we can't."

"I know." She licks her lips. "I know we can't."

"We had last night. Nobody can take that from us."

Her voice is quieter than a whisper now, a sultry purr, dragging me way the fuck down a path I shouldn't even be on. "I'll always have that memory of you making me feel good. I'll think about it tonight."

Fuck me. I stroke her cheek. "Good. I want you to think about it often. And when you do…." I lean all the way in and brush my lips against her ear. "Daddy wants you to touch yourself and remember when he was a stranger."

She shudders against the door, and I step back, just enough to put space between us.

Her gaze immediately drops to my obvious erection.

I desperately put my hand to her mouth, stopping her from saying anything else. But that's a mistake because her lips are endlessly soft, plump pink reminders of what I cannot have because of who I am.

Who she is.

"We can't do this," she breathes. A reminder to me. A goad to make me do something, anyway.

"We're not doing anything." I brush my fingers to the side of her mouth, that sweet disappearing corner of her smile that's almost a dimple.

She parts her lips, and my middle finger slips into her mouth.

Hot, wet, sweet.

"What time do you go to bed?" I rasp.

"Eleven." She forms the word slowly around my invading finger, then smiles. My finger slides out of her mouth, shiny and wet. Her mouth looks like it needs a cock in it next. "Why? Are you going to be in bed at the same time? Maybe thinking about last night?"

"No." I press my thumb against the other side of her jaw and squeeze, then release her and step all the way back. "That would be a mistake. But I hope you have sweet dreams tonight, Lily."

Sweet, impossible dreams.

———

At ten thirty, I tell myself I'm going out for a run. Hard, punishing exercise is what I need to do. *Turn myself into the authorities is what I actually need to do.*

I'm playing with fire, though, and it turns out I like it.

Lily's hot gaze as I touched her mouth… Fuck, that is enough right there. That's all I need.

So, of course, I'm lurking in the forest at ten to eleven. Not running. Not punishing myself. I'm watching her instead and not feeling bad about it at-fucking-all. Her light is on, and her curtains only half-closed, so I can see her working at her desk. She's changed out of her uniform. I can't tell from this distance, but it looks like she's wearing a T-shirt, and when she stands up, I see bare legs.

Getting ready for bed in a T-shirt and panties.

Ready for Daddy to tuck her in.

Daddy.

I'd give her a goodnight kiss. On her mouth, and when she sighs, on her neck. Her tits. Over the shirt, just to see if she likes it. When she sighs again and arches her back, I'd push her shirt up. Just enough to kiss her sweet belly. Push it up a little higher, find her breasts, just the underside of them, and kiss her there.

More sighs.

Restless legs.

Sweet girl wants more kisses from Daddy, but she'll have to ask me for them.

In the shadows of the forest, I palm my dick, then squeeze it roughly. I will not jerk off here, staring at the dorms.

Oh, the fucking lies I tell myself.

Lily is a dirty, beautifully filthy woman.

I watch as she moves around her room, then comes to the window and closes the drapes.

There's a momentary pause, then her body moves away. The light turns out. I imagine her burrowing under the covers and sliding her hand into her panties.

Eager, hot panting. Her clit is hard and aching to be touched. Legs falling open, stroking herself as she thinks about how I licked her there.

I would do it again. Swallow every drop of her pleasure, then kiss her on the forehead as she drifted off.

Good girl. Go to sleep.

I ease deeper into the forest where it's dark and forbidden, like my thoughts. I palm myself as I think about her humping her hand, slim little fingers working faster and faster.

My hand is her virgin cunt, too tight to fuck. My fingers are at the fluttering lips of her pussy, where I could just rub against her and come like that. Spilling my seed where she's wet. Not inside her, just at the entrance.

Daddy.

I can't.

Not yet.

Turning on my heel, I let myself stay frustrated. But those two words—*not yet*—carry me all the way to my house on the other side of the woods.

It's time for me to think long and hard about what I want after this term is over. And I need to find out more about Lily's parents.

7
lily

I FALL ASLEEP, dreaming of Sebastian jerking off between my legs. I wake up in the middle of the night, covered in a cold sweat.

Guilt.

It's a familiar feeling to the girl who's been kicked out of several schools and disappointed her parents in endless other ways. My whole life, I just haven't fit in.

Fucking the headmaster is a new and unexpected way for me to self-sabotage a new situation. At least I waited until I was legal, so it's just morally gray, not absolutely wrong.

It's pretty fucking wrong.

Well, they shouldn't make headmasters that hot. It's not my fault.

But that stubborn refusal to accept blame doesn't help me fall back asleep, and I toss and turn until dawn.

———

After breakfast, I meet my advisor for my thesis, the English Lit department head, Mrs. Taylor.

She says I can do most of my work independently, but she

wants me to check in more frequently over the first couple of weeks, just to make sure I'm on the right track. Fine, whatever. I just want to get my credits and get out of here.

At lunch, Stacey tells me Mrs. Taylor is the school mom to Sebastian's role as school dad. I burn with jealousy at the thought there might be something to that. She's not off-limits the way I am. She's pretty and grown-up, and they have lots in common.

I think.

I don't actually know anything about what Sebastian likes, other than pressing me hard against walls and mirrors occasionally.

After lunch, I go to the library, get out my tablet, and start reading. When I finally finish my research for the day, it's well past dinner.

I head to the dining hall anyway, knowing the drill from every other school I've gone to—snacks will be available until the dining hall closes at curfew.

What's different from every other school is that this dining hall has a hot headmaster sprawled out on a chair, eating an orange and talking to a group of kids.

Maybe I can grab a sandwich before he sees me. That's my best intentions plan. But once I grab food from the fridge, I make a hot chocolate and settle in at a table.

Go back to your room, Lily. I don't move. I pull out my work instead, and I read. Fifty percent of my attention is on the book. The other half is tracking how his hands work the peel off the orange, the way he laughs before sliding a segment into his mouth.

I want to lick the taste of that orange off his lips.

Go back—

He stands up.

I jerk my attention back to the page, re-reading the passage I didn't actually absorb before, and pretend to be surprised when he slides onto the chair across from me. "Studying?"

I nod. "I met with Mrs. Taylor today. We have a game plan."

"She told me."

Ah. So they talk frequently. Of course, they do; they're colleagues. It's her job to tell him about the new girl's thesis plans. I nod again, pretending I'm not sizzling with misplaced jealousy on the inside. "Good."

He glances at the sandwich. "Did you miss dinner?"

"I was in the library."

He frowns. "Do you want me to see if there's any leftover stew in the kitchen?"

"I'm fine with this."

"It's important to eat."

I smile against my will at the concern. "I know."

"It's my job to make sure you're well taken care of." While this is probably true, it also sounds filthy.

"I'm... thank you."

His voice lowers. "How did you sleep?"

Shame rolls through me. "Uh..."

"Sorry."

"No, it's okay." I make a face. "I went to bed just fine. Very sweet dreams. But then I woke up feeling guilty."

His own expression tightens into concern. "That's my fault."

"Funny, I was thinking the same thing. I'm a bit of a...." I hesitate to swear in front of the headmaster, but I can't think of another label. "Fuck up?"

"You are not." His voice is immediately stern. "Lily, I can't let you think that."

"Don't know how you'll stop me."

"If I had my way, it would be with a spanking," he mutters. And he doesn't even look embarrassed when he locks his gaze on me. "Which isn't on the table. But maybe you should know that's how I feel."

"Oh." A funny heat replaces the shame inside me. "You would really spank me?"

He crosses his arms over his chest. "If you needed it."

I lean in, the tension in his body captivating me. "Why would I need it?"

"I don't know exactly." He clenches his jaw. "Forget I said that."

"I don't think I can." I pick up my tablet and type in *Why would someone need to be spanked?*

Sebastian's eyes go wide. "What are you doing?"

"Research." I poke the tip of my tongue into the corner of my mouth as I scroll. "This is really quite the mix of adults being horny and terrible parenting advice, isn't it?"

"Put that away."

"Why?" But I do as he says.

"We should talk about something else. Your thesis, for example."

I let him change the subject, but I know what I'm reading more of when I get back to my room.

8
sebastian

I DON'T KNOW what's wrong with me. I should be able to go an entire conversation with Lily without saying something inappropriate. But apparently, I have zero restraint with her. And she gives as good as I do. Pulling out her tablet and looking up spanking? Pointing out that it's either about being horny or terrible parenting?

I wanted to drag her over the table and promise it could be the best kind of caregiving she might ever receive and threaten to spank the brat right out of her. Except we weren't alone in the dining hall, and I have never in my life spanked a woman. I'm not sure why I'm threatening to start now.

But the threat felt like a heady promise.

I'm a grown man. I know what kink is.

That it might be *for me* is a brand new concept, though. When curfew falls and the campus goes dark, I head through the forest to my private residence. I don't stand in the shadows and watch Lily get ready for bed. I head straight home instead and have a cold shower that does nothing for the dark thoughts that don't feel nearly wrong enough.

———

Every day for the next month, we have encounters like that. Brief, public conversations that look innocent enough to outside observers, but each time I can't help but lower my voice to a private, husky note.

I love the way her eyes light up at my attention. And I crave those moments myself. There's no denying it, so I don't even try. I stop myself from touching her but can't completely stay away.

Our creative writing group is my favorite hour of the entire week. I often jerk off to the image of her slowly consuming an apple as she works. And she's not just sex fodder for me. I love the look of concentration on her face as she scribbles in her notebook, the careful and earnest way she listens to her class-mates. The thoughtful feedback she gives and the surprising way she blushes when others like her work.

She's a complicated woman, a tangle of contradictions. Brazenly cocky and stubbornly uninterested in authority, yet secretly unsure of herself and desperate for the right kind of attention.

I give her as much as is appropriate given our roles. I take perverse pleasure in writing her critique notes on lined paper, folding them in half, and handing them over to her. She reads them all in front of me, squirming in delight at the praise I give her.

Your scene-setting is very well done here. I can imagine myself there, touching and hearing everything.

Entirely innocent.

I want more from you in this character sketch. Show me what's inside her. I know you can do it. You've done it before.

Nothing wrong with that.

I want to take you away from here and fuck you until neither of us can stand properly... I don't write that one down. It wouldn't be constructive because we can't. It would just make her feel bad, and that's the last thing I want.

And as we flirt, I slowly gain her trust. She tells me she's nervous about her father trying to interfere with her studies here. I promise her that nothing will get in the way of her graduating at the end of the term.

It takes a few weeks to convince her I won't betray her trust.

Then one day after class, Lily asks me to read something new she's written. "It's not ready for group feedback," she says before scampering out the door. "Just for you."

I know I started this version of our game, a dangerous flirtation under the guise of classwork, but I'm not prepared for the handwritten essay title:

Virginity is just a social construct

It's satire and clearly over the top, but at the core is a thesis that rips away all the pretending I've been doing about our relationship. And what I've already done to her.

9
lily

SEBASTIAN FINDS me in the library that night. I'm on the third floor in the stacks, looking for a book on Sherlock Holmes. He appears at the end of the row, blocking the light. "You skipped dinner," he rumbles.

"That's not why you're here, though."

"No?" He glances at his watch, then glances up.

The lights blink out.

His voice rumbles toward me again, this time in the dark. "Maybe I'm here to tell you the library is closing."

My pulse jumps as he tugs me deeper into the stacks and presses his hand over my mouth. My eyes go wide. Not that he can see that. We can't see anything.

We're all alone in the dark, and he's gently pressing me up against a hard, wooden bookshelf.

He groans my name as my eyes adjust to the darkness, finding his face hovering above mine. I smile. "Is this about the essay?"

"It can be. It can also be about the fact you didn't eat, and curfew is in half an hour."

"Oooh, sounds like we don't have a lot of time to cover all of those bases, so let me reassure you that I have an apple and some crackers back in my room and jump right to my essay."

"Sure. The essay." He clears his throat. "It doesn't exactly meet the brief of the creative writing assignment."

"Really?" My pulse is dancing right now, a skittering flutter under my skin. "I thought it was pretty creative. The idea that you took my virginity that night. That some people would say that I've already had sex for the first time." My breath brushes against his cheek. "With you. In a truck stop bathroom."

"You can't write that shit down."

"I didn't put it on the computer. I didn't print it out. Your copy is the only copy."

He groans again. "Why now?"

"Because it's been a long, lonely month." It's the truth. "And you're close enough to touch, but I'm not allowed to touch. It makes me sad."

"We don't always get what we want," he points out.

Don't I know it. "But you said you would spank me for not eating. I think that means that you care about what I need."

"I do." Two desperate, growled words.

I grin triumphantly. "Then you agree. Now that I know how good sex is—and we agree that we've already had sex, so to speak—it's cruel to expect me to not have more of it. You don't need to hold back, Sebastian. You've already taken my virginity. You just didn't know it because you weren't using the right terms."

"That was your first time doing *anything*?"

"I was such a good girl before you shot your load between my legs, Sebastian." I lick his cheek for good measure to show him I'm a bad girl now. To give him a taste of just how much he's ruined me. "And now I want that all the time. It's all I can think about when I'm supposed to be researching Sherlock Holmes re-tellings. I think about how hot the headmaster looks when I'm stroking his cock, and the sounds he makes when his come hits my bare pussy."

"Jesus, Lily." He huffs a frustrated laugh. "Yeah? That's what you think about?"

"It's terrible, I know."

He brushes his knuckles against my cheek. "It's not, though. You didn't know who I was. We came into this as equals. We found each other and didn't get enough to quench our needs." His body tenses against mine. "I think about you all the time, too. And that is wrong."

"Why is it wrong for you and not for me?" I know the answer, but I want him to say it. I want him to say it because I like it. Because I love this forbidden dynamic, but I also want to slay it.

All my life, I've bumped into stupid rules that have made no sense, and every time, they have knocked me down.

Not this time.

I am going to have Sebastian. I don't care what the rules are. This time, I'm trusting my heart and doing what feels right.

"Because I'm a grown-up, entrusted with your care."

I take his hand and guide it down to my waist, shivering as his fingers clench against my skin. I push his touch into my butt, forcing our hips together. "So take care of me."

"There are rules, Lily."

"I know. But we're the exception."

"There is no exception to this rule."

"It didn't apply that first night. And we can't unring that bell." I writhe inside his grip. "We tried pretending this isn't a thing. That didn't work. If you want to take care of me, let's be honest about what I need."

"We can't do this."

"I know you think that."

But he doesn't let me go; he can't. I feel that in his body. He's vibrating with tension.

Just like that first night, he needs a release. I've been studying him. Listening to people talk about him. He never dates, never leaves campus. That night on the highway was probably an aberration. My poor, horny headmaster. Stuck in the middle of nowhere without a safe hole to rut all his delicious tension into.

I can't fuck him in the library. It would be wrong. And it would start us down a path that would ruin us both. His career, my future. I cannot fuck him. That wasn't my plan tonight. *I didn't even bring him to the library. I just wrote something down and gave it to him. He sought me out.* That's how I justify what I do next.

With a shaky exhale, I sink to my knees and press my face to the thick bulge behind his fly.

Above me, he swears, then breathes my name. Coarse and then soft. That's who he is, and I'm the only one who knows it.

I can't fuck him, but I can help take the edge off his desperate need. Show him what is possible, and then he'll make the next move.

He doesn't stop me when I fumble with his zipper. As I reach my little fingers into his pants and find his erection.

I glance up at him as I stroke him, familiarizing myself with the hot, heavy length. The marvelous silky feel of his skin here, so different from everywhere else on him. I didn't notice that the first time, but now I'm memorizing every detail for when I touch myself later.

And he smells good, too. I breathe him in as I find his gaze locked on mine. "Are you going to tell me to stop?"

"No." A hoarse confession.

I smile. "Why not?"

"Because my cock is yours. It belongs in your mouth."

Nodding, I lick the flared crown, tasting him for the first time. "Because this is right."

"Fuck. Yes."

"Good." I take his cock into my mouth, and the guttural sound he makes matches the desperate wave of relief that rolls through me.

"Lily, your mouth." He grunts as I swallow, savoring the taste of him. "You're such a good girl."

I squirm. The way he says that makes my thighs shake.

"You like that, don't you? I see you, sweet girl. I see you need me to tell you how smart you are. Your essay was perfect. That's why I...." He trails off because I'm bobbing my head, trying to find a rhythm. "Yes, like that. Slower. Suck me harder, if you like. It feels so good. You can lick me or swallow me. Whatever you like. You're perfect."

I'm floating on his praise now, eager to make him happy that he knows I'm trying to be good at this.

"I've missed you," he whispers. "Told myself I didn't need you, but it was a lie."

I cry out and move my mouth faster.

"Yes," he hisses above me. "Make Daddy come. Use your naughty little mouth the way I used mine between your legs. Make me come, and I'll make you feel good, too."

Make Daddy come.

I press up on my legs, shoving his cock deep into my throat, and make myself gag.

"Shh," he murmurs. "Slow down. It's okay. Take just as much as you can handle. I'm too big to fit the whole thing in your sweet little mouth."

Daddy. Sweet girl. Good girl. Little mouth.

I shove my hand between my legs and grind my fingers against my clit.

He wants to spank me.

Daddy's cock.

This is definitely on the horny grown-up side of the Google search.

"Lily," he growls. "Hands off your pussy." I cry out in protest, and he pulls his cock out of my mouth. "I'm serious. I want to feel you come on my fingers."

I lift my hands in the air.

"Good girl." He smiles. "Put them behind your head."

I do as I'm told, which feels good in a new and unexpected way. There's a happy warmth in my chest that makes the angsty ache between my legs bearable.

He rubs the head of his cock against my lips, telling me to open for Daddy again, and I part my lips.

"Do you like that?" He thrusts slowly, just the tip, back and forth over my tongue. "Can I be your Daddy? Take care of you in every way?"

I nod, my mouth full. Maybe that's why he's asking me now. I'll have questions, but they can come later. Now it's just a yes or no, and my answer is an emotionally charged *yes*, without needing to think about it at all.

I don't know why.

I just know it's right.

He strokes my cheek as he works his cock in and out of my mouth. "You're going to make me come like this. Do you think you can swallow it?"

My eyes flare wide, but I nod again.

He speeds up, rocking more of his erection over my lips, making them stretch. I panic a little, my breath coming in short, fearful pants, but it's a good kind of fear. He grabs my hands, linked behind my head, holding me still with one fist tight around my fingers, the other pressed against my jaw. It's exciting, and then he's growling my name.

I feel a hot burst at first, a thick spurt against the roof of my mouth, and then his whole cock jerks against my tongue. He's not moving, just his erection is. A slow pulse of flesh that delivers more of his come.

First, he decorated my skin with it. Now it's filling my mouth. I try to swallow, but I choke, and he tells me to open my mouth, to let him go.

I didn't know I latched on to his cock. I gasp, and he slides out of my mouth with a wet sound.

He tips my chin up, wipes the corner of my mouth with his

thumb, and then slides that into my mouth. I suckle on it as I swallow down everything that was in my mouth.

"Are you okay?"

"It was more than I expected."

He reaches down and picks me up with ease. Then he perches me on the window ledge at the end of the row. "You did an outstanding job." Then he nudges my thighs apart with his fingers. Gentle. "Can Daddy touch you here?"

I nod.

"Tell me in your words, Lily."

My voice shakes with desire as I spread my legs even wider for him. "Yes, you can touch me there." I lick my lips. "If you're my Daddy, then you can touch me anywhere you want."

"You like that?"

"Yes."

"Do you know what I mean when I say that?"

"It's a dirty thing."

He nods. "I've never been anyone's Daddy before. It's special. Just you and me. I don't know why, but that's how I feel about you. It's all I can think about."

"What does that make me?"

"My sweet girl." His voice catches on the third word. "Or whatever you want me to call you."

"I like that." I pull my legs up, resting my heels on the ledge so my knees are bent, and my legs wiggle back and forth. "I like it when you called me good girl, too. But I always want to be...."

He watches me intently. "Say it. Anything."

"I want to be a woman for you. I found this... sex... with you. And that's meaningful to me."

"You're my woman, all right." He leans in and brushes a hard kiss against my mouth. I catch his lips with mine, not letting him go. Begging him to deepen it, and he does, his tongue rough against mine. Claiming.

And as we kiss, one of his hands slides up my inner thigh,

and he strokes me through my soaking wet panties. Instantly, my body reacts. It's a wild kind of tension, where I feel all stiff and yet liquid at the same time. I need him to touch me everywhere, be inside me in every way, and I don't know how to ask for it.

"Tell me what you want," he whispers, but I can't.

I don't know.

"Do you want my fingers inside your panties?"

"Yes."

"Tell me."

"Pull them to the side. Touch me." I gasp as he tugs the wet cotton out of the way, and I feel moisture roll down my bare skin, slicking my butt where it meets the window sill.

I close my eyes, dead from mortification.

I'm going to leave a mess in the library. I'll have to pack up my stuff and leave in the middle of the night because this is so wrong, and we can't stop. I need him to touch me more, spread that wetness everywhere, use it to shove inside me.

"Tell me more."

"Can you put your fingers inside me?"

He groans. "Yes. Hold on tight."

I cling to his broad shoulders as he finds my entrance and slowly eases one finger in, stretching me open. I buck my hips, making it sting. But yes, oh that. I want more of *that full feeling*. Of Daddy's fingers inside me, of Sebastian fucking me with his hand. Oh, God.

"More," I pant. "Deeper."

"You're so perfect." He kisses me again as his finger pulses just inside my entrance. "One day, I'm going to fuck this sweet little pink pussy. You're going to climb on my cock and work it into you, just like you're working on my finger. Yes, just like that. Good girl. So good. Take it. See? You're fucking me. Feel that? Your body is making room for more."

"I want it." I lick my lips, feverish now. "I want your cock. Fuck me."

"Not here."

"Then where?" God, I'm whining, it's embarrassing, but I need him.

"I'm not sure where yet. We'll figure it out." He rubs his thumb against my aching clit, then slowly teases a second finger at my entrance. That's enough to make me see stars. I cry out, and he covers my mouth with his. I come on his hand as his thumb rubs a reassuring circle over my clit. His lips seal in the sounds I'm making, and his other arm circles around me, holding me tight.

"My beautiful Lily." He groans; that's the best name of all that he can call me.

He's my Daddy.

And I'm his Lily.

He stays inside me as I pulse around him, only withdrawing his fingers after I've finished my orgasm. Then he carefully licks my taste off his fingers before leaning in and brushing another kiss on my mouth. "Be patient," he whispers. "We'll be together, eventually. But you have to be good, okay? No more dirty stories pretending to be writing assignments. That isn't safe."

"I know." But my chest aches as he steps away from me.

There are eight more weeks in this term. I need to finish my thesis project, write some non-horny creative writing things, and do my best to not jump the headmaster again.

It's an impossible to-do list.

10
sebastian

I'VE IGNORED a few messages from Lily's father—as headmaster of an expensive private school, I'm used to dodging meddling parents—but his last contact came curiously.

To an email address that is attached to my name but not really accessible to the public. Definitely not through an official channel.

We would like our daughter to stay at Edgewood for another term. We must talk about this soon.

It's an innocuous line, a seemingly reasonable request from a parent. The most parent-like request Mr. Murphy has made in all of his efforts to get in touch with me.

I don't like it.

So when I'm alone at my residence on Saturday afternoon, I call him. I need to hear his voice and figure out his angle. Man to man.

His tone is hard when he answers the phone, but it turns jovial as soon as I introduce myself. Like he's handling me instead of the other way around. Interesting.

"You're a hard man to get ahold of," he says.

"You found a way."

"I had my assistant do some digging."

I can imagine how frustrating it must have been to only find a private email address I use for online purchases. I'm a pretty boring guy, outside of the fact I'm having a secret affair with his daughter. "There are proper channels for academic inquiries, Mr. Murphy."

"I tried those."

"The lack of a response should have been a clue." I wince at my tone. This isn't how I should be acting. But part of me doesn't care.

"Delilah isn't ready to graduate."

"Her transcripts say otherwise."

"She has struggled at past schools," he replies silkily. "And those headmasters agreed she needed more time. We're happy to make another donation if that is needed."

He's bribing me. "You would pay Edgewood to keep Delilah here another term?"

I stop talking as I hear a rustle of footsteps, and Lily steps into view. She's dressed for a run and breathing hard like she's nearly at the end of it, and this wasn't how she planned for it to finish. *Me neither, sweet girl.* Fuck. Her face is tight with a hurt expression, and I wince at what she's just heard.

I hold up my hand as if to compel her to stay and clear my throat. "That is not an option, actually. She's already completed enough school work to ensure she will graduate at Christmas."

Lily watches me as I finish biting out those words, for her ears as much as his, and her expression shifts from hurt to wary. It's slightly better.

"Of course, it's an option." His voice is tight. "It's always an option."

I bet it has been in the past.

"If you won't cooperate, Mr. Craig, we can remove her from your institution."

"She's legally an adult. You don't have guardianship over her in that regard. You might think you know—"

"We may not be her legal guardians anymore," he snarls. "But we're the named beneficiaries of her trust fund allowance. So if we say her tuition needs to go somewhere else, it will go somewhere else. Do you understand me?"

That is not fucking happening. I need her here, with me, until we can leave Edgewood behind—together. "Let me be crystal clear, Mr. Murphy. Tuition at Edgewood is non-refundable. And we always make decisions that are in the best interests of our students, not their parents."

I end the call before saying something else, something I might regret, and Lily and I stare at each other in silence.

"So that was my father, huh?" She shrugs. "He's nice, right?"

"Do you want to tell me about your trust fund?"

She shakes her head. "No."

"Why not?"

She doesn't answer.

I gesture for her to come closer. She cautiously climbs onto the porch, and I duck so we're the same height so she can see that I'm not angry at her. I never would be. "He doesn't have any say over what happens next, Lily. You will graduate at the end of term."

She shudders in relief. "Thank you."

"If you tell me more about what you know, then I can help you even more." I suspect her father is misappropriating her money, but I don't want to tell her that. Not yet.

"My father is a wannabe businessman. He's also a part-time criminal, but I don't think he's good at that, either. My trust fund comes from my grandfather, and it pays for my education —it's tied up in that, so I need to be a private school, or nobody gets any money from it."

"You went to a public school for part of last year."

"They hated that. That's when I figured out they were taking some of my annual allowance. And they're allowed to, as long as they pay for my schooling. It's kind of messed up. My grandfather set it up, and I don't think this is what he intended. Before he died, he told me I would get access to it when I graduate high school. But that's been harder than it should be because my...."

When she trails off, I come to a horrible conclusion. Her parents are deliberately delaying her graduation. Somehow. It's madness. Maybe even criminal. But she doesn't need to worry about that anymore.

Those people have never taken care of her properly. Now I will.

I growl under my breath, and she gives me a look that says she likes it when I get all possessive.

I like it too.

She cranes her neck around me, looking at my house. "Is this where you live? It's private."

It sure is. And just like that, my blood heats. I should tell her she can't be here. Make her go back to the dorms and wait a little longer. But she heard the sharp end of a conversation she doesn't understand, and I need to make that right first. "This is the headmaster's residence, yes."

"It's nice." She's angling for an invite inside.

I want to carry her over the damn threshold. But first, I need to make something crystal clear to her. I catch her wrist, bringing her hand to my chest and her attention to my face. "Lily, I need you to know that when I called your father, it was so I could better understand the situation. I want to protect you so we can be together for real."

She blinks. "Together?"

Forever, if she'll have me. "If you want me, when this term ends, I will follow you wherever you go."

"No way."

I smile at that. "Would you like that?"

"I was thinking of going to the West Coast." Her eyes narrow. Testing me. "Pretty far from here."

The echo of my own fantasy escape isn't lost on me. "Sounds great."

She rolls her bottom lip between her teeth. "Why?"

The first answer that rolls through my head is, *I don't know*. But that's a lie. "Because there's been something between us since that first moment. I walked into that truck stop, and I thought, I want to be with that woman for the rest of my life. And if that scares you, I'll choke on those words until it doesn't. But if you'll—"

She leaps into my arms.

Fuck, she feels good. I carry her inside and lock the door behind us. Then I crush my mouth against hers, tasting the craving on her lips. She tangles her fingers in my hair, holding us together as I work my hands under her tight, damp running shirt. Her skin is impossibly soft, her body slight and strong at the same time. I need to see all of her this time. I need to stretch her out in my bed and take my time.

But the bed is all the way upstairs. So I settle for the stairs, sprawling on the first landing with her perched in my lap.

The raw, sweet scent of her fresh sweat makes me feral. I peel her shirt up just enough to bare her belly. My fingertips brush the bottom of her breasts. She's not wearing a bra, and my cock stiffens with another jolt of adrenaline. I ease her back a little, so she's still perched on my lap, but I can see my big, off-limit hands groping her under her bright pink running shirt.

She whimpers as I stroke her sweet flesh. "Sebastian, I need a shower."

"The fuck you do." I press my face to her trembling neck and breathe her in. My cock strains against my jeans, thick with the need to be inside her. To claim her and have her claim me in equal measure. I wish I could wear the mark of her scent on my body.

She's going to be the death of me, and I won't mind even a little. I rock my erection up into the soft, sweet cradle of her tight ass. My hands slide the rest of the way up her shirt, finally cupping the sweet, slight swells of her innocent tits. Her perfect, tiny breasts that I should never touch, never put my filthy mouth on, never suck on, and definitely never cover in my come.

I'm going to do all of that and more today because I cannot stop myself.

Ducking my head, I breathe in another lung full of her scent, then lick a careful circle around one nipple. The soft, puffy peak tightens, and I pull the newly hardened bud into my mouth. She arches her back as I suck on her flesh, her hips moving unconsciously to find my cock.

My sweet, innocent girl needs me inside her.

I let her grind as I taste my fill of one breast and then the other. I go back and forth until she tightens her fingers in my hair and pulls me off. Her mouth comes crashing down on mine, hungry and wet.

Together, we strip naked on the landing, and when we finally stand, still kissing, we're bare-assed, revealing all of ourselves for the first time.

She skims her hands over my chest and down the sides of my torso. "You're bigger naked." She blinks up at me shyly. "And you were already big."

My cock rises in the air between us, approving of the compliment. Lily wraps her fingers around it and slides her hand down to the base, making a bead of pre-come appear at the tip. "It's different like this. It feels real."

"We don't have to do anything you aren't comfortable with."

She twists in front of me, a lithe siren. "Oh, I want to do everything." She squeezes my dick firmly, then lets go. She walks up the stairs, turning just enough to give me another look at her mouth-watering nude profile. "Which way to the bedroom?"

"To the right." My voice sounds rough as I give the direction. I follow her, my gaze locked on the hypnotic sway of her slim hips.

She pauses in the doorway, long enough for me to catch up to her. I wrap my arms around her from behind, my cock nestled in the cleft of her bare bottom.

"This is your room," she whispers.

I duck my head so I can whisper back. Our secret. "Daddy's room."

She grins. "That, too."

I let her go, and she scampers forward, jumping onto the bed. I stalk after her in my own version of being playful. I fall on top of her, kissing her mouth first, then move down to her breasts again. Her belly. The bare stretch of skin above her slit, her perfect hairless mound, shaved for Daddy.

That's new. She had a little patch of hair that night at the truck stop and again in the library.

I move down her body, wanting to see all of her before I return to that delta between her legs, where I could lose myself for hours.

At her knees, I lick the curve of her thigh, then slide back up, her limbs falling open for me.

One day, I'll be able to do this all the time. In the future, this will be how I wake Lily up in the morning and the last thing I do before I tuck us in for the night.

Daddy's kisses where she likes them the most.

Special kisses for her beautiful pussy.

It's been too long since I've gazed upon her secret wonder, and I reacquaint myself with the delicate folds of her sex. I remember she likes a lick between her pussy lips, and she gasps the same way when I circle her clit.

"We have all evening. There's no rush here."

"No?" She smiles as I slide fingers along the wet path I've just licked, circling her tight entrance. "Maybe I'm eager to have you inside me. I've waited long enough."

"You've been very good."

"Patient?"

I chuckle and climb up her body, leaving my hand between her legs for her to rub against as I kiss her.

I don't stop until her lips are swollen and her legs wrap around me, her pussy wet against the length of my cock. In theory, she could roll her hips and take me inside her like this. But there's no just slipping into a woman who hasn't done this before.

I rear up between her legs and reach for a condom from the same pack I bought our first night together.

She watches, her lower lip caught between her teeth as I roll the protection down my length, which I then slide between her puffy pussy lips. She reaches down between us and wraps her hand around mine. We're both rubbing the tip between her folds, then dragging it up to her clit. She moans with each press against her hole, gasping at each flick up.

Those little gasps and moans are the only sound in my house, and it's the most erotic thing I've ever experienced.

As we move our bodies together, our hands become slick with her arousal. Her fingers slip around mine to the base of my cock.

In a mix of horror and deeply pleasing perversion, I realize she's rolling the condom off me with each stroke.

"Lily." The way I growl her name is a warning.

"Please?" She spreads her legs wide in wanton invitation, her words a dangerous drip of honey. "Just this once. I want to feel you inside me."

It won't be just this once. If she gives me a taste of her bare, that will be all I'll ever want. "I might want to plant my seed there, sweet girl. It's a dangerous game."

She shakes her head. "Not dangerous with you. You make me want all sorts of things." She licks her lips. "But it's not a good time for that." She blushes. "I mean, in my cycle."

Fuck. I buck my hips, letting her get rid of the protection.

"You have to be sure."

"Do you want it?"

I cover her with my entire body, imagining all the ways we'll do this in our lifetime. "Yes, Lily. I want to be inside you, nothing between us, very much."

She kisses me this time, hungry nibbles at my mouth, and I work my cock against her tight pussy again.

"Deeper," she begs as I rub against her entrance. "Just a bit more, Sebastian. I want it."

"I want it, too. Want to see my cock slide into this sweet pussy so much it hurts, but I can't hurt you. You gotta be ready. You're too little, and Daddy's too big."

"You're perfect," she gasps. "It feels good, I promise."

"Tell me, then. Tell me what you want." I feel my control slip away as the warm, wet opening sucks at my cock.

"Fuck me," she whispers. "Put your cock in me."

I groan and push in another inch, my balls pulling tight as I watch her pink hole stretch around my girth.

"More," she pants, but the look on her face tells me she's not ready.

"No," I protest.

"Daddy," she whines, and something inside me snaps. With a grunt, I tip her hips up, changing the angle, but she wraps her legs around my waist before I can stop her.

She cries out as my cock spears into her body. I brace myself against the bed, but it's done. I've buried my cook in her untouched pussy, and I've hurt her.

It feels so fucking good.

My tight virgin queen.

My sexy fucking secret.

Mine.

My Lily.

My good girl.

My pure girl, wrapped around my cock.

I roll my hips, forcing myself to ease back. I drag my length out an inch at a time, but it's not possible to go slowly enough, carefully enough.

She cries out again, a sound perilously close to *no*, and I freeze with my cock still halfway in her body.

"Shhh," I croon. I want her to tell me it's good, but I know it's not.

"It's too much." Her voice catches.

"I know."

She whimpers and tries to wrap her legs tighter around me, but that moves me inside her, and a tear rolls down her cheek.

I brace myself on my arms and lean in, kissing the tear away. "Don't move. Just take a minute and breathe. Let me make you feel good."

"You can't."

"I can." I kiss the corner of her mouth. "Shhh. Just listen to your body."

"My body is a lying bitch."

I grin. "I'll hold still and kiss you, and you find where it feels good."

"Nowhere."

I laugh.

"Don't laugh!"

"You wanted this." I lick from one corner of her bottom lip to the other, and on the way back, she sighs and shifts against me.

I lick deeper into her mouth, and she moves again.

She might make me come like this, her tiny movements on the head of my cock, and that's fine. Even if she makes me come, I can still keep fucking her. As tight as she is, I'll never lose my erection. Fine by me. I never want to leave her perfect pussy.

When she rolls her hips in a regular pattern, I shift my weight to one arm and use the other hand to touch her all over. I stroke her breasts, then her side. I squeeze her hip, curving around to her ass and letting my fingers drift between her cheeks. I rub against the nerve endings there just enough to light a new path of pleasure for her to discover.

She grinds faster against me, and I shift to the other side, squeezing her breast harder this time, then sliding my hand between us. I cover her belly, where I'll plant my seed, and then lower so my thumb can rub against her clit with each roll of our bodies.

It's a beautiful, slow start, but suddenly she's flying, discovering what her body can do, and she cries out my name.

"Sebastian…" It's music to my ears. Permission, too, and I take over. Matching the rhythm she set, I move in shallow little pulses, finally fucking her.

My cock drags in and out of her virgin pussy, and she loves it.

"It feels good," she gasps. "Thank God."

"I wasn't worried."

"You're too old to remember," she mutters.

I exhale a confession. "It's been a long time."

She makes a little sound, a squeak of surprise, and throws her arms around my neck, dragging me in for a kiss. "Good," she breathes against my mouth. "Welcome back to sex. It's very good with me."

I laugh out loud, then groan. Because, oh God, that's an understatement. "It's perfect. You're perfect."

She nods happily and runs her hands up and down between our bodies, touching me at first, then herself.

The sight of her little hands on her small breasts is enough to undo me. I growl as she squeezes her own flesh.

"Yes?"

I grunt and fuck her harder.

"Oh." It's a tiny sound. So fucking hot. Her eyes go wide. "Oh, yes. That."

Oh.

"Come for me," I beg at the same time as she tips her head back and cries out, her hands on her tits, my thumb on her clit.

My cock buried to the hilt in her perfect little body.

She gasps, her orgasm in my ear, then falls back against the bed, temporarily drained. She blinks up at me, her eyes wide as she catches her breath. "Don't stop. I want to feel you come, Daddy."

The way she says it unleashes the beast inside me. I growl and let loose, planting my hands on the mattress, my body hunching on top of hers, wild now. My thighs strain as I drive my hips, burying my cock deep inside her over and over again. Her wet little cunt is taking me easily now, and I can't stop myself. My balls pull tight, the corners of my vision go black, and I grunt out her name as the climax rips out of me.

My hands are clamped to her hips when I come to, and my cock is pulsing in her belly. She's so fucking little beneath me, and I swear and try to apologize, but she giggles and kisses my face.

"Wow," she whispers. "That was awesome."

My heart thumps painfully in my chest. Awesome is one word for it.

Fucking life-changing is another way to put it.

My Lily. My sweet girl. These feelings for her are deeply primal and shock me but in a good way. I feel alive for the first time in a long time. This is the feeling I was chasing on the highway. I was looking for Lily this whole time.

I clean her up and then tuck us under the blankets so she doesn't get cold. But cuddling only lasts long enough for recovery, and before long, we're making out again.

I pull her on top of me, all the way up, and after making sure she has a good hold on the headboard, I gently start licking her tender pussy. "You're not too sore?"

"Nope." She wriggles above me. "Can I tell you a secret?"

"Of course."

"I was hoping to find you today."

I pause my careful kissing. "That's very naughty."

"Does it make you want to spank me?"

I laugh and gently bite the inside of her thigh. "No."

She stretches above me in tempting perfection. "What would make Daddy want to spank me?"

I abandon my licking because I have a serious answer. And it makes my cock thicken even more against my thigh. "You not eating dinner."

"I'll miss it tonight." She lets go of the headboard, and I sit up. She immediately rolls over on my lap, presenting her bottom. "I came here knowing I might miss dinner."

"And how did you feel when you made that decision?"

"Reckless. Wild." Her body tightens up. "Scared but determined to find you, anyway."

We can't have her being scared. I squeeze one firm ass cheek, then the other, and my cock flexes beneath her. "Do you think you should have made a different decision?"

"You think I should wait until the term is over to spend time with you."

"It would be safest, but I won't tell you this was a mistake." I rub her flesh. "But maybe you need a reminder that it's good to be safe. Would you like a spanking? Because you were reckless instead of being safe, even though we both enjoyed it?"

She shrugs, indifferent teen attitude in full force. "I dunno."

I give her a light swat, barely a taste. "Honesty, please."

Her breath hitches, and she shifts in my lap. "I guess it sounds… interesting."

This time, I bring the flat of my palm down hard on the fleshiest part of her right cheek, instantly turning it red.

"Ouch!"

I rub a gentle circle over what I can imagine is smarting flesh. My hand tingles a bit, too. "How does that make you feel?"

"Like a silly fool," she mutters. She rocks her hips. "People like that?"

I grin. "I liked it."

She groans and presses her hips in the air. "Do it again,

then."

"Not if you don't want it."

"I do." She huffs a frustrated breath. "I need it." Another pause, and then her voice goes silky and pleading. "Daddy."

Fuck me.

I spank her again, softer this time, and she gasps. "Oh."

"Maybe I need to remind you why you wanted this. Do you remember?"

"Yes. I should be safe and careful."

I want to hear the name again. "Yes, *Daddy*. I should be safe and careful."

She bobs her head. "Yes, Daddy."

"If you don't eat, you get cranky. If you get cranky, you're more likely to talk back in class."

"I don't talk back in class!"

"Because I give you apples."

She twists in my lap and glares at me. "Seriously?"

"It works."

"But how—"

"I read your file, remember? And I'm good at reading between the lines. You aren't the first kid—" I cut myself off. "You aren't the first student to need that kind of care. But you are the first woman to make me want to be this explicit about it. And the only woman to be over my knee as we have this conversation, that's for damn sure."

"The apples aren't for everyone?"

"Of course they are."

Her lower lip pushes out in a pout. "Okay."

"Would you rather they were just for you?"

"I don't know!" She laughs and rolls away from me. I follow, covering her with my body. Eventually, we'll get to dinner. And then I need to send her scampering back to her dorm room before curfew.

But first, I need to kiss her and show her she is safe, wanted, and adored.

11
lily

I ARRIVE at Sunday brunch in the dining hall a changed person. Despite all my bluster that Sebastian had already taken my virginity—or maybe that it didn't even exist or wasn't even a real thing—yesterday was A Big Deal.

Can people tell that I'm different?

I feel different. Literally, because I'm deliciously sore in all the right places. I even have a bit of a bruise on my right butt cheek, which feels good when I push on it.

I shouldn't want it, but I can't wait to sneak over to his house again and get another spanking.

When I sit down at the table next to Stacey, I find out that won't happen.

Sebastian apparently has a new house guest—a visiting teacher from another private academy. I hate that so much because I'm already horny for him.

They introduced the guest just before I sauntered in late. Even though we're in a massive dining hall, I can feel Sebastian deliberately not making eye contact with me as Stacey fills me in on the details.

He knew last night that we wouldn't get another chance for a while.

"How long is this guy here?" I ask Stacey, who's eating oatmeal next to me.

"Usually, the visiting scholars stay for a few weeks."

Un-fucking-acceptable. I just discovered how good dick is, and now the headmaster's bedroom is off-limits?

I sulk all day. And then that night, for the first time since I've arrived here, he texts me.

I'm sorry I didn't tell you

I don't reply.

And the next day, when it comes time for my creative writing seminar, I refuse to make eye contact with him. As soon as class ends, I'm out of my seat, one of the first students out the door.

I avoid him until the end of the day. He's casually walking in the same direction as me when I step out of the dining hall.

"Miss Murphy." The only evidence he's not *that* casual about the conversation, or me, is a muscle tick in his temple.

"Headmaster."

He falls into step beside me.

"You're grumpy," he says under his breath.

I glance around. We're alone. "I'm horny. And you cock blocked me."

His eyebrows curve high. The headmaster in him desperately wants to caution me for the brazen language, but his mouth is curving into a reluctant smile because the man likes my smutty, wild mouth. He stops next to the path to my dorm and loosens his tie. End of the day. Time to take the headmaster outfit off.

I wish I could do it for him. "You better get back to your guest."

"He's in the library for a while." He shrugs out of his jacket, then slings that over one arm as he works on the buttons at his wrist.

What is this, a teacher version of a striptease?

"Just so you know, we've planned his visit for some time. I didn't tell you about it Saturday night because I honestly forgot." His voice, already low and private, drops another note. "I was consumed with wanting you."

"Oh." I scuff my toe on the ground. "Well, that's nice."

He finishes rolling up one shirt sleeve and starts on the other side. "Did you know that seniors over the age of eighteen can sign themselves out for the weekend with the headmaster's permission?"

Shock rolls through me. "No."

"Put in a request, Lily." He slings his jacket over his shoulder and takes a step in the direction of the forest. "And then we'll go away this weekend. Just the two of us."

12

sebastian

LILY IS WAITING for me next to a silver Lexus at the carpool lot next to the truck stop where we first met. When I pull in beside her, she grabs a bag from the back seat.

For the first time in a month and a half, she's dressed as she was when I first met her. Bright red lipstick, slicked straight hair, and that same mini skirt that short-circuited my brain. The woman I fell for at first sight.

I'm glad it's a nice day. Perfect for her bare little legs. Maybe the last nice week we get before the weather cools more.

My blood thickens in my veins, a heady need for her consuming me all over again. As soon as she's in the passenger seat of my Jeep, I slide my hands into her hair, holding her close so I can kiss her. When I pull back, she rubs a thumb over my lips.

"Did you mark me?" I ask huskily, not caring at all if she did.

She grins. "Just a tiny smudge. It's the good stuff." She glances around the car. "You drive more than a motorcycle."

"This is my winter set of wheels."

"Do I have to wait until the spring to ride on the back of your bike?"

I grin. "You sure do. I like that you're thinking about the spring, and me, though. That's nice."

She rolls her eyes. But she blushes, too.

"Where are we going?" she asks as I navigate the car onto the highway.

"I promised you brunch."

She looks at me with a mix of suspicion and delight. I'm going to spend the rest of my life delivering experiences that build the latter and doing my damnedest to get rid of her fear. "We can't go out in public."

"Not yet." Not here. "But we can have brunch in private."

She twists in the passenger seat, folding her leg beneath her as she turns to face me. Her skirt rides up in her lap, distracting me.

I reach across and tug it back down, letting my fingers graze her inner thigh.

She shivers. "How private?"

"Very."

"And... how far away is it?"

"Not far."

"You're just full of information," she snaps with no heat. Her eyes are sparkling.

I take her hand and squeeze her fingers. "Is it okay if it's a surprise?"

She nods.

"Did you tell anyone where you were going?"

She makes a strangled sound that turns into a coughing laugh. "Sort of."

"What did you say?"

"Uh..." She reaches across the gearshift and rests her hand on my thigh. "I said I was spending the weekend with my stepdad."

Blood pools low in my belly. I've memorized her file. Her parents are still married. Dysfunctionally so, but very much together.

There's no stepfather.

There's just me. I grunt. "Did you?"

"Mm-hmm."

"Did you say anything else?"

"I said he was my favorite person in the whole world, and I don't get to see him very often—"

"We see each other every day."

"This is my fantasy, shh." She giggles. "He travels a lot for work, but when he's in a city near me, he books a suite in a hotel so we can have some quality time."

"You didn't tell people that."

She laughs longer now, a lovely sweet lilt. "And corrupt some of your innocent students? No, of course not. That part is just for you."

I take the next exit off the highway. "A suite in a big city hotel, huh?"

"Yep."

"And what if your stepdad booked something a little more private?" I take the next turn, following the directions on my GPS.

"I don't care where we are," she whispers as I pull into the lane for the house I've rented. "As long as I get his undivided attention."

As soon as I park, she climbs over the gearshift and onto my lap. She will have all of my attention for the next thirty-six hours. We both need this. I smooth my hand over her hair as she buries her face in my neck.

"That fantasy is older than our relationship," she mutters. "For the record."

"Did you call him Daddy in your dreams?"

"No." A pause. "That's just for you."

I didn't have any specific fantasies like that one that pre-date Lily, but in hindsight, I can see how I was waiting for her. "When I saw you at the truck stop, you looked exactly like a woman I had seen before. In my dreams."

"Really?" She lifts her head, and her expression matches how I feel, too. Confused, amazed, and relieved. "This last month has been so hard. Even with the pull between us, you're the headmaster, and I'm a student. And I wanted to tell you…."

"Tell me everything. Anything." I grip her by the arms, then release her. God, I could be so rough, too rough with her if I'm not careful.

"I felt like, I can't tell you I met a guy who changed my world, and he's all I can think about. That's not something I can tell my *headmaster*."

"Then tell *me*. Tell Sebastian."

She makes a wounded noise, then kisses me instead. I let her because I want her mouth endlessly. I want her hands and her scent and body, too, but I want her heart more. I want her mind and her soul.

"Let's go inside," I murmur after she makes me hard. "But we'll keep talking."

The property is on the edge of a small lake, a two-and-a-half-story modern lake house. And we have it all to ourselves. Inside, there is an open concept main floor, with glass windows overlooking a deck and the water beyond. There's a hot tub, an indoor/outdoor fireplace, and an oversized sectional that looks perfect for both naps and fucking.

The rental company has even stocked the fridge as I requested.

Lily twirls around in the open space as I pull out the makings of our brunch. Strawberries, croissants, hard-boiled eggs, a tray of vegetables, various cheeses, and a few jars of fancy jams.

"Brunch, a month delayed." We curl up in the breakfast nook. "I have wanted this date with you since the moment I laid eyes on you."

She takes a big bite out of a juicy strawberry. "I didn't understand that at the time. I just wanted…."

I brush her pink cheek. "You're my horny little minx."

"There's something about you." She feeds me a berry next. "I still feel guilty, you know."

Guilt—now that's spank-worthy. I can't have my sweet girl feeling guilty. "Why?"

"I dunno. Maybe you should be with someone like Mrs. Taylor."

I blink at her. "Madeline?"

"Yes." Her lower lip trembles for a second, but her gaze is unwavering. She's honest, and that's all I've ever asked of her. "I could destroy you. We could get caught, and it will be my fault because I pushed you."

"We both need this. But I'm the only person who can decide about my career and assume that risk. Not you. That's on me." I rub my jaw. "I want to know more about why you think I should be with Mrs. Taylor, though."

"Sebastian." My name rolls off her lips like fire, with a bit of growl, and fuck me, but I like my girl jealous. "Don't make me say it."

"Say what?"

"She's perfect for you. Smart, your own age, pretty—"

"Married," I point out.

That stops her. "What?"

"Madeline is married. Where did you think the *Mrs.* came from?"

"Stacey said she was the campus mom, like…." She trails off in an embarrassed whisper. "Okay, I didn't think that through."

"I don't care about her age, or yours, for that matter. But for the record, you are also smart and pretty, which I appreciate. That's not why I love you, though."

"You… *love*… me?"

"I wasn't supposed to say that during brunch," I say gruffly.

She squeals and throws herself at me, and we abandon our food as I carry her up the stairs to the largest bedroom, which has a king-sized bed overlooking the lake.

I can't get enough of her. The sweet jiggle of her ass, the

sway of her young tits as she climbs on top of me. How gloriously, immediately wet she is for me, and the ease at which she sinks onto my throbbing cock.

She rides me slowly as I play with her sensitive nipples. Her weight leans into my hands, and I'm cupping her flesh, rubbing and squeezing and tugging to make her whine and grind against me.

I tell her to touch herself, to show me how she likes her clit rubbed, and I watch with rapt amazement as her pink slit slides up and down my rigid cock, her cream making us both glisten.

It doesn't take long before her thighs tremble, and she squeezes her eyes shut as her whole body shudders. Her climax squeezes me tight, milking my dripping dick straight into her body.

I feel the first spurt before I can think of pulling out. I lock my gaze to where her sex wraps around my pulsing cock. I watch as the engorged flesh twitches, and I should ease her off me, but my shaft stays firmly planted where it shouldn't be.

For the second time, I'm pouring my seed into her hot, tight, off-limits pussy. Her forbidden bare cunt, now red and swollen and full of my come.

No condom. *Again.* I should know better. I can't stop myself. And I want there to be consequences. I will make us a life where the fruit of our fucking is a blessing, not a curse.

It's only after we're both finished that I roll her onto her back and collapse between her legs. My head rests on her inner thigh, and I gaze in wonder at her bare mound, glistening with the product of both of our orgasms. Sticky, messy perfection.

"You like looking at me there," she murmurs, running her fingers through my hair.

I grunt. "Yeah."

"And you sound like a caveman when I point it out."

"I feel like a caveman when I'm doing it." I climb off the bed and sweep her into my arms. "Shower time, then I want to kick your butt at backgammon."

"Can I run around naked?"

"You sure can."

She wraps herself in a blanket for our game—which she wins. After, as I read in the den, she roams around the house without a stitch of clothing on.

We take a long nap in the afternoon, and when I wake up with her in my arms, I'm the happiest man in the world.

"This has been the best day ever," she tells me as we eat ice cream sandwiches at midnight, curled up together on the couch, all the lights in the house off so we can see the stars in the sky. "This is just so gorgeous."

It is. But all I can see is her. "The most amazing view," I agree, gazing at her profile.

She glances at me and grins. "Stop."

"Never. You have a little...." I wipe a drop of ice cream from the corner of her lips with my thumb.

She catches my wrist with her free hand, holding me in place as she takes my thumb into her mouth. "Yummy."

The sweet, gentle happiness in the middle of my chest right now has to be the best part of the weekend.

"I love you," she whispers, her eyes big and luminous, better than any night sky. "I can't wait until we can be together all the time."

I press my forehead against hers. "Soon, sweet girl. Very soon."

13
lily

I AM on my best behavior for the entire month of November. We sneak away for Thanksgiving when everyone else leaves campus, anyway. It's a reward for me not crawling into his bed on campus, and suddenly there are only three more weeks left in the term.

We've almost done it. By some small miracle, nobody has even caught a whiff of the secret connection between us. Of course, this moment, when everything actually feels safe and perfect and wonderful, is when the cracks appear.

Not in the form of my parents. Sebastian has kept his promise to me and put measures into place that ensure they stay far away. But in the unexpected form of a surprising discovery.

Stacey staring at Sebastian's forearms during class.

I get it. He's insanely hot.

But those are *my* forearms to stare at, not hers, and she never has before.

Later that same day, we meet in the dining hall to have snacks and read over each other's latest creative writing assignments.

"Can I tell you something?" Stacey asks.

I should say *no, don't tell me,* but I've never had a friend want to confide in me before. "Sure."

She blushes. "It's not school related."

I shrug and stretch my legs out on the chair in front of me. "I can keep a secret."

More than she'll ever know.

She takes a deep breath. "I think Mr. Craig might leave the school soon."

My feet fall off the chair and thunk against the floor. "What?"

"I overheard him in the office." Her pink cheeks turn red. "He's asked the board of governors to appoint Mrs. Taylor the interim headmaster. And I'm thinking of...." She drops her voice and glances around the empty hall. "Offering myself to him."

This time my *"What?"* is more of a screech. I can keep secrets, but I cannot keep chill.

She shifts nervously in her chair. "You can't tell anyone."

I'm telling Sebastian as soon as I can find him. "Yeah, of course." No, maybe I won't tell him. It depends on what she says next. He's an exception to my normal vault-like persona.

But also, people trusting me? That's a new and novel concept. I should be a good friend and keep her secret, right? Except... That's my boyfriend. Hands-fucking-off.

I press my lips together and try to just listen to her wild plan.

"He doesn't date. Ever. My sister came here before I did, and she said he maybe had a girlfriend when he first became head-master, and they broke up? Ever since, he's been all about the school. So if he's leaving, it might be because he's lonely, and honestly, he's the most fuckable man in the universe, so—"

"I didn't know you knew the word fuckable," I mutter.

She smiles shyly. "I keep it under wraps."

Yeah, me too. "Has he ever…" I swallow around the lump in my throat. "Shown that kind of interest in you?"

She makes a face. "No. But sex-starved men don't say no to eighteen-year-old virgins, right?"

She's not wrong. Bile rises in my throat. "And you like Mr. Craig enough to give him your virginity?"

"Hell yes. Have you seen his hands? I bet they would be so—"

I cut her off. I know all about his hands. "What if he turns you down? Won't that be awkward?"

"I'll do it right when he's leaving." She shifts in her seat, clearly pressing her thighs together. Oh, God. No.

He better turn her down.

He will.

The doubt makes my stomach tremble with a wave of gross, low-grade nausea.

"How about you?" she asks, her curiosity sharp like a knife.

"What about me?"

She gives me a knowing look. "You'd totally sleep with him, too, right? I can tell. You stare at him sometimes."

That's it, I'm skipping the next three weeks of class. Fuck. Fucking hell. Fuckstick. "Uh…"

"Is that too personal?" She shrugs. "Sorry."

But somehow, I'm the one who feels full of guilt and regret because it's probably normal to have a crush on your teacher and tell your friend about it. Less normal for your friend to not take part in that conversation honestly because she's secretly banging that teacher.

When people pile into the dining hall for dinner, I excuse myself and dash back to my room. I pull on leggings, a couple of layers on top, and head into the forest to squeeze in some exercise before losing the light.

I tell myself that I'm just going for a run. I'm not planning to go to his house, not in the middle of the week. He has evening responsibilities, and I need to respect that. By Christmas, he will be all mine with no limits. I can wait that long.

But then I come across him in a clearing, not near his house at all, and he's chopping wood.

It is not my fault that I spontaneously combust at the sight of my much older lover looking every inch a fucking lumberjack. As in, a lumberjack who should fuck me. A lumberjack who would look even better with my mouth wrapped around his dick or my pussy on his face.

A Daddy Lumberjack with a big, mean, monster cock.

I already knew I had a type—Sebastian. No other man has even remotely interested me. But Sebastian wearing a plaid shirt over a sweat-dampened, white T-shirt?

My panties evaporate. I step into the clearing, and he immediately pivots in my direction. The spark that arcs between us is immediate and intense. He huffs a breath and sets down his ax. "Lily."

That's it. He just says my name, and I know we're going to break the rules again because we can't help ourselves.

"I was just… for real…."

He picks up a pile of sticks and hands them to me. "It's okay. Come back with me. You can carry the kindling."

I trot after him with glee. He's got his ax over one shoulder and three split logs in the other arm. We're not that far from his house, I realize, when he takes a path on the other side of the clearing. He stacks the logs on top of a significant pile on the porch.

"You've been busy," I remark as he takes the kindling bundle and shoves it in a bucket.

He hauls me inside. "I had to find some way to burn off this energy I desperately wish I could use to make love to you."

The way he says that makes me melt. But the next thing he says makes me pout.

He lets go of me and leads the way into the kitchen instead of his bedroom. "What do you want for dinner?"

I pull off my long-sleeve outer layer top. "Daddy's cock."

"Lily." He gives me a stern look. "You're skipping dinner to be here. I need to feed you."

I shrug. "Whatever. And how do you know I skipped dinner?"

He doesn't explain. "What do you like?"

"Pasta?"

"Is that a question?" He pins his best headmaster look on me. "You know I'd prefer an honest answer."

"I do like pasta. A lot. With cheese is good."

"I have… spaghetti and elbow noodles. If you like cheese, I could do macaroni?"

"That's little kid food." I scoff. But it also sounds perfect, and my stomach grumbles at the same time.

He grins. "Well, I like it. Are you calling me a little kid?"

"No."

He hauls me into his body and kisses my pouting lower lip. "I think you're all woman, Lily. Never fear that. But there's nothing wrong with feeding the little kid inside you, too." His gaze darkens. "Do you want Daddy to make you macaroni while you tell him how your day was?"

I shouldn't want that. I shouldn't lean into our age gap that much. But I *do* want that, and he told me he wanted me to be honest. "Yes," I whisper. And then I start shaking.

"Hey." His touch instantly gentles, soothing as he lifts me onto the counter and wraps his arms around me. "It's okay."

"It's stupid."

"I don't even know what *it* is, but I promise it's not stupid." He kisses my temple, his breath warm and steady.

I'm horrified to realize I'm crying.

He smooths his hand over my back and waits. Just holding me. Not asking me again what *it* is, which is good. Because I don't know.

Dragging in a rough breath, I try to make sense of the weird feelings in my head. I want Sebastian to make me mac and cheese. It's sweet and kind and a little dirty, the way everything he does for me is. The way he's holding me right now, with his big body between my legs, his arms wrapped around me. Caging me. I can make that dirty, too.

I can make anything dirty.

And nothing remains sweet.

I hiccup.

But Sebastian makes all sorts of things sweet. He takes care of me, even as I try to push sex all the time.

He wants to fuck me and love me, and it's more than my heart can handle. Add a layer of *why the fuck does an eighteen-year-old get emotional about macaroni*, and I think I might be too much for him.

With a shaky voice, I repeat that thought for him. Bare honesty. That's what he wanted. "I'm worried I'm too much. For you."

He exhales. Long and slow. And then his arms tighten around me. "Never. You could be a wild storm of a teenager forever, and I will always love that. Your big feelings bring me out of my shell. Your impulsive, hungry needs give me something to do. I've been missing you in my life for a very long time. You're worried that you're too much? Lily, I worry that I'm not enough for you."

I gasp. "No."

"Right? That's how I feel about *you*. We're perfect for each other. It sometimes feels hard to believe, but that's when the outside world intrudes. When we're letting it inside our hearts."

"We shouldn't do that," I whisper, arching inside the tight confines of his arms. "I want you to make me macaroni. I want to call you Daddy, and be your teenager forever, and make you horny in a hundred inappropriate ways."

"A thousand."

"A million." I giggle.

He kisses me on my nose. "Can I cook now?"

"Yes."

He makes the macaroni from scratch, and I tell him I finished my lit review. "I'm meeting with Madeline tomorrow to go over the last part of my project. I need to keep my head down to work for two more weeks and then… done."

"Good girl."

I will never tire of hearing him say that to me.

"What else are you working on? One more creative writing assignment?"

That question reminds me of the conversation with Stacey, and I wince.

He immediately sets aside the spatula he was holding and gets right in front of me. "What is it?"

"I don't know if I can tell you. It's a student thing. But it's also kinda an us thing, and I'm…."

"Can you talk about it as a hypothetical?"

I take a deep breath. "Yeah. Okay. Uh… hypothetically, someone I know has a crush on my boyfriend."

Now it's his turn to wince. "A student?"

"Don't ask me who."

"I won't." He groans and kisses my mouth. "You know your boyfriend isn't interested in anyone other than you, right?"

"Yeah."

He kisses me again for good measure. "Good. Because Daddy doesn't want his little girl to be jealous. There's nobody else for him. Ever. But crushes are normal, and if anyone ever tried to act on that, I would politely and privately shut it down."

"Good."

He dishes up our food, and I follow him to the table.

After we eat, I crawl into his lap. "Do we have time for a quickie?"

He groans. "Yes."

I run ahead of him upstairs, peeling off my clothes.

He stops in the doorway to his bedroom and watches as I stretch out naked on his bed. He cups his erection through his jeans and growls something at me about being patient. I spread my legs and show him how wet I am instead.

It works.

As he crawls on top of me, he grabs a condom. I do the math and think about telling him I'm at the end of my cycle, and it's probably fine, but the condoms make a quickie easier. And they have another advantage, too—they help him fit in me better when we don't have a lot of time. We discovered that on our second weekend away, and oh my God, I love it.

He rubs his cock against me, the condom making it easier to push the thick, flared crown into my slick but tiny slit.

When I whine at the blunt intrusion, he makes this unholy sound that sends fire up my spine and makes me rock my hips. I love that I make him feel that good, that I've tapped into this deeply primal need in him to conquer my body. But it's not just the effect I have on him. *I* like the struggle, too. Why do I want more of that edge-of-pain plunge into my body? What does it do to my brain that lights up the *gimme more* button?

I don't understand why, but it just feels right. I want him to pin me down and make me take it. Just thinking about that floods my pussy with a wave of welcoming honey. I can feel it, my traitorous cunt, making room for him when my insides aren't sure yet. They haven't made room for Mr. Monster Cock, but here he is, seated deeply inside me.

Causing ache and ecstasy in equal measure.

I cry out at the bruising feel of him *inside* me, at the way my body feels like it's splitting in two as I fight to take his cock, and he kisses me gently.

"Shh, sweet girl. So good for Daddy."

I shudder and nod.

"You took it like a brave girl, and you made me feel so good."

That makes me smile even as I still tremble. "Mmm."

"I want you to feel good, too," he murmurs, rocking his hips as I did just a minute ago. His heavy length drags back and forth inside me, lighting up nerve endings along my entrance and deeper inside.

But this won't be a simple missionary fuck. Sebastian barely lets me catch my breath before he rolls me onto all fours, rearranging me with brute efficiency. He palms my ass, spreading my sex open for his appraisal. As my body reacts, trembling and turning wet under his gaze, he growls. "Your pussy is peeking out at me, begging to be licked." To prove his point, he buries his face between my legs and licks me obscenely. His next words are hot against my inner thigh. "Needing to be fucked, too. A needy pink slit, that's what you have."

I shake and nod, pressing my face to the bed. The next thing I hear is the sound of my body welcoming his heavy length. The wet sounds of fucking.

And then he slows down and starts saying the sweetest things, which undo me in a whole new way. "We're going to do this forever, sweet girl. I'll always make it good for you. God, you look so pretty like this. Daddy loves you."

I cry and come at the same time, and he pulls out, turning me over. I reach for his cock, mumbling that I'm fine, and it's fine, and I just love him, too. As I yank the condom off him and wrap my fingers around his bare shaft, he comes in my hands, warm seed all over my fingers, and then we're kissing and laughing.

It's messy and perfect.

After he cleans up my hands and belly, I reluctantly pull on my clothes and head into the darkness to finish my run. He follows at a distance, making sure I get back to the field behind the dorms, then he fades away.

The following morning, I wake up and feel *off*. The thought of going to the dining hall and dealing with the scent of all those breakfast foods mingling in the air makes my head spin.

And when I crawl out of bed and brushing my teeth makes me want to throw up, too?

I wouldn't be a star student if I couldn't figure out what that was a potential sign of.

Fuck me.

Did the headmaster knock me up?

14
sebastian

SOMETHING'S WRONG.

Lily misses the next creative writing seminar. I know she's on campus because people have seen her, but it's always that she "just left" or "is around here somewhere."

She's dodging me, and I don't like it.

We have two weeks to go.

We have a plan. I've given my notice, and Madeline Taylor has agreed to take over as the interim headmaster in the new year.

So why is my little girl hiding from me now?

But she doesn't hide forever. Just as I'm thinking of using my headmaster powers and summoning her to my office, she appears there the next morning. I hear her voice asking if I'm available, and I stalk to my office door, swinging it the rest of the way open as she approaches.

She doesn't make eye contact with me.

Instead, she carefully closes the door, then flattens herself against it, her face pale. "Sorry," she whispers. "I needed to see you."

I lower my voice so it's just for her. "I've missed you. What's wrong?"

I gesture for her to sit, but she doesn't move. I swallow around the now-familiar lump of regret in my throat. Not because we've complicated our relationship—which is wild and perfect and inevitable, because she's mine, and I'm hers. But that she can't come to this office and find the support she needs. That any other student would get.

"It's… uh…." She takes a long, steadying breath, then squares her shoulders. Her face is set in a new and unreadable expression. Not Stubborn Lily or Loving Lily, but… Resolved Lily.

Like she thinks I'm going to change her mind about something, and she doesn't want to give me a chance.

I don't like it.

Frowning, I lean in. "What is it?"

She moves around me toward my desk, then glances over her shoulder as if making sure the door is solidly closed. Then she grips her hands together, her knuckles turning white. "I'm—"

A knock interrupts her, and one of the student helpers of the day opens the door just as a fire alarm goes off in the distance. "Excuse me, Headmaster Craig. We have a situation in the quad."

I'm already moving, pausing next to Lily only long enough to squeeze her shoulder. *Later*, I try to tell her with my eyes.

She gives me a tight smile.

———

She's still in my office when I get back—curled up on the leather couch under the window, fast asleep. I lock the door so we won't be disturbed, then cover her with a blanket and go to my desk. Something tells me we might need to move up the timeline of Lily and Sebastian hitting the road. I don't know what's wrong, but whatever it is, we can make it right.

If my sweet girl isn't happy here, we'll need to leave. It's just that simple.

I'm halfway through reviewing the term grades already submitted when she wakes up with a start.

Throwing off the blanket, she swings her feet to the floor, but when she tries to stand, she goes pale. "Nope," she mutters. "Ugh. Gross."

Alarmed, I move to her side, crouching in front of her. "What's wrong? Are you sick? Should I call the school nurse?"

She shakes her head, her messy waves extra cute today, even with her pale, pinched expression. "I'm not sick. Not exactly."

I take a minute and search her face, but it's when I reach for her hand, and she trembles, pulling it toward her belly, that I figure it out.

"You're pregnant," I whisper.

She nods, and a tear slips down her cheek. "I'm having a baby."

"My baby."

"Yes."

My heart leaps in my chest. "That's fucking fantastic."

"What?"

Goddamn it. I need to contain my reaction. "Unless it isn't what you want...?"

"No, it is, but—" She blinks at me. Wide-eyed, unsure.

I wipe away her tear and kiss her mouth, not caring at all where we are or officially what my role is. "I put a baby in your belly?"

A tremulous smile spreads across her face. "You did."

"I'm the luckiest man in the world, Lily. Fucking hell."

"You swear a lot for a headmaster."

"I'm not a headmaster when I'm with you. I'm the man who got to put a baby in your belly."

"You keep saying that." She giggles, then covers my hand as we both stroke her still flat tummy.

"And I'm going to do it again, and again, and—" I cut myself off.

"I don't know. I want to go to school, too."

"You'll do that. I'll take care of the kids while you study your little heart out."

"You'd do that for me?"

"I'd do anything and everything to make your dreams come true." I shift my position so I'm properly on one knee in front of her. The solitaire ring I got her is carefully tucked away in my house, so for now, I can only offer her my promise. "Tell me this is your dream, too. Tell me you want to wear my ring and have my babies."

She nods. "I do."

There's a crash in the outer office, and I reluctantly stand up, knowing that I still need to do my job for a few more weeks.

Outside, I find the secretary chastising Stacey for making a mess of the student files. I hold my hands out and glance between the two of them. "Is everything all right?"

"Yes, sir," Stacey mutters, not meeting my gaze. "I—" She turns on her heel and runs out the door.

I exchange a look with the secretary, who mutters something about hissy fits. I wince apologetically, then go back into my office.

Lily is standing in front of the couch, the blanket in her hands. "What was it?"

I want to tell her it was nothing, convince her to go back to napping. But her expression warns me she won't be put off. "Stacey had a quarrel with—"

The blanket falls to her feet, forgotten. Her face is pale. "Stacey knows I'm pregnant. She heard me throwing up this morning. I swear, that girl has superhuman ears. And I bet she heard us talking just now. I have to find her."

15
lily

STACEY ISN'T in the outer office or the main hallway. I run out the back door and across the quad, making a beeline to our dorm. Her room is one floor up from mine, and when I get there, I find her door ajar.

I knock first, then push it open.

She's lying on her bed, facing the window.

"Can I come in?"

She doesn't answer. Which is not a no, I guess.

Stepping inside, I close the door behind me so we have some privacy. "Did you… hear something today?"

"Go away."

"I will. But can I say something first?"

She flops onto her back and glares at me. "You lied to me."

"I couldn't tell you the truth."

"You shouldn't be sleeping with him."

"You wanted to!"

"That was stupid!" She swipes at her eyes. "You're pregnant with his baby?"

"It's complicated."

"How?"

"We met before he was my headmaster," I whisper. "We've been keeping a secret this whole time. I couldn't tell you."

"This is so embarrassing." She groans. "You let me tell you I wanted to give him my virginity? How gross is that?"

"It's not. It was awkward AF, but it wasn't gross. And I felt bad. Oh my God, so much, and I couldn't tell you the truth."

"No, I get it." She gives me a rueful look. "You're having *his* baby?"

I nod. "Mm-hmm."

"Holy crap. I thought you slept with some townie and didn't know his name."

That makes me laugh so hard I snort. "When I met him, that's what I thought Sebastian was." I take a deep breath and decide to trust her. A leap of faith. "We met at a truck stop."

"Shut up." She shifts and makes room for me on her bed. "What? Tell me everything. Except the sex parts."

I sit next to her, my body a twist of emotions. Excited to confide in someone but nervous that to do so could throw everything into peril. "You can't tell anyone. I swear up and down that Sebastian would never have touched me if we hadn't met outside of school first."

She holds out her hand, baby finger extended. "Pinky swear. I was sad for a hot minute because I'm going through some kind of sexual awakening or something—"

"You're horny all the time?" When she nods, I lean in. "Me too, I get it. Don't worry, I'm sure you'll find someone to help you with that just as soon as you leave this place. I promise life will get better once you graduate."

Her eyes go wide. "Which you get to do in a few weeks. Are you the reason he's leaving at Christmas?"

Warmth blooms in my chest. "Yeah. I am."

It's the first time in my entire life anyone has ever put me first.

"Where are you going to go?"

"I don't know yet. Far away from here. We're going to settle somewhere near a college, and I'll enroll in a school after I have the baby."

"I can't believe it." She glances at my belly. "You're going to get fat."

I laugh out loud. "Maybe. That'll be okay."

"He'll love you no matter what." She says it wistfully. "I've heard him say that, too."

"How do you hear these things?"

She chews on her lower lip. "Uh… There's a hole in the office wall behind the filing cabinet. When the file drawers are open, it's like a wind tunnel of information."

"Holy shit."

"I never heard him talk about a woman like the way he talks about you. Except I didn't know it was you until today."

"Wow."

"Does he know… about my crush?"

I shake my head. "No. And that will be our secret forever."

She throws her arms around me. "You're such a lucky bitch."

I squeeze her into a tight hug. "Because I have a friend like you, maybe."

"Shut up."

I hug her even tighter. I will not shut up about being lucky to know her. Not ever. "I'll tell you where we land," I whisper in her ear. "If you feel like heading west at some point, too."

———

I don't go back to Sebastian's office. Instead, I go downstairs to my room and text him.

S is okay. I'm going into town for some fresh air.

I need to clear my head. But when I get to my car in the

parking lot, Sebastian is waiting for me. "You can't leave campus." His face is drawn tight with concern.

"Why not?"

"It's not safe."

"What's going on?"

"Come into my office; let me explain everything."

"Your office has a hole in the wall," I tell him. "Behind the filing cabinet. So anyone can overhear whatever we talk about in there if putting student files away."

He scrubs a hand over his face. "Great."

Instead of going inside, we walk around the main building to the quad. To anyone watching, we probably just look like a headmaster and student talking about school things. Nobody knows that he's explaining that my grandfather's lawyer has had to hire a private investigator to look into my parents' misuse of my trust fund resources.

And now they're angry—with me, who had no idea.

"They haven't tried to contact me," I point out.

"Your phone's been restricted to only accept incoming calls from a certain set of numbers."

I pull it out of my purse. "No, it's not...."

His face is tight, his arms taut as he crosses them over his chest. "It is now."

"Since when?"

"Thanksgiving."

"Sebastian!" I bark his name out loud, and he raises an eyebrow. Right. "Headmaster Craig," I say sarcastically. "That's something you should have told me. Or asked my permission to do."

"I didn't want you to worry."

"I'm not worried," I snap. Except... I shiver, and Sebastian rakes his gaze down my arms, which I wrap around myself.

"We can leave early. I'll pack us up tonight, and we can hit the road."

I glance around the beautiful green space. "This has been the best school experience I've ever had. I kind of want to finish it properly. And maybe not leave a scandal in our wake, you know?"

He nods. "Just don't leave campus. Promise me?"

"I promise."

"Two weeks, Lily. And then you're going to get one hell of a graduation present."

"What are you talking about?" I drop my voice to a whisper. "Is that a dirty thing? Because I like it."

He chuckles. "Oh, well, yes. You'll get the celebration of your life that night. Our first night on the road. Daddy's going to book the best hotel suite he can find. But no..." he trails off, his eyes warm. "There will be a surprise. That's all I'm saying. So get your work done and prepare to be rewarded."

16
sebastian

THE LAST DAY of term is always a joyous one. It's a bittersweet one this year, too, because it's my last day as a teacher.

I've decided not to look for a new school position when Lily and I go out West. I don't want to explain our relationship in anything but the most glowing, perfect terms. I refuse to feel shame for how much I love her or risk putting her in the spotlight.

I may teach online or at a postsecondary school. Being a college instructor has a lot of appeal. But most of all, I want to spend the next six months tending to my wife-to-be as she blossoms with our child inside her.

That's what is next.

Today, though, I have the smallest graduation in Edgewood Academy's history to preside over. We have one graduate, one cap and gown to organize, and there is only one guest: her grandfather's lawyer, who came to campus.

We do it at the end of the creative writing seminar. Eight students, one headmaster, and a little parade to the auditorium, where that lawyer now sits in the front row.

Lily's classmates applaud as she crosses the stage, shakes my hand, and receives her diploma.

I follow her down the stairs, then introduce her to her grandfather's attorney, who draws her to the side.

"Miss Murphy, it is my pleasure to inform you that you have met the conditions of your trust fund. Your headmaster and I have communicated about the irregular circumstances of your previous allowance dispersal. I want to assure you that you will now begin receiving your annual allowance directly. When you graduate from college, you will get access to the entire trust. There are some documents for you to sign."

Lily glances at me, and I point them to a room just off the stage.

Once we're in the private space, he details the current balance on the accounts and the payment options. All I can see is Lily's face, her eyes wide as saucers, as she realizes just how much money is in her inheritance.

Money her parents can never touch. That will provide for her and her children for the rest of her life. I will do that, too, but she doesn't *need* me. She's an incredibly wealthy young woman in her own right.

My greatest hope is that she will *want* me by her side, but it will always be her choice to stay with this old guy because he loves her with all of his heart.

Once the legalities are out of the way, I leave her to celebrate with her classmates. I planned the rest of the afternoon out in exacting detail: she will take her time packing up her room. I'll finish putting my belongings in my Jeep. I've already shipped my bike to California. And as soon as the last student leaves campus today, she's hopping in my passenger seat, and we're hitting the highway. She's selling her car, wanting nothing to do with that memory of how her parents doled out small parts of a trust that was rightfully hers all along.

My last stop before going to my house is the office. Madeline is drinking a glass of sherry on my couch.

"Helping yourself already?"

She grins and checks her watch. "My husband is picking me up today, but I had a few minutes to say goodbye."

"I hope you enjoy your time as head of the school."

"Did you?" She tilts her head to the side. "Now that you're no longer my boss, I think I can say out loud that I wonder if you did."

I nod. "At one time, it was the most meaningful part of my life."

"And now you're on to greener pastures." She searches my face for a clue, but that's my secret.

Lily's and mine.

I'm her man, her partner, her mate for life. Everything else pales compared to the fact that we're going to have a family together.

"I am," I say simply.

"Good luck."

I won't need luck. I have love. But I thank her anyway, gather the last of my personal effects, and head into the forest.

17
lily

IT'S dark when we pull off the highway. Nobody saw us leave Edgewood together—a Christmas miracle—and now it's our first night on the road.

We're taking our time. We should be in California by New Year's Eve, so we'll start the new year in our new home state. But for the next week, it's a road trip with my Daddy. A week of truck stops and creating naughty memories to keep us warm for the rest of our life together.

"Why don't you go inside and grab some juice while I fuel up." Sebastian drops his hand to my knee and squeezes. Maybe he's thinking of the night we met, too.

Inside, I buy a pack of strawberry-flavored bubble gum and pop a piece in my mouth as I saunter down the juice and soda aisle.

Out the window, I see him finish at the pump and move the Jeep in front of the store.

My whole body tingles with awareness as he saunters inside. Tall, broad-shouldered, and wrapped in a leather jacket that makes my panties wet. Maybe it'll smell like me by the time we're done in the shower stall.

He stalks over to me. This time, there's no conversation. He holds my gaze, hot and bright and electric, as he grabs a Coke for himself. My hands tremble as I select an orange juice. He takes it from me, our fingers brushing, then jerks his head to the shower stalls.

This time, he doesn't buy a pack of condoms.

This time, he goes straight to perching me on the edge of the counter. I'm wearing thick tights under my skirt, and we work together to pull them down my hips. As soon as my pussy is accessible, he's pawing at me, his fingers big and thick and urgent.

"Your sweet little pussy smells so good." He grunts and pushes my legs up against my torso and tugs my skimpy underwear to the side. I'm a panting mess, a mix of horny girl and constricting clothes. I can barely move, but it doesn't matter because he finds my slit easily and then my slippery hole, ready and eager for his cock.

We both cry out as he slides one finger into me, then two.

"I saw you as soon as I stepped inside the doors." His voice is rough as he whispers in my ear. "Knew I wanted to bury my face between your innocent legs. Needed to hear the way you sound when you come on Daddy's face. That was all I wanted to do to you. I took one look at you and knew you were too innocent for my cock. But I take that back now because this horny cunt needs it, doesn't she?"

I whimper and nod my head. "Yes, Daddy."

"Good girl. So fucking brave. Tell me you need me to fuck you."

"Put it in me," I plead. "Fuck me. I need it. I need you."

"We're going to do this every night. In truck stops all across America, I'm going to mark you as mine. Get my Daddy dick covered in your scent so when we check-in at the nice hotels, they know I'm yours. Then I'll fuck you all over again when it's just you and Daddy alone in the hotel room."

My fantasy, and his fantasy, smashed together. Over and over again.

There's a heavy clunk as his belt buckle hits the edge of the counter. Then his cock is free, and he's rubbing it against my hole.

"Gonna put a baby in you," he growls.

He already did. I smile and throw my head back. His mouth falls to the stretch of bare skin there, sucking at my flesh as he works himself in and out of my tight little pussy. Each thick thrust makes me cry out, wanting more. Once upon a time, I worried this would hurt. Now I want it to, just a bit. I want this big beast of a man to claim me as his every single time.

It doesn't take long for him to make me come. The fifth complete thrust, that deep feeling of him filling me to the brim, and I shudder around him. He follows me over the brink, muttering my name and the most beautiful string of filthy words under his breath as his cock swells and spurts inside me.

Exactly what I needed.

He presses his forehead against mine. We're both hot, sweaty messes. "You're so fucking beautiful," he whispers as I grin at him. "And all mine."

"I love you," I whisper back.

He captures my mouth hungrily, and I feel him harden inside me again.

With a dark glance between us, he growls. "Oh, I love you too, sweet girl. Hang on tight."

And I do.

epilogue

ten years later

lily

"YOUR HUSBAND IS SO good with the boys," my neighbor says to me as I lean against her porch, drinking the glass of lemonade she offered me when she saw us playing outside.

She took pity on the heavily pregnant woman, and the heavily pregnant woman happily accepted the generosity.

"He's a great dad." I brush a sticky strand of hair off my cheek.

"He'll take good care of you when you're home after the baby arrives." She keeps going on about things I already know but never tire of hearing.

Adoration for Sebastian is a very understandable situation.

My husband is an absolute gem. A pillar in our community, Conception Ridge. A brilliant father, a caring friend. A college administrator. And after everyone goes to sleep, when it's just the two of us, he's still the deeply dirty Daddy to my eternally feisty inner teenager.

I'll be thirty next year. A grown-up with a career, three beautiful kids, and a fourth son on the way.

Daddy keeps knocking me up, something he started even before he was my husband.

I'm Lily Craig now, legally. I even changed my first name. It would be hard for my parents to find me, even if they had the resources to try—which they don't.

One of the philanthropic causes I support is a charity that helps teens emancipate themselves from their parents. I wish I had known that was an option, but a lot has changed since I was a kid. There's more information available online now.

As if he can sense I'm thinking about that time long ago, Sebastian looks up and catches me watching him. He tosses the football to our oldest one more time, then tells the kids it's time to head inside to clean up for dinner.

"Mommy needs a rest," he says as he saunters over. I love the way the sunshine makes the silver in his hair glint.

"Do I?" I finish my lemonade and hand the glass back to our neighbor, who winks at me. "I guess I do."

"You take good care of that one," she says to my husband.

He wraps his arm around me. "I always do."

Ten minutes later, he's peeling my panties down my thighs.

I tumble back on the bed and giggle as he kisses his way to where I'm already wet for him.

"Shhh." He lifts his head from between my legs. "Be quiet for Daddy."

I blush and bite my lip, nodding. Then I need to cover my mouth with my hand as he goes to town, licking and sucking up all my juices, working his way to my eager clit. He swirls his tongue around the hard bud, then kisses it with his open mouth, a dirty move that gives him more slickness every time. It's the combination of his hot breath and his talented tongue. Like Daddy is both licking me and looking at me at the same time.

A decade in, and our shared desires have never waned.
I roll onto all fours and shamelessly present myself for him.
I need him inside me—now. Again.
Always.

above the shop

a Conception Ridge novel

above the shop

He was my mom's high school boyfriend.

I have seventeen dollars to my name and a one-way bus ticket to my new college town—two months early. Oh, and the name of a man I've never met scrawled on a piece of paper. Henry Wilde.

But when I show up on his doorstep, he has no idea that my mom said I could stay with him. And he only has one bed.

It's eight weeks until I can move onto campus.

Eight weeks of living with him above his barbershop. So I'm going to make myself useful. Help him out and try not to pester him about what it will be like at college. Because this home-schooled girl has a lot of questions, but they're not appropriate for my de facto guardian. Not even if we're both consenting adults…

1
summer

THE BARBERSHOP IS ONLY a block from the bus station. But when I arrive, there's a sign in the window.

Closed, Back Soon.

I stay in the shade of the brightly colored awning covering the front door and glance up and down Main Street.

This is my new home for the next four years. I'm attending Ridge College on a full scholarship, and in eight weeks, I'll move onto campus. So why am I here almost two months early? It's a great question. One I asked my mother repeatedly when she bought me a one-way bus ticket to my future college town and bundled me out of California with a hundred and fifty dollars in my pocket.

She promises she'll send more money soon. But until then, I have the name of her friend I can stay with. A barber. Her ex-boyfriend, sort of. From once upon a time, before she had me.

Henry Wilde.

The only man my mama ever trusted, apparently.

I squint, trying to determine if I can see the college in the distance. I'd like to put my bags in the barbershop before exploring, but I am so excited to see the campus. This is my first time in Conception Ridge.

Where, ironically, I was conceived nineteen years ago. Not a fact most people know about themselves, but Mama and I have a weird relationship. I know way too much about some things and not nearly enough about other things. She homeschooled me so I wouldn't get into the same kind of trouble she did, but now that I'm eighteen, it's time for me to go to college. And for my mom to have her freedom, too.

She has the most beautiful singing voice, and right now, she's getting on a cruise ship to work as a lounge singer. I'm proud of her.

"Are you looking for a haircut, miss?"

I spin, my attention changing from the college in the distance to a man who came out of nowhere. Or maybe, if the takeout coffee cup in his hand is any clue, from the coffee shop next to the bus station.

He's tall and burly, all chest and close-cropped beard. Dark eyes and thick arms. Thick thighs, too, when I drop my gaze because looking at him is a lot to take in.

This hulking guy is the only man my mother ever trusted? No. I scurry down the steps and into the blazing sun.

He gives me a look like I'm the strange one—obviously. I'm used to that. He's not wrong. Then he moves around me and unlocks the barbershop.

Once the door is open and he's changed the sign around to a cheery *Open*, he holds it for me like he knows I need to follow him inside.

Even though I don't.

"Are you Henry?"

"Sure am."

"I'm Jennifer Figaro's daughter."

He rocks back on his heels. "That's a name I haven't heard in a while."

"Didn't she tell you I was coming?" Panic rises in my throat.

His thick brows pull together. "Come on in."

I have a terrible feeling I'm not going to like what he says next. My heart sinks as I follow him inside.

It's a retro-looking place. In L.A., I'd say it was a deliberate aesthetic. But in this town, it might just be original. Two brown, leather barber chairs dominate the space in front of a long mirror. There's a beaded curtain over a door in the back and a counter with a cash register.

A very small waiting area completes the space.

It's too small for him.

Definitely too small for both of us. I can't breathe.

"Whoa," he says quietly, moving fast for a big man. "No fainting, little girl." He reaches for me, and I stumble back.

"I'm fine." I'm not. I feel lightheaded, but I'm not going to faint in a strange place with this very strange man who has the biggest hands I've ever seen.

I drop my bags on the floor and stumble to the creaky, plastic chairs in the waiting area.

"What's your name, daughter of Jennifer Figaro?"

"Summer."

Out of the corner of my eye, I see him approach again, his big body folding into the furthest plastic chair. It creaks as he spreads his legs wide and leans forward, forearms braced against his thighs. It's like he's trying to make himself small enough to sit next to me and not be. . . too big.

Like he's being extra careful because he has to give me bad news.

"You didn't know I was coming." It's a statement because I don't need him to confirm it as true.

He shakes his head anyway. "Sorry, miss. This is a surprise to me."

"Mama said she would email you. It was on her to-do list all week."

"Where's your mom now?"

"On a cruise ship."

"She went on vacation and dropped you in Oregon?"

"I took a bus. And it's not a vacation. She's working on the ship."

"Who's taking care of you?"

I sit up straighter, affronted. "Excuse me, I'm eighteen. I can take care of myself." Except for the pesky minor detail of not having a job or money because Mama said I could stay with Henry until school started. "I'm going to get a job here, and then I start at the college in September."

He nods slowly. "Uh-huh."

"Would you mind if I leave my bags here for the day? I'm going to. . ." I glance outside. Probably go cry in a park or something. "I'm going to look for a job and a place to stay today, and it would be easier if I didn't have to carry my stuff with me."

"Of course." He wipes his hand over his face. "Jennifer's little girl is ready for college? Time flies."

"Mama said she emailed you."

"She does, from time to time. But this detail seems to have slipped through the cracks. What kind of job are you looking for? Conception Ridge isn't that big. The college is the biggest employer, and it's quiet over the summer."

"I don't know." I ignore the swell of panic in my chest. "I can do anything. I'm a hard worker."

"Hey. It's okay. I bet you are." His hand shoves into his hair now, and I wonder if there's something wrong with him. Like my presence is giving him a headache.

I move toward the door.

"Wait." He gives me a pained look. Definitely a headache. "You can stay here. You don't need to look for a place to live. Looking for a job will be hard enough. Can you wait here for five minutes? I need to go and get the apartment ready for you. It won't take long—I'm not a slob."

"Oh. Okay."

"If anyone comes in, tell them I'll be right back."

I nod mutely as he disappears through the beaded curtain. I can see the shape of him turn a corner and disappear.

Up a flight of stairs. I guess he must live up there.

Above the shop.

Sure enough, I hear his footsteps. To the front of the building, then back and forth a bit, before returning.

"Nobody came in," I report when he's in front of me again.

He nods and picks up my suitcase.

I follow him through the curtain, where there's a staircase to the left and a short hallway to the right leading to a back door. Upstairs, there's a small kitchen, a decent-sized living room with two couches, a wall of bookcases, and a TV hanging next to a window overlooking the alley behind the shop.

A small hallway toward the front of the building goes to a bedroom and a bathroom behind the kitchen. Both have frosted windows that, I guess, look onto the street I was standing on less than half an hour ago. The whole space is big and bright, with tall ceilings, and it's the nicest apartment I've ever been in.

I didn't expect that.

I also didn't expect it to only have one bed.

"You'll sleep in here," Henry says, putting my suitcase on a bench under the window in the bedroom. "I'll sleep on the couch out there."

"No," I gasp. "I can't kick you out of your room."

"It's fine." His mouth quirks up at the corner. "I fall asleep on the couch half the time anyway. And I'll wake up earlier than you, I expect."

"I can wake up early." I feel a little lost. And grateful, but also, embarrassed. "Henry, I don't want to put you out. I really don't. This was terrible of my mother to suggest. I should have stayed in L.A. and gotten a job there for the summer."

"Your mama was always a dreamer. That's okay. I bet she had a good reason for wanting you to come here early."

Yeah, because she's worried about me making the same mistake she did—getting knocked up before I even get to college. But that's not going to happen. I've never dated anyone. Never kissed a boy.

I don't even want to. I just want to curl up in a ball and wake up on the first day of college, when I can move into my dorm room and begin the next stage of my life.

"You won't even notice that I'm here," I promise him. "I'll make myself useful and invisible."

He gives me a funny smile. "Hard to be both of those at the same time."

"I might surprise you." But even as I say it, I'm not so sure. There's something about the way his gaze bores into me, searching my face, that makes me worry there's no way I'll be invisible around Henry.

Can I survive two months of having a man like him be this *aware* of me? When that intense assessment sears my skin and makes me tremble on the inside. . .

Oh.

Well, hello, inconvenient hormones. I cut my attention away from him. "I might lie down—"

"I need to get back downstairs," he says brusquely.

"Thanks," I whisper as I scurry into his bedroom—his *bedroom*—and quietly flop on top of the blankets.

His footsteps are slow down the stars. Careful.

My heart rate is the opposite—wild and reckless and fast— and doesn't start to settle until I imagine he's well through the beaded curtain.

My mom's high school boyfriend—a big, burly man twice my age—should not be the first man to stir *feelings* inside me. I know that. But now, all I can see as I close my eyes is his hot, scrutinizing gaze. The rest of him is seared on my retinas, too but in a fuzzier way.

He's big.

Thick through the chest and then solid all the way down. Nothing like men in my mother's music circles. Nothing like the men at the pool I used to swim at.

I'm downright little compared to Henry, and that difference makes my thighs ache.

I want him on top of me.

It's a shocking thought. And then followed by an even worse idea.

I want him inside me.

No.

Mama would kill me. I cannot touch Henry. I cannot have sex—with anyone, but especially not the guardian she's sent me to stay with.

I cannot repeat her mistakes, even if *I* am that mistake, and I don't feel like a mistake at all.

2
henry

FOR THE FIRST eleven hours of having a house guest, I convince myself it's going to be just fine.

Summer's a bit of a mouse. How much of an inconvenience could she be while trying to be absolutely still in my space? I let her get settled in my room while I go back downstairs and work for the afternoon. When I return, she's asleep on the bed. On top of the blankets, shoes off and neatly stacked against the wall.

I pull a light blanket over her, and she murmurs thanks in her sleep.

A sweet little mouse. A polite little girl in a grown-up body.

I'm still shook at the idea of my high school crush having a daughter who is now older than Jennifer was when I saw her last. Yes, we've kept in touch, but I don't do social media. We exchange emails and the odd letter, and she's mentioned Summer in passing, but always in the royal *we*. As if Summer was a part of her. Which she was.

And now here she is, in my bed, while I cook her dinner.

I don't know what she likes, so I make a simple tomato pasta, some sausages on the side, and a green salad.

When she wakes up and comes out of my room, hair all

mussed up and cheeks flushed from sleep, she gives me a shy smile. "Something smells good."

I tell her what I'm cooking, and she rubs her tummy.

How did someone this innocent and adorable come out of L.A. and the sometimes wild life Jennifer lived in the music scene? "So your mom is working on a cruise ship, huh?"

"Yeah." She glances at her phone. "I sent her an email letting her know you didn't know I was coming, but it's worked out. It's a very. . . Mom thing to do. She's flighty. But she means well."

"I get it. It's fine." And it is, but I still don't understand exactly how this all came to be.

Summer frowns at me. "Why are you looking at me like that?"

I jerk my attention back to the food, setting it up so she can serve herself. I don't entertain often, and never someone so young—or direct. "Uh. . ." I wince. "How was I looking at you?"

"Like I'm a puzzle you're trying to solve."

Fuck me. I laugh a little. "I guess because you *are* a puzzle I'm trying to figure out. Sorry if it was that obvious. You're just. . . not what I expected."

"Nothing like my mom?"

"Yeah."

"That's by design." She moves closer, and I hand her a plate.

"What do you mean?"

"Some people would say my mom sheltered me, but that's not exactly it. She *told* me what life was like. And she tried to protect me from it as much as possible, precisely because she. . ." Summer sighs. "She struggles sometimes. Which I think you know about."

"Yep, I think I do." We plate up our dinner, then I gesture to the stools at the island or over to the couch. "Those are our options for dinner. Pick your seating choice."

She pulls up a stool at the island and digs in. The sounds she makes as she eats—happy little hums and the occasional groan of delight—are. . . well, they could be filthy, coming out of another mouth, but I won't think of them like that. If things had gone differently, I could have been her father. Even though I'm not, I'm old enough to be.

So her little sounds are *not* filthy. They're fun.

She's fun, and by the time dinner is over, we're both laughing as we compare stories about her mom.

After we wash up and put the leftovers away, I lean against the counter and try to make myself look as relaxed and easygoing as a six-foot-four burly fucker can look. "Listen, Summer. . . It really is fine that you're here. I know how hard it was for your mom to raise you all by herself, and if I can help out for the summer, I'm happy to be of service to her. And you."

Her face lights up. "Thank you. And I, in turn, will be helpful to you. I promise."

———

It's a bit strange hearing someone else get settled for the night in my apartment that has been my solitary space for so long.

Summer takes the washroom first, and once she's done brushing her teeth, she gives me a sparkling good night and retreats to my bedroom, closing the door between us.

Earlier today, I moved some of my clothes to the closet in the hallway. I retrieve a pair of sleep pants I bought a few winters ago when it was extra cold and change in the bathroom.

Then I make myself a bed on the couch, turn out the lights in the rest of the apartment, and grab my tablet. But sleep proves elusive. Even as I flip through news stories and webcomics, my thoughts race with how to make this work. To the best of my knowledge, there aren't any vacant apartments above the other stores on Main Street. I'll look into that as a backup option just in case the next eight weeks get to be too much.

A dark, troubling thought threatens to form itself around what *too much* might be. I push it away.

This is going to be just fine.

She's a sweet girl.

It was nice to have someone to laugh with over dinner. She might be a help in the shop, too.

You've never wanted help before.

Well, I didn't have Summer sleeping in my bed, being grateful as fuck for some basic human decency before, either.

I close my eyes and set the tablet down on my chest, making my mind blank. I'm thinking about counting sheep when I hear the bedroom door creak open. I crack one eye open to make sure she's all right.

The dimly lit hallway is in my line of sight. Summer probably doesn't realize this as she pads across the hallway to the bathroom wearing nothing but a cropped T-shirt and a tiny scrap of white cotton, sort of passing for panties, stretched across her hips.

As she steps into the bathroom and turns on the light, the shape of her body is perfectly silhouetted for the basest part of my primal animal brain to absorb like a perverted record. Permanently seared on my retinas.

Curvy hips.

A tight waist.

A round little belly above her panties. Thick thighs that taper down to long, toned calves.

Her cropped top disguises her breasts, but my brain fills in a best guess at the perfect shape of them, too.

And just like that, my cock is thick, rising against my hand.

No.

But yes. Fuck. *Yes.* Carefully blanked-out thoughts roar to life in my mind, fully formed and clearly dangerous. What if being around this goddess of a young woman gets to be too much? What if Henry Wilde's imagination gets to be too much?

What if I *want* too much of her flesh, her body, her sweet, virginal perfection?

———

"I'll take you shopping today," I tell Summer over breakfast. She's wearing a sundress that falls all the way to the floor, a flowery drape of fabric that should be demure, but one strap is threatening to slide off her shoulder, and I can see the swells of the top of her breasts.

I'm not supposed to look at her breasts.

Not supposed to see that press of flesh and remember how juicy her ass looked in the hallway, all of her flesh seemingly made for sinking teeth into.

"I don't need anything," she says, her gaze wary.

I'm making her nervous. "You need pajamas."

She frowns. "Why?"

Because the first thing I did this morning was to check the local rental board, and there's no apartment I can sub-let for two months. My first plan—get her another place to stay—has already failed.

So it's on to plan number two.

"We're sharing this small space for the next two months, and you'll be sharing spaces when you go to the college dorms, too. Bathrooms in hallways, that sort of thing."

Her confused look just grows. "So?"

"You can't walk around in. . . uh. . ." My mouth goes dry. "Maybe a bathrobe to put on if you don't want pajamas."

She blinks at me.

"I saw you last night. In the hall. Wearing just your panties and, uh, a shirt."

"Oh." Her eyes go wide. "I thought you were asleep."

"I was drifting off." A lie.

"I like PJs." She shrugs. "But I don't want you to buy me anything. I'm already enough of an inconvenience."

"How about you work for me for a few hours? Then I'm not buying you anything. I'm paying you for your time, and you can use that money instead."

She brightens right up. "Okay."

Before we open the shop, I show her where the broom and dustpan are and how to use the cash register. If she can sweep up and ring customers out, that would actually be a big help.

And sure enough, eight hours later, when I flip the sign in the window around to *Closed*, the shop is already spotless. There's no need to spend the next hour cleaning it myself, and that right there is a gift from Summer.

I go to the till, close it out for the night, and take the cash tray upstairs.

She follows along, perching on the couch as I quickly reconcile the receipts—all correct, all monies accounted for—and put the cash in my safe. All of it except two hundred dollars, which I hand to her.

Her eyes go as wide as saucers. "I can't take this."

"You need some clothes. Even if we go to Walmart, you'll need at least this much."

"Walmart's fine." She gives me a small smile. "Thank you. I'll work extra-hard for you next week."

"I know you will." And I do. From the moment Summer walked into my shop, there's just been something about her that makes me trust her. She's guileless and eager.

"Do you want to grab something to eat on the way?"

She catches her bottom lip between her teeth and worries it for a moment before replying. "I don't want—"

"I like to go The Roadhouse a few nights a week. It's not expensive. You're not— Summer, your mama sent you here because she knew I could take care of you. All right? I can give you money for shopping *and* take you out for dinner. More than once, even. So no more protesting."

She blushes. "All right. Thank you. I'll just grab a sweater."

She disappears into the bedroom and returns with a little

white cardigan over her sundress. A purse is slung across her body. The way she clutches it, I imagine her earnings are tucked safely inside.

Something in my chest squeezes tight, and my voice is gruff when I tell her my truck is parked out back.

It's a short drive to the edge of town, where the big box stores get a better tax rate on the other side of the freeway. The Roadhouse is just this side of the highway and a popular stop for travelers and locals alike.

The parking lot is full. Usually, I don't care because I'll sit at the bar, but it occurs to me that sweet little Summer might not want to rub elbows with the usual crowd here.

"If they don't have a table for us, we can go to one of the chain restaurants on the other side of the freeway."

She shrugs. "This is great."

Inside, my unease grows as every male in the place seems to look our way and check out my new ward.

I scowl at the way they look at her like she's ripe for the picking. She's oblivious, but I'm not, and they need to know she's off-limits. I wrap my arm around her shoulders and turn us toward the hostess stand, putting my big, burly don't-fuck-with-me body between her and their hungry eyes.

"We need a booth," I bark when one of the waitresses swings by.

"Hey, Henry," she says smoothly. "We're a bit full up at the moment."

Behind her, I see a family pack up, clearing a table against the window. "Or that table will work."

"Okay, okay. You're usually a stool at the bar guy, but I guess if you have your niece with you. . ." She trails off.

"I'm not his niece," Summer offers.

I tighten my grip on her shoulders. She's not wrong to correct the assumption. But it's a little early in her return to Conception Ridge to start spelling out for the world who she is and why she's staying with me.

Luckily this waitress isn't a nosy gossip. She just nods, then grabs two menus. "Follow me, then."

After we're seated, Summer glances around.

"This place is nice," she says happily.

All I can see are the assholes at the bar who sized her up and saw fresh meat. "It can be dangerous. Don't come here without me."

She laughs. "Why would I want to do that?"

I grunt. Because in two months, you'll move into the dorms, and I won't be able to protect you from old men like myself. "Just remember what I said."

"Okay. What's good?" She opens her menu.

"Everything."

"Even the burger with a fried egg on it?"

I shrug. "I'm not a picky eater."

"I'm not either." Even if she were, I don't think she'd tell me. Summer's so damn eager to please.

I change the subject. "You were really helpful today."

Her eyebrows lift in surprise.

"I bet working in a barbershop isn't exciting for a smart girl like you, thinking about college in the fall."

"Oh no," she hurries to correct me. "It's fine. Good. Great, even."

I chuckle. "It's fine. You won't hurt my feelings. But if there's anything I can do to help you prepare for school. . . if there's anything that aligns with what you'll be studying, for example?"

"I haven't picked an area to focus on yet. I'm taking their recommended first-year courses." She nibbles on her lower lip. "Going to college is Mama's idea for me. Not mine."

I frown. "An education is a good thing."

"It's the big campus I'm not sure about," she confesses. "All the people."

"They probably have some online classes. Maybe not for next year, but once you get the basics down, you'll be able to pick. . ." I trail off, remembering my own years at college. "School is what you make it. I had a small circle of friends, didn't party too much, and at the end of it, I had the business knowledge to pick a career path."

"Is that when you became a barber? After college?"

I shook my head. "I sold insurance for five years and saved up money while I searched for someone to apprentice with. Built a business plan."

She counts on her fingers. The years of college. Five years of working. "So you've been a barber for ten years?"

"Almost eleven."

"That's pretty cool." Her eyes are warm and bright as she smiles at me. "I think I'm going to get the deluxe grilled cheese."

All right. I guess we're back to the question of food. "Good choice."

The waitress appears a minute later, and I order the roast beef sandwich after Summer relays what she wants.

"What about drinks for you folks?"

I glance at Summer. "Do you want a pop?"

She shakes her head. "Do you have juice? Orange or cranberry?"

"Sure thing, sweetie. And you, Henry? A beer?"

3
summer

HENRY HAS LOOKED uncomfortable since we walked in, but his face goes all tight at the offer of alcohol. "Just water."

"Is something wrong?" I ask after the waitress leaves.

He frowns. "No."

"You look upset."

His expression softens, his eyebrows lifting in surprise. "You're direct, aren't you?"

Now I'm the one frowning. "Shouldn't I be?"

A grin spreads across his face. "No, it's fine. It's good, in fact. I'm not upset. I'm very aware that there are men in here who see you as an attractive young thing, and I take my role in protecting you from them seriously."

I roll my eyes. "You sound like my mom."

"She's my oldest friend," he points out. "We're cut from the same cloth."

"Does that mean you won't let me have any fun, either?"

The pained expression is back. "I don't think I have that kind of power over you, Summer. You're a grown woman."

"You just said—"

"I want to protect you from unwanted advances. That's not

the same thing." He clears his throat. "What fun you have on campus. . . when you get there. . . that's different."

The truth is, I have no idea what fun I might want to have on campus. The only person I've ever had lecherous thoughts about is the man sitting opposite. Oh, the irony. He's focused on protecting me from unwanted advances while I'm only thinking about him.

Speaking of unwanted.

I drop my gaze to the table, my face hot now. If he's cut from the same cloth as my mom, he'll think it's horrible that I have the thoughts I do. I'll never forget the day my mom realized I was touching myself.

Absolutely mortifying. A conversation I never want to repeat, but especially not with *Henry*.

"And now I've embarrassed you." He sighs. "Summer, I'm—"

"There's nothing wrong with sex." I jerk my head up again.

Now he looks slightly panicked. "I didn't say there was."

"I may not be ready to have sex with someone else, but there's nothing wrong with thinking about it."

His eyes are comically wide. I should laugh. I want to cry instead. "I've made it even more awkward now, haven't I?"

"Fuck. No." He reaches across the table and grabs my hands, his big paws rough around my wrists. Like a grizzly bear trying to soothe a rabbit. "Stop. It's fine. Jesus Christ, I don't know how to respond to that, but yeah, nothing wrong with thinking about sex, okay?"

I jut my chin up at him in a stubborn nod.

"Just don't cry, okay?"

To my horror, I realize I *am* about to cry, my eyes shimmering with unshed tears. He grabs a napkin and dabs at the corners of my eyes.

"Teenage girls, huh? Is this why your mama sent you to me?"

"I'm starting to get the impression that she sent me to you because she knows you're just as puritanical as she is," I mutter.

He drops the napkin and catches my chin in his hand. His thumb strokes my cheek and along my jaw, making my breath hitch and my skin sizzle at the warm touch. His whole face softens. "I'm not puritanical at all, Summer. I don't know where you got that idea, but I promise you, I won't ever judge you for being a human being or having human desire."

I swipe my tongue against my lower lip. "My mom. . . she struggled with some of that."

He nods. "All right. I promise I won't. Even if I'm caught off guard, give me a minute to adjust, okay?"

I nod, too, and he eases away, leaning back against his side of the booth. He cracks a smile, I laugh nervously, and the moment shifts.

But as our food arrives, I think about his thumb on my face and how good it felt for him to pin his gaze on me and promise he'd never judge me for what I want.

He didn't say that in so many words, of course. And I don't know that he'd still promise it if he knew *who* I wanted. But it's nice to know I don't have to hide every part of myself from my roommate.

Just the parts where I want to climb him like a tree.

4
henry

"YOU SAID I should buy something to sleep in." Summer grabs my hand as soon as we walk into Walmart. "Let's go get that first."

The Ladies' sleep section has more satin than I expected for a discount superstore.

She holds up a white negligee that looks like some knock-off wedding night get up. "How about this?"

I imagine her generous hips making the satin sway in the hall light and how the fabric would feel under my hands as I pushed it up to her waist. Fuck, no. I look around and grab a T-shirt and shorts set instead. It's a peachy pink color and covered in hideous green flamingos. "This. It's cotton and comfortable."

She shrugs and takes it from me. "All right." Then she flips through the same rack and picks another cotton set, this one turquoise and covered in lemons and oranges. "This one is cute, too. It looks comfy, right?" She held it up against her body. "Should I try them on?"

The answer should be yes. But I am a stupid man who doesn't want to risk being dragged into a dressing room to watch a barely legal teenage girl get changed on the other side of a particleboard half-door. So I say no, they're fine, and we keep shopping.

I watch her pick out two sundresses—shorter than the one she's wearing now—before she drags me into the underwear aisle.

When she reaches for a perfectly innocent pack of white bikini briefs, I nearly fall over myself to get out of there. Not my finest hour. "I'm gonna grab some groceries," I mutter.

It's not until we get home and she puts on her PJs—ones I told her to buy—that I realize I should have suffered through the potential changing room embarrassment.

Because the woman who comes tripping out of the bedroom in the cotton set covered in fucking ugly flamingos is the sexiest person I've ever seen in my entire life. The shorts are no better than the panties she wore the night before; they just have an added frill around the leg holes. And the stretchy T-shirt is thin enough that not only can I see the shape of her round and full breasts but also the individual bumps of the areola around her nipples.

She looks like a serving of peach sorbet.

I want to gobble her up.

"Is this better than me wandering around in my underwear?"

God, yes. And fuck, no. I grab a cushion and cover my junk. "You like it?"

She rubs her hands over her hips, then grins. "It's so comfortable. You were right."

I was fucking wrong.

And I'm going to hell.

5
summer

ONCE WE GET over the sleep clothes snafu, Henry and I settle into a pretty good roommate situation. I work for him in the shop when it's busy and stay out of his hair when it's not.

At first, I'd sit in the barber chair and pepper him with questions. But after a while, he would give me a look, somewhere between exasperation and reluctant amusement, and send me upstairs.

Now, two weeks into our new normal, he sends me upstairs as soon as it's not busy. He has three busy periods in the day. First thing in the morning, around lunch, and then late afternoon through closing time.

Sometimes he sends me out to pick up treats from the coffee shop, and twice I've gone to the college to just walk around.

On my second visit, I pick up the summer edition of the student paper and see that they're hiring for the fall. I race back to the barbershop, my heart pounding.

"Do you think I could apply for this job?" I shove the paper into his hands and crowd close, pointing to the listing. *Summer residents are encouraged to come in for an in-person interview.* "Will you practice with me?"

He tugs on my ponytail. "Sure."

There's a lull before lunch, then he's busy for an hour straight. Just as we're talking about walking down the block to the coffee shop, Wake Up Call, someone comes in for a shave.

Henry gets them sitting in the chair, then pulls a twenty from his pocket. "Summer, do you mind getting the drinks? An iced coffee for me, please, and something for yourself."

"Sure."

I clutch the money Henry gave me and race down the block. It's scorching hot today, the temperature rising as the afternoon progresses, and the cool of the coffee shop is a welcome relief.

There's a short line, and a couple girls my age are ahead of me. As we wait, I can't help but overhear their conversation.

"Are you going to stay on campus for orientation week?"

"Nah, my mom wants me to come home. But I don't have a curfew. You?"

"My cousin is in the dorms, so I'll crash with her. Or hopefully with someone else." They both giggle at that.

The one who will go home at night flicks her hair over her shoulder. "I don't want to actually *sleep* with anyone. Just fuck them and go home to my own bed where I can spread out. Boys aren't fun to sleep next to."

That makes me frown. Henry would be lovely to sleep next to. He's big and warm. But maybe after you have sex with someone, it's different?

The girls make it to the counter and order their drinks. Then it's my turn. I get Henry's iced coffee and a blended strawberry smoothie for myself. The barista points me to the end of the counter for drink pick-up, then helps the customer behind me.

I slide down, hoping to catch more of their conversation, but they've moved on to chatting about a TV show I haven't seen.

Back in the shop, Henry has his customer's head tilted back with warm towels on his face, and he's prepping shave cream in a bowl with a brush. They're chatting away about music, so I put Henry's iced coffee on the ledge nearby and head for the stairs.

But Henry calls out my name. "I won't be long if you want to practice the job interview questions next."

I stop and turn around. "You don't mind if I hang out?"

He gives me a funny look. "Not at all."

I busy myself at the till making everything nice and neat while I sip my smoothie. Out of the corner of my eye, I watch Henry shave his customer. For a big guy, he's really careful with his hands, and his fingers are nimble, flicking the straight razor this way and that.

Once the customer is finished, I ring him out, and he leaves a tip for Henry. As soon as he's gone, Henry hands that to me.

"I didn't earn that," I protest.

He doesn't say anything, just holds it out until I take it, our fingers brushing as I accept the gift. I tuck it away in my purse, then grab my smoothie and hop up in the barber chair. "Henry, can I ask you a question?"

"Sure."

"Do you like it when the people you have sex with sleep over?"

He blinks at me, his cheeks darkening. "Excuse me?"

"After you have sex. Do you like them to stay? You have such a big bed. Surely it's big enough for two."

His chest puffs out, and he rocks back on his heels. "You can't ask me that."

"Why not?"

"It's inappropriate."

"Oh." I frown.

He frowns right back. "Where did that question come from?"

"I overheard two girls at the coffee shop talking about not wanting to stay, you know. After. They were talking about orientation week, and. . . that part hadn't occurred to me."

"Ah." His face twists in a pained expression. "That's different. That's hooking up, and I don't do that. If I have someone in my bed, I want them to stay there. But you don't need to hook up with anyone, understand?"

That's the end of the conversation because he's uncomfortable, and I don't want to push it. But now I have more questions. Like, why he said *if* he has someone in his bed, and not *when* he has someone in his bed.

———

The next week, I go to the college for the whole day. There's a new-student orientation that starts with a guided tour of campus while it's quiet, and then we're given a choice of three summer school classes to audit.

I go to an astronomy class that easily has two hundred students in it, the most popular summer school class they offer apparently, and it's overwhelming.

Wonderful, but a lot to take in.

I have no idea how I'll take notes and people watch and *learn anything* when school actually begins, but I'm excited all the same.

At lunch, our group goes to the main cafeteria. I spend some of the money Henry gave me on a sandwich and a sparkling pineapple juice that feels like a real treat.

Finally, I go to the student newspaper office for a job interview. I think I do okay, but it's hard to know.

When I get home at the end of the day, Henry teases me about being all tuckered out from excitement, and I blush. "It's a weekly thing. I may need to go to all of them to prepare myself for being a full-time student."

"You had fun, though, didn't you?"

"Yep."

"I'm glad." He pushes a mug of hot chocolate into my hands. "Are you hungry? What did you eat for lunch?"

"A big sandwich."

"I'll make a snack tray for dinner, then."

"Okay." I take a slow sip of the cocoa, then yawn.

He wraps one arm around my shoulders and points me to the couch. "Go sit."

I'd rather lean into his warmth. There's something about the way his hand covers all of my upper arm that spikes a feeling that won't go away. I want him to touch me all over.

I don't move.

He sets both hands on my shoulders now and nudges me forward. It's so inappropriate to turn an entirely innocent care-taking effort into something dirty in my head. He made me hot chocolate, for goodness sake. But I like the way he takes charge when I'm recalcitrant.

It makes me want to try being a bit of a brat with him. My mother always hated my lip, took it personally, and forced me to be a grown-up equal to her.

I bet Henry would be more indulgent than that.

You can't lust after him and *want him to take care of you like you're a little kid.* Obviously not. That would be deeply weird. Or would it?

He leaves me on the sofa, and I watch him stalk back to the kitchen, filled with the most delicious warmth that I don't care if it's weird. I like this feeling, and I want more of it.

6
henry

SUMMER HAS A LOT OF MOODS. Sometimes she's nervous, smart-ass other times, occasionally really serious, and every so often painfully direct. Tonight I'm seeing yet another facet to her personality, but I can't quite put my finger on it.

It's cute, whatever it is. Like, instead of college, today was her first day of kindergarten or something like that.

The innocence of it all is endearing.

I chop some veggies for a dip, then add crackers and cheese and some grapes, too. We don't need to eat this at the island. After a full day of people interaction, I'm guessing she'd rather zone out in front of the TV.

Sure enough, I bring the tray over, and she gives me a grateful smile when I ask her if she wants me to put on a show.

"You can choose," she says. "I'm kind of tired."

After she eats, I'm not surprised when she stretches out and puts her head on a pillow at the far end of the couch. I move to get up and give her the whole space.

"You can stay," she mumbles, her eyes already closed.

I wrap my hand around her top foot. "Do you want to put these things up on me?"

One eyelid cracks open. "These things? What, my goblin feet?"

I laugh out loud and pull them into my lap. "Your feet are beautiful."

She smiles and closes her eyes again. The smile stays, the corners of her mouth turned up for quite some time. I know because I don't stop watching her until she's well and truly asleep.

After the show ends, I get out from under her feet and take a shower, drying off and changing in the bathroom before coming back to the main room. Summer's still out cold, so I tidy up and go downstairs to make sure the shop is locked.

When I return, I realize I'm puttering aimlessly. I don't want to disturb her, I guess. But she's sleeping where I usually spend my evenings, so if I'm going to do anything else before going to bed myself, I need to move her.

And I definitely need to move her before I sleep.

I gently nudge her shoulder, then give her a shake. Nothing.

Sighing, I scoop her into my arms and carry her to the bedroom.

I don't come in here. It's her space now. As I set her down in the unmade mess of blankets, I realize my sheets now smell like her.

"This bed was never left unmade before you stormed into my life." I mutter this to myself as if pretending to be grumpy will ward off other feelings I don't want to acknowledge. Like how much I enjoy her scent marking up my bedding.

She doesn't stir at my reprimand.

She doesn't let go of my neck, either.

I wrap my hand around her wrist and gently pry her arm off my body.

But as soon as I go for the other one, she latches on again, whining in her sleep.

"Do you miss your mom, sweet pea?" I stroke her hair.

"Yeah, I bet you do." I ease myself more fully onto my back, letting her cling to my side like a limpet.

I remember what she said about sharing a bed with Jennifer. In her sleepy state, she's probably confused me with her mother.

That's all right. She can hold me if she needs a warm body.

———

At some point, I fall asleep. I wake up with a start around midnight and extract myself from the sweet, warm cuddle monster that Summer turns into when she's unconscious.

I go to the couch, which is extra uncomfortable after a few hours in my own bed, and force myself out of twenty years of habit to go the fuck to sleep.

Do not think about anything, do not pass GO.

The next thing I hear is the coffee maker hissing. It's still dark out when I sit up and blearily look out the back window.

Summer's in the kitchen. She's changed out of the dress I put her to bed in, and her hair is damp.

"Someone woke up early," I mutter as I join her.

She hands me a cup of coffee. "Did I wake you?"

"It's all right. My alarm will go off in five minutes."

"I slept so well last night."

"I can tell."

She's that well-rested, she's practically glowing.

Me, on the other hand. . . I'm growling every word.

She wraps one arm around my waist and gives me a half-hug. "You're so grumpy in the morning. I had no idea."

"You've never been up this early before." I extract myself from the soft press of her flesh against mine.

It's too early for thoughts of how sweet her thighs would taste, fresh out of the shower. How good the damp tendrils of her hair would feel wrapped around my hand as I guide her mouth up and down my cock.

"Does food help?"

I lift my cup. "Coffee helps."

She frowns, and before I can apologize for being curt, she disappears into her room.

Fuck.

———

Summer avoids me for the rest of the day. It's painful—for both of us—but there's no time to talk between customers. When I close up the store, she announces she's going to Wake Up Call for a poetry reading she saw on a poster on campus.

"I could come with you." But the offer sounds gruff and forced, and she shakes her head.

"No, you don't have to."

I want to. I think I want to, anyway. I've never been into the artsy stuff happening around town, preferring to go to a bar for a break from the four walls of my apartment above the shop. But I don't want to intrude on her plans.

So I go to The Roadhouse while she goes to the coffee shop.

I'm miserable the whole time. My chest feels tight in a weird way that doesn't ease until I'm home again, and I see her strolling towards me on the street.

"Did you have fun?" I ask when she reaches the shop door. I hold it open for her.

She shrugs.

I frown.

She walks through the door and straight through the shop, heading for the stairs.

I call her name, and she stops. Counting to ten, I slowly lock the door, then cross my arms over my chest. "I think we need to talk."

7
summer

I DON'T WANT to talk. I want to change into my pajamas, curl up in bed, and be alone with my loneliness.

Even as I think that, I realize how self-sabotaging that is. *Alone with my loneliness.* This is stupid.

Even Henry is being stupid today, and I don't know why. I wait for him to tell me, but he doesn't say anything.

"Well?"

He raises one eyebrow. "Excuse me?"

"You want to talk. I don't. So I guess, it's—"

"Don't speak to me like that." He frowns. "Do I speak to you like that? Ever?"

"No." Hot embarrassment rolls over me. "I'm sorry."

"Did you eat at the poetry reading?"

I shake my head.

"Let's go upstairs. You can eat something and tell me how it was."

I burst into tears.

He crosses the room and takes me in his arms. "Oh, honey."

"I don't know how to talk to people," I wail, the truth coming out of me. "And I didn't mean to be rude to you."

He strokes his hand over the back of my head. "I see you, baby girl. It's okay. I'm not mad."

"You looked mad, with your arms crossed like that."

"Maybe I'm feeling bad myself."

I wipe the tears from my eyes and look up at him. "About what?"

He turns me around and nudges me up the stairs. "I think I should have gone with you to the poetry reading."

He says it to my back, and when I try to twist to see him, he gently pushes me, keeping me moving up the stairs.

Why would he feel bad about not going to the coffee shop with me? That doesn't make any sense.

He makes me a sandwich, then takes me by the hand and sits me at the island to eat.

It's only when I finish that he leans in, bracing his forearms on the counter next to me, and whispers, "Now tell me about not being able to talk to people."

All those weird emotions stir up again, and I feel like I'm going to cry. Henry slides his hand up and down my back. Warm, soothing.

"Take a deep breath," he murmurs.

I nod and do as he tells me. "I thought today was going to be a really good day," I finally tell him. "I slept so well last night. Like I haven't in. . ."

Since I arrived.

Henry puts two and two together. "Have you been struggling since you got here?"

"I didn't know I was, but maybe. Yes."

"Ah, baby." He kisses me on the temple. It's a kind gesture, nothing more, but it makes my pulse jack up.

And it annoys me. "I'm not a little kid," I mutter.

He pauses. I feel his whole body tense up. "I don't think you are."

"You're treating me—"

"Like a young woman. Which you are. This is your first time

away from home, and you're starting a whole new life. There are going to be bumps along the way. Keep breathing. And stop snapping at me unless you want me to treat you like a child and take you over my knee."

I gasp, heat twirling wildly and inappropriately inside me. I giggle and shake my head to cover up how much I like that idea. *Not the time or the place, Summer.* "You wouldn't."

"Just because I haven't done something before doesn't mean I'm not willing to give it a try." He grunts and moves away from me. "Finish your sandwich."

I pick at it as I watch him aggressively change the laundry over, and I try to think about why I'm being so obnoxious. It's not that people didn't magically talk to me tonight. I don't even like people that much, so it's fine if they don't talk to me most of the time. Why would I want to—

I stop and mentally count backward.

Then I get out my phone and check my app.

"Oooh. . ." I say loud enough that I get Henry's attention.

"What is it?"

"Nothing." I quickly finish my sandwich.

"Is something wrong?" He sets the laundry basket on top of the washing machine and comes back to where I'm sitting.

I scoot off the stool and rinse my plate at the sink.

He's right there when I turn around, looking concerned. "You can tell me anything."

Not this.

He doesn't look away. A gentle, misplaced understanding settles in his gaze. "Is it that time of the month? It's fine. If you need anything. . ."

I roll my lower lip through my teeth. "No. The opposite, actually."

I love the way his brows tug together in confusion. I like that I can shock him.

"I'm ovulating," I whisper.

He recoils like I've hit him, and my glee falls away.

"Oh shit." I wave my hands in jerky, get-it-off motions. "Ignore I said that. That was weird. Right? I shouldn't share that?"

"It was unexpected, that's all." He clears his throat, trying not to look pained. "How do you know you're ovulating?"

"My mood was a tip-off, and now that I think about it, I can feel it in my body." I wrap my arms over my sensitive chest, then think better of sharing that detail. "I, uh, get a cramp in my side."

"Your mom teach you that?"

"Yeah."

The corner of his mouth tugs up into a half-smile. "She was always blunt about how our bodies work."

"With you?"

He exhales roughly. "We had a weird relationship. Your mom never saw me as a love interest, not really. I was her. . . like a girlfriend, I guess. Her confidant."

"She said you were her first boyfriend."

"I wanted to be. But she didn't have those feelings for me. We went out a few times, but we never did more than kiss. She told me when she got her period and when it didn't show up. Because she was pregnant with you."

"Oh, wow." I poke my tongue in the corner of my cheek. A new curiosity drives me forward. "Do you know who my dad is, then?"

He shakes his head. "She never told me."

"I knew it was a long shot." I make a face. "I don't need to know."

"But it makes sense that you'd want to."

"I think it's great you were a good friend to her," I mumble.

As I try to look away, he catches my chin with his knuckle and gives me another gentle look. "If I can be a friend to you, too, that would make me really happy."

But I don't want Henry to be my friend. I don't understand

how my mom could have passed him over for some asshole who would knock her up and then abandon her.

If Henry got me pregnant, he would do the right thing and marry me. I'm sure of it.

Even if he only sees me as his Jennifer's little girl right now.

Instead of saying any of that, I just shrug.

"Maybe you'll feel better in the morning," he finally says. "A good night's sleep fixes a lot."

I would have said that this morning, too, but now I'm not so sure. "Then why am I so grumpy now, after having the best sleep of the summer so far?"

8
henry

I FLUSH HOT, awkward, and uncomfortable. "I don't think it's because you slept well. I was abrupt this morning. That set both of our days off on the wrong foot. Had I known how badly you've been sleeping, I'd have been, I dunno. Less of a dickhead."

That makes her laugh. "You're never that."

"It's okay to tell me I was too curt, too rough with your sweet girl feelings."

She rolls her eyes, but she's smiling now. "All right."

"Maybe we need to get you a body pillow to snuggle with at night, so I. . ." I trail off as her eyes go wide.

"You, what?" She frowns. The way her eyebrows pull together and her lips purse when she's thinking. . . fucking beautiful. "Henry?"

Fuck. Me.

"Last night. . ." She inhales with a little hitch in her breath before she licks her lips. "Henry, did you sleep in the big bed with me last night? Did I? Did you. . .?"

"It's not—You wouldn't let go of me when I moved you. I didn't—"

"I liked it," she whispers. Her eyes are big as saucers. "I remember now. Is that why you were short with me this morning?"

This time, my curse is out loud. "Fuck. Yeah, maybe. I thought I'd crossed a line. I don't want to make you uncomfortable."

She shakes her head vigorously. "You would never. Is that why I slept so well?"

I cannot be the answer to her restless nights. Cannot. Will not.

And she doesn't care. She presses on. "Would you sleep with me again tonight?"

I shake my head. "I can't."

"Why not?"

I open my mouth to tell her it's not fucking appropriate. That I'm an old man, and she's too innocent for the filthy thoughts I have about her. Then I realize I didn't have any of those last night.

Not one. I didn't get a fucking hard-on as I held her. I just worried about her and wanted her to be safe.

If she needs me, I can do whatever she wants. "No good reason," I say gruffly. "Just trying to be a good guy."

"You are the best." She stretches. "I'll put my PJs on. And I know you might not be tired yet, but if you just lie down with me, I'll fall asleep fast, and then you can get back up. Is that okay?"

How can I say no? "Yeah. That's fine."

But I won't get back up. I know it in my bones. I've missed holding her all day, and if she knows I might be there all night, I'm going to fucking take it.

This is fine, I tell myself as she crawls into bed. Unlike last night, where she was exhausted and unconscious, this time, she's nervous and unsure of how to hold on to me.

She launches herself against me as I'm still settling in, then laughs as I push her back, just a little, until I'm lying down. Then she pounces again.

And fuck if that eager uncertainty doesn't wake a part of me that stayed dormant last night.

My cock thickens as she wriggles against me, her top leg creeping onto mine. A heavy need pulses deep inside me as I think about the innocent need to wrap herself around another person.

Before her leg slides too high and discovers my growing erection under the blanket, I shift my hand across my body, stopping her thigh just in time.

Of course, now I'm fucking holding her bare leg.

Danger is an understatement.

She makes a happy, contented sound and then yawns. It's a big, tired gasp for air, and her eyes fluttering shut, then stay closed when she settles again.

My hand covers most of her thigh, and her flesh is cool and soft and plump at the top where my thumb rests. I need to release her, move my hand to somewhere, anywhere else.

Stop touching her bare fucking skin. But I can't. She threw herself against me. The feelings of vague, shadowy want constantly looming in my mind now threaten to coalesce into clear images that—if imprinted—could ruin me forever. Even worse, they would ruin Summer.

Let go of her. But I can't.

I tell myself it's because she might nudge my cock. I'm not holding her against me; I'm holding her back from being too close.

It's both a truth and a lie at the same time.

And then my thumb strokes back and forth. I want to pretend it's not of my own volition, but *I* do that. *I* make the fucking choice to touch more of her, even as my heart pounds in my chest.

She won't want you mauling her. But that shadowy want is stronger now, more confident.

When this is over, and she moves into her dorm, I'll look back and recognize that mistakes were made. But right now? I can't let myself think about this as wrong, not when she clings to me as if her life depends on it.

So I hold my breath and wait for her to fall asleep.

9

summer

HENRY GOES BACK to the couch after that night, but something has shifted between us. I find myself drawn to him. I can't stop looking at him, like he's full of mysteries I need to know.

The next night, I make another foray out of the apartment for another student event.

Henry wants to come with me, but I need to do it myself. "I'll only be gone for an hour," I tell him. "And it's. . ."

"People your own age?"

I stick my tongue out at him. "Yes."

"Go. Have a good time, and tell me about it when you get back."

This time, I bump into a heavily pregnant girl my own age, and when she smiles at me, I screw up the courage to introduce myself. "I'm Summer."

"Lily. Are you a first-year student?"

"Yep."

"Same. I'll be. . ." She gestures at her belly. "Not around for the first few weeks, but I got permission to bring the baby with me after that."

"That's awesome."

She smiles shyly. "Yeah. I really like it here."

"Are you new in town? Me, too."

We exchange phone numbers, and I wish her luck with the rest of her pregnancy.

Back at the apartment, Henry hears me run up the stairs, and he's waiting for me with his arms wide open. "It was good?"

I leap into his embrace and squeeze him tight. "It was great. I made a friend."

"Oh, baby, that's awesome. Good job."

"Thanks."

He twirls me around, then sets me down and brushes a strand of hair off my face. For a second, I think he might kiss me, but then it passes.

"I was just, uh, watching. . ." He trails off.

I throw myself onto the couch.

He grins. "Do you want to watch with me?"

We each take a corner of the couch, but I stretch my legs out in his direction as the show progresses.

When my feet brush his thigh, he drops his hand around my ankle, his fingers wrapping all the way around, and he tugs.

I wiggle into position for a foot rub, and the corner of his mouth pulls up into a half-smile. "Sore little feet?"

"Maybe."

"Next time you want something, just ask." He's looking straight ahead at the TV, but when I grin bashfully, his smile grows, too. "Okay?"

"Okay," I whisper back. Then I wiggle my toes deeper into his grip.

As we close a few days later, I'm sweeping up while he's resetting his two stations for the next morning.

Our conversations have shifted to more adult topics, so I

decide to bring up something that's been on my mind. "Remember when you said you don't do hook-ups?"

In the mirror, I see him take a slow breath in and square his shoulders. "Sure. Why are you asking?"

"I'm wondering if you date people."

"I have dated people."

"Girlfriends?"

He presses his lips together, then meets my gaze in the mirror. "I'm forty years old, Summer. Yes, I've had girlfriends."

"But you don't have one now."

"No."

"Do you want one?"

He frowns. "Why are you asking?"

"I'm curious."

"That's an understatement."

"It'll be awkward if you go on a date and can't bring her home because I'm in your bed."

His eyes narrow, and his jaw works back and forth. A vein pulses in his forehead. "I'm not bringing a woman home this summer."

"You'd go to her place?"

He turns around and grabs me around the waist. The broom clatters to the floor. "I see that someone wants attention."

"No," I protest, but I squirm into his grip instead of away from it.

"Yes," he counters, tickling my side with his free hand. "You act like a brat when you want attention. And that's just fine by me because I like giving you all of my attention, just. . . like. . . this. . ."

I laugh and feign, trying to get away, but his arms tighten, and he pulls me right up against his body.

Then he stiffens, and as I exhale, still giggling, I relax, and my bottom settles against what is obviously an erection.

Henry is hard.

A thick, unmistakable ridge pushes against me, and I jolt.

My legs flex against his thick thighs, and I make a sound, something surprised. *Oh.*

Everything stops. I swear I can feel his pulse stop, his breath sucks in, and then nothing.

Just the pulse of his *cock*, Henry's *dick*, and how it feels to be trapped in his arms.

Then he exhales, his breath brushing against my neck, and time starts again.

He lets me go, and I finish sweeping up. I don't look at him, just finish the task. No more teasing. No more tickling. We're not going to talk about it, I know that much. I'm not going to bring up dating again, either. Because if I did that, we'd have to talk about attraction, and how men get erections, and what that means.

What it means is that Henry got an erection while tickling me and calling me a brat.

What it means is that he caught me in his arms, held me tight, and I rubbed my butt against his cock—and how it felt.

And now I know what power I have—when I misbehave and am precocious—and what that does to my temporary guardian.

10
henry

JUST WHEN I think the worst thing to happen this summer is Summer bumping up against my hard-as-fuck cock—definitely not tickling her again. *What the fuck was I thinking?* We get another heatwave at the end of July.

Summer is slowly coming out of her shell and spending half her time on campus.

I pretend to be okay with that because she'll be moving out in another month. This is temporary, I remind myself constantly. And that's for the best.

Do not get attached.

Summer drifts downstairs more often now, even when I don't need her help because the living room upstairs doesn't have air conditioning. There's only so long a teenage girl can spend in a bedroom, apparently.

On the hottest afternoon yet, when there aren't enough iced coffees in the world to fight off the slow slide of sweat down my back, Summer is sitting in the barber chair, her head in the clouds.

"What are you thinking about?" I ask as I tidy up around her.

"Boys." The guileless way she says it hits me straight in the chest. I don't want her thinking about walking hormone machines.

She's a walking hormone machine herself, though. It's the age. I remember it well.

She's looking at me like she can read my mind. "Is that what you were like when you wanted to date my mom?"

"Was I like what?"

"A. . ." she lowers her voice, mimicking me. *"Walking hormone machine."*

"Did I say that out loud?"

"You muttered it under your breath."

"I should have more self-control than that."

"Do you?"

What kind of a question is that? A Summer kind of question. Raw, unvarnished, and dangerously curious. "I usually do."

"You didn't answer my question."

"Which one?" I poke her in the side to lighten the mood. "You're full of questions."

"Were you a walking hormone machine when you dated my mom? Or after that, with anyone else?"

I shrug. "Sure. We're all human."

"When was the last time you had a crush on someone?"

Right fucking now, because I'm a pervert. Instead of that off-limits truth, I lie. It's far too easy. "It's been a while."

"You said my mom wasn't into you, but she told me you were the only man she ever trusted. I dunno, it sounds like she really liked you."

That's an old wound, well-healed over, so I shake my head. "Nope. I told you, we went out a few times. She didn't even let me kiss her for real, just a few pecks. Which was more than fine —girls should call the shots about things like that."

"Kissing?"

"Yep."

"And other stuff?"

"I'm not talking to you about that."

"Why not?"

"Because—"

She crosses her arms over her chest. "I'm a grown-up."

Just fucking barely.

She unfolds from the chair and saunters to the stairs. "Are you going to be a while down here?"

Why? The question jumps into my throat, but I can't ask it out loud. I don't need to know why she wants privacy upstairs. I glance at the clock. "I've got paperwork to do. I probably won't come up until at least seven."

Her eyelashes sweep against her cheeks as she blinks slowly. "Wanna make dinner together when you come up?"

"Yep."

"I'm going to lie down until then."

I swallow thickly. "Good. Get some rest."

As she disappears through the curtain and I hear her footsteps on the stairs, I imagine her stretching out on my bed—her bed, now—and sliding her fingers between her legs.

The opposite of rest.

Slow, rhythmic movements as she thinks about kissing and other stuff.

I give her a full hour to herself, then drag myself upstairs, already missing the air-conditioned splendor of the shop.

"I might head out to Walmart after we eat," I tell Summer. "Get an air mattress."

She gives me a confused look. "What's wrong with the couch?"

"With this heat. . ."

Her eyes flare wide in alarm. "Oh, shit. No, Henry, you take the bed."

"I'm not going to make you sweat all night."

"Well, same right back at you." She crosses her arms. "And how does an air mattress make the situation better?"

"I'll sleep downstairs in the shop."

Her mouth drops open, then snaps shut again as she shakes

her head vigorously. "No. Nope. Not going to happen. We can share the bed. It's plenty big, and if you're worried about me cuddling up against you in the night, we'll make a pillow barrier between us." She exhales, a breathy, confident sound like she knows she's won the argument. "Besides, this way we can talk late into the night about girl things."

I groan. "Stop."

"Boy things?" She grins.

"We can talk about school stuff."

She nods sagely. "Like chemistry. And biology."

"Yep," I agree, a beat too fast.

I realize that she's being subtle, but not that subtle, and her eyes gleam like she's planning something.

Am I really accepting the invitation back into her bed, my bed, *to share a bed* because it's unusually hot in Oregon?

Or are we both using this as an excuse to poke that line and see what happens?

———

The answer comes sooner than I expect.

We take turns showering, then lie down next to each other in the cool darkness of the bedroom.

Her hand finds mine. "Henry?"

"Mmm."

"Can I tell you a secret?"

No is the only answer here. No, because I can't be trusted. No, because she's on a path moving away from me, and secrets could yank her off that journey. No, because I can't be sure I'll be a good enough man to only hold those secrets and not exploit them.

I don't say no. I don't say anything.

"Henry?"

"Your mother wants—"

"She's not here. And I'm a grown-up with wants of my own." She moves closer. "And I want you."

I know.

I've known for weeks, probably, and yet hearing it sends a new kind of panic racing through my bloodstream. A dull roar fills my ears.

Her breath is warm and soft on my jaw. "Henry. . ."

"No." I clear my throat. "We can't do this."

"Why not?" It's a simple question with a very complicated answer.

"Because you're young enough to be my daughter."

"But I'm not your daughter." She has an ethereal sweetness, an innocence that makes all the complicated layers fuzzy. "We're friends. That's what you said."

We are friends. But it's more than that. I feel a sense of responsibility for her well-being. I have money, and she doesn't. I have world knowledge that she doesn't have. "It's a power imbalance," I say gently. "I'm much older than you. I know things you don't."

"I know," she whispers. "But you could teach me. Then I'll know those things, too, and we'll be on equal footing."

I don't push her away. My lack of a reply is enough. I've left an opening I should close firmly, but I can't. I tried, and I failed.

Happiness radiates off her as she exhales, softening against me. I hold my breath as I listen to her fall asleep.

And then I lay there in the dark, thinking about how I might teach her about being a woman.

The next morning, I wake up to her wriggling her bum against my erection. One of my hands is inside her shirt, flat against her smooth, soft belly, and my other hand is tangled in her hair.

She's holding her breath.

Slowly, I kiss the back of her neck, my pulse heavy. I feel drugged.

My cock is drooling to be inside her, or even just between her lush little thighs.

But this cannot be about me and my base desires.

I exhale roughly and roll away from her, ignoring her small protest.

"Coffee," I mutter.

"So you're not a morning sex person?" she calls after me.

"No sex!" I bark back, already halfway to the kitchen.

She giggles, and I hear her little footsteps following me. She hops onto the counter, watching me. An eager shadow. I remember how much it upset her when I didn't give her attention first thing in the morning, so I stop in front of her and let her tug me into the vee of her legs. I press a kiss to her forehead.

The happy noise she makes when my lips hit her skin makes me want to fuck her into next week.

No sex.

I cup her face in my hands, holding her still. Making her look at me. "Summer, we can't. . . there are lines we can't cross."

"But you want to."

I groan. "Yes, damn it. I want to."

"So why can't we?"

"Because it would be wrong."

"Sounds simplistic."

"I'm a simple man."

"Then what *isn't* wrong?" Her sharp little eyes don't leave my face. "Can we hug?"

An innocent question. But I know better now. Summer is far from innocent. She's a fully formed woman with complicated wants and desires. I play her game, though. "Yes."

"Can we kiss?" The yearning in her voice hits me square in the chest.

The need to taste her soft mouth is overwhelming. "Yes. Forehead kisses are definitely allowed."

She rolls her eyes."And what about my. . . cheek?"

"That's fine, too."

"And my mouth?"

"Summer. . ."

"For educational purposes only."

Could I teach her how to kiss a man? I nod, feeling like the worst kind of animal. Not feeling bad enough to take it back, though. All of me is throbbing for her now.

Her whole face lights up. "There's a lot we can do with hugging and kissing. I bet we can make that *very* filthy."

"I have no doubt. But let's do our best not to because we can't go too far."

She chews on the corner of her lip, a determined expression settling on her face. "What about. . . other kinds of education? Can you teach me—"

I press my finger to her mouth. "Let's leave it at hugging and kissing."

"Cuddling?" She glares at me. "We're both grown-ups."

"Barely."

"I'd rather learn from you than some fumbling—"

"I don't want those boys touching you, either." I wipe my hand across my mouth. "What exactly do you want me to teach you? I need you to be specific."

She holds my gaze, steady and calm, as she ticks off a clearly thought-out list on her fingers. It starts sweet and goes to places that almost break my brain.

"I definitely want to learn how to kiss," she says softly. One finger. "And how to give pleasure. How to turn a man on." Another finger.

She gives me an angelic smile as she ticks the third finger in the air. "I want to know about sex, of course, but that's off the table, so maybe. . . fingers? And, of course, orgasms. What it looks like when a man, you know."

I'm speechless.

And fucking hard. Painfully swollen and ready to show her

all of that. Starting with how men like it when innocent girls wrap their tiny fingers around dripping cocks and make them spray come all over sweet little mouths.

The coffee maker beeps.

She brushes her lips at the corner of my mouth and pushes me away from her counter perch. "Time to get caffeinated."

11
summer

AFTER I BRUSH my teeth and get dressed for the day—a sundress, light as air—I return to the living room and find Henry brooding in the armchair.

I glance over at the couch. That's where I should go sit. That was the point of him taking the chair, to put some distance between us. But I don't want distance. So I close the gap between us and walk right up to his chair, nudging his dangling hand with my knee.

His fingertips are still against my skin as he looks up at me.

The silence of the room is heavy. Secret.

I slowly twist on the spot, still brushing my knee against his hand. Guiding his fingers to my inner thigh.

He flexes his arm when I stop and presses against my skin just a little before dropping his hand away. It's a reluctant move, though. I can see in his face that he wanted to slide it up under my skirt, to where I'm warm and willing.

"Time for work?" I ask.

He nods.

I help him open the shop, then skip down the street for an iced coffee and some treats for breakfast. Over the month I've worked for him, I've saved almost a thousand dollars. He pays me too much and gives me his tips, so the least I can do is keep the man well nourished.

When I return, he has customers in both chairs but still gives me his attention—all of it—for a long, hot beat. Like he can't stop looking at me, drinking me in, and that feels better than the kiss I so desperately want from him.

Instead of going upstairs or heading to the college, I stick around all day. I'm as helpful as I can be, anticipating whatever Henry needs. And when he closes up for the day, the first thing he does after locking the door is crook his finger, beckoning me over to him.

"You've been a very good girl today." His voice rumbles in the silent shop. Deep, rich, sexy. "Thank you for your help."

I sway against him. "Always."

"What would you like for a reward?"

He knows.

I know.

I smile. "A kiss."

"What kind of kiss?"

"A grown-up kiss. My first real one."

His gaze drops to my lips, and I suck in a breath. "Your first kiss should be special. Gentle."

I nod.

"I don't know if I can be gentle with you, Summer." He licks his lips. "Maybe that's what's been holding me back."

"Maybe I don't need gentle." I push up on my tiptoes, searching for his mouth, but he takes hold of me and pulls me in against his body instead.

His arms are solid and heavy. Comforting, even as I want to protest that it's not a hug I want. Except I can feel the tension in his body, and I will myself to be patient.

I breathe in the scent of him and soften into his embrace. There's something perfect about the way I fit against his body. And when he rubs his hands up and down my back, they cover all of me, all at once. In Henry's arms, I feel safe and protected.

Little and hidden in his embrace, like he's a cloak against the outside world.

And when I'm a pliable puddle of happy goo, he slowly tips my head back, one of his hands cradling the side of my face, and brings our lips together.

After weeks of wanting this, my first real kiss is a beautiful surprise.

His lips feel wonderful—warm and firm—and then he moves them. Just that little shift sends a bolt of sensation through my body, making me press in for more. His mouth slants against mine, fitting us together in careful ways, different each time.

It makes my mouth water.

Then I feel the steady pressure of his tongue at the seam of my lips, tracing a line to the corner of my mouth, almost tickling. But not quite because this feels so good, better than a tickle.

It makes me feel alive.

Like I can see the world in technicolor even though my eyes have drifted shut.

My lips part, and he's back to those shifting kisses all over my mouth, now with just the hint of a firm, wet tongue.

Little sips.

Tasting me.

When our tongues meet, I start to get the feel of it. He tastes me, then it's my turn to venture into his mouth, getting to know the power of sliding my tongue against his and the sounds he makes.

I whimper, I think, some kind of noise, and he picks me up. I wrap my legs around his back, and he carries me to the wall, pressing me against it.

I twist my fingers into his hair and hold him still so I can do what he was doing, little kisses all over. The corner of his mouth is my favorite spot. The grunt he makes when I lick there makes me want to cry out in joy.

My thighs tighten around his waist, and he rocks against me, giving me the pressure of his firm belly to grind against.

We're making out now. That's what this is. It's not just a kiss; it's two people sucking face and getting so turned on we won't be able to walk straight when we stop.

Maybe we should never stop.

But when I trail my mouth down his neck, to where there's a hint of chest hair peeking out from his open collar, he eases me off him.

I slide down the wall, feeling boneless and aching for more. "Henry. . ."

He kisses me gently when my feet are fully underneath me. "That's enough for now."

For now.

Those two words float me through the rest of the day and mollify me when we go to sleep that night, and all he lets me do is cuddle against his big, warm body after a single, scorching good night kiss.

Everything changes after that kiss. I see things differently. I know that I don't want this to just be a game we play over the summer, and I know Henry doesn't want it to end when I go to college, either.

But he's not going to admit that because he's stuck in some misguided sense of chivalry or responsibility.

So I'll need to trick him.

Is it really manipulation if we both know what I'm doing when I tell him I want to know how to date people?

I ask him one night when we get home from another shopping trip. I'm modeling the clothes I bought with him because he refused to watch me try them on at the store.

I twirl in front of him in a peasant blouse and a pair of jean shorts. "Would this be a good outfit to wear on a date?"

He grunts.

"Henry, you need to help me. It's a central part of college life."

He gives me a glare that's far too sexy. "Aren't you supposed to be focused on school?"

"Life is all about balance."

"I think you should seek balance in a black turtleneck."

That makes me laugh. "Well, I think you should take me on a date."

"Summer. . ."

"For educational purposes. So I can practice."

"You don't need to practice that. You're enchanting exactly as you are."

"You have to say that."

"I really don't. What I have to say is, your mother doesn't want you dating anyone."

"But she's not the boss of me. And neither are you."

"I'm very aware of that. If you were mine, you wouldn't be allowed to date, ever."

"Spoken like a man who secretly wants to date me himself."

He laughs. "Come here."

I crawl into his lap and kiss him before he can tell me to get off. It's a sweet kiss, just my lips against his, and then he eases me back. Not off his lap, just away from his mouth.

Progress.

His hands are holding my wrists, pinning my arms to my sides, and he leaves them there as he regards me with a slow, critical look. Not mean. Just. . . searching.

I smile at him. "I know, you keep saying we can't be together. But then you kiss me, and I get all wound up. Henry, I've been waiting for you to make a move all summer. If you aren't going to, that's okay, but at some point, I'll. . ."

His grip tightens, and one of his thumbs strokes my skin slowly, making me crave so much more than I can ever have. "Is that what you really want? To start dating people?"

"No," I moan. "I don't want anyone else. Just you."

He groans. "No, Summer. Not even me."

"But I like it when you—" I wrench my hands free of his light grasp and twist my fingers so I'm the one holding *his* wrists. I drag his hands up my body to where my breasts throb in need. "Please, Henry. They hurt."

"I shouldn't touch them, then. Or ever. But especially if they're tender, baby girl. You don't want my big hands all over you."

"I do." I gasp as his fingertips hook against my neckline, the weight of his touch testing the stretch of the fabric.

His gaze darkens, his eyes hooded as he slowly drags the fabric down, revealing my swollen flesh. He stops short of my nipples, keeping those covered, but the way he licks his lips at what he *can* see is enough to make me moan.

"We're not going to do whatever you think we might do," he mutters.

"I just want you to touch me."

"Not below the belt."

"Just my breasts," I breathe. "And if you want me to touch you—"

"No." He clears his throat. "I do, but no. This is just for you." He strokes the pebbling flesh of my chest. "You're sore?"

"It's happening more frequently now. When I think about kissing you. . ."

"Your body is working hard." He exhales and flexes his thighs beneath me. The movement rocks me forward a little, and the warm, wet space between my legs settles firmly on a very thick erection. "I told myself I wasn't allowed to want you, but God damn, it's hard to deny how good you feel in my lap."

"I dream of you," I whisper. "More now than before."

His gaze softens as he cups my breasts through my shirt. "Do you?"

I breathe his name.

He tugs the elastic neckline down off my shoulders, the

whole blouse dangerously low now, and then it's around my waist, and he has my bare breasts in his hands.

I rock against him as he rolls delicate circles around my nipples with his thumbs, and then he dips his head.

Henry's kisses drive me wild.

His mouth on my breast? Transcendent.

I grind harder, desperate now, each gentle pull of his mouth sending a signal directly to my clit. I'm hot and slick now, I can feel it, and the hard press of his erection against my denim-clad sex is enough friction that I'm going to get there, I'm going to come. I can feel it, I can—

"Henry," I whine as I grip his head, holding him against my chest. One of his hands lands on my thigh, curving around to the back of my leg, and then he's moving me, both of us, his body rutting against me as hard as I'm grinding down.

Time slows, and everything slides into individual pieces. How I feel. How he sounds. The wet suck of his mouth. My aching nipples. How hot and wet I am, impossibly sloppy. Can he feel that? Am I making a mess of these new shorts?

And then it all comes back together in a blinding crash, and I'm flying, rolling over his erection, and he's clamping me down against him as he jerks his hips.

"Fuck," he gasps.

My pulse is going a mile a minute. Between us, I can feel him go a bit soft. Still big, but? "Was that?"

He kisses me, wild and wet and hard. "Yes."

"It wasn't just for me?"

"I couldn't resist you." His voice cracks.

I love you. The words are so close to spilling out of my mouth, but I can't put that on him. He won't know what to do with that, so I kiss him instead, softly, right on the corner of his mouth.

And I burrow my face into his neck and smile so he knows how much I liked what we just did.

12
henry

THERE'S a calendar hanging in the kitchen. Summer has written reminders on it for the end of August.

Pick up welcome package

And then the one that I can't think about too hard or it hurts.

Residence move-in day

Time is sliding faster and faster now. And she's pushing my buttons every day now. I can't fault her for being clear about what she wants, not when she knows I want her, too.

Because the next thing she picks as an "educational learning experience" is far too tempting.

"I want to know how to give a blowjob."

"You don't need to give any boys a blowjob."

"Why not? I'm an adult."

"So you keep telling me."

"I'm starting to think you want me to be a little girl forever." She smirks at me, but goddamn it, that's a little too close to home. "Daddy. . ."

I give her a warning growl.

"Your little girl is all grown up, though. Ready to learn about sex. And if you won't teach her. . ."

I haul her in and savage her mouth with a kiss that probably hurts, but fuck it. I need her to stop talking in that sing-song voice that makes me want to bust her in half with my cock.

"No blowjob lessons."

"I don't like that answer." She pouts, and that just makes me kiss her again.

I tangle my hands in her hair and give her a stern look. "I have to open the shop."

"So what you're saying is, I should ask again tonight."

"What I'm saying is, little girls shouldn't be in a rush to grow up." But when she sways against me, I dip my mouth, and we're kissing *again*, her tongue wet and slick against my lips.

Not a little girl at all.

An eager woman who likes to play at being innocent. Who gets me hard as fuck and makes me want to drag her back to bed, a bed we're sharing now, and a bed in which I'm *not* fucking her.

I deserve a gold medal.

I need a cold shower.

And I have customers to get to because real life waits for no horny man.

"I'll wait until you're ready," she whispers as she pushes me toward the stairs.

I rake my gaze down her body, from her bare legs sticking out from the bottom of her sundress, then back up again to the tits I want to decorate with come, and that mouth—still wet from my mouth—she's offering up.

I'm ready.

I'm fucked, but I'm ready.

13
summer

AFTER DINNER THAT NIGHT, we move to the couch without any discussion.

Henry sprawls out and tugs me in against him, so we're both lying down as we watch a show he likes.

I don't pay any attention to it. I'm more interested in his body. I slide my hand under the hem of his T-shirt. "Is this okay?"

His muscles tense under my touch. "Yes."

But he hesitates before he says it. I don't want him to regret this later. "Henry..."

"It's okay," he says quietly. "You can touch me."

I play with the soft hairs below his belly button, then run my palm flat down the front of his pants. To the heavy cock I want to explore.

I stroke him through the fabric of his pants. I like how he grows under my touch, getting harder and flexing. I trace the shape of him with my fingertip, loving the change in his breathing.

My touch does that to him. Makes his exhales ragged, and his inhales slower and more deliberate. Like he's gotta hold on really hard to his control.

I could make him slide out of control.

I flatten my palm again, covering as much of his cock as I can, and I try to imagine what it would be like to have him bare in my hand. To jerk him off and make him come.

"That's enough."

I squeeze. "Doesn't feel like enough."

"We should go to bed."

"Mmm, yes."

"To sleep, Summer."

"Buzzkill." I launch myself onto his body, loving the way he catches me and holds me against his big chest. I give him a serious look. "You know I'm just teasing, right? I'm okay with the slow stuff if that's what you want. I'm having fun."

"I can tell."

"You didn't finish watching your show."

"I was watching you." He holds my chin between his fingers. "Better than anything on TV."

I wriggle against him, and he lets me kiss him, then kisses me back. Slow and deep, with lots of tongue. My legs rub against his, my pelvis pressing against the cock I raised to a hard erection.

He's still rock solid, and he's not stopping me from grinding against him.

"You make me feel good," I whisper.

"I'm glad."

"Do you want to come like this?"

He groans and rolls us off the couch, his big arms holding me until my feet find the floor. "And that's enough of that."

"Why?"

He ignores me and stalks into the bathroom. I follow him and watch as he brushes his teeth.

Wordlessly, he hands me my toothbrush. We clean up together, then he leaves when I say I have to pee.

"You could stay," I tease through the closed door.

When I come out, he's lying flat on his back on the bed,

blankets folded down to the bottom of the bed. His cock is in relief against his sweatpants, like a thick, beautiful, and vulgar sculpture.

"Was that too much?"

"No," he says thickly. "It's never too much."

"You'd watch me pee?"

He swears under his breath. "Come to bed."

I curl up next to him, and he turns out the light, tugging the blanket up and over my body.

"Yes," he says in the darkness. "I would."

"That's fascinating."

"Is it?"

"I mean, I know people on the Internet—"

"Don't look that shit up."

"It's not something I *sought out*," I say hotly. "Sometimes it just appears when you're looking up normal stuff."

"What kind of normal stuff were you looking up?"

I press my lips together, trying to contain my glee that Henry asks me about sex stuff for once and not the other way around. "Taking virginity videos. Big man, little girl. . . that sort of thing. How it works. With the size difference, and—"

He rolls over and kisses me, his hand in my hair, his mouth urgent.

I kiss him back, soft and welcoming. *Show me*, I try to say. *Who needs porn when you have a real-life Henry.*

"It's not like that. Whatever you've seen. It's not. . ." He stops and drags in a breath.

"Show me."

"I can't."

"Why not?"

"Because I want to do bad things to you." He tucks me into his side, a big, soft giant who could never hurt me even if he tried.

"How bad?"

He chuckles in the dark. "Can't trick me."

"But maybe you're wrong, and they aren't actually bad." I stretch one leg up into the air, a flash of pale skin, then lower it down and repeat it on the other side. "Mama taught me that it's not the act that's wrong; it's just the timing. And maybe the person, too, although she didn't say that part out loud. But if it's just a matter of timing, it figures that there will be the right person at the right time. And when it's the right person, all the bad things will be good things because—"

"I'm not your right person."

I smile at the ceiling. "Yes, you are. But it'll take you some time to realize."

"God, I love your confidence. Now go to sleep."

I roll onto my side, away from him. "Scratch my back?"

"Sure."

He draws lazy figures on the bare skin between my tank top straps.

I don't fall asleep. I usually do, really fast; it's a gift. But not tonight. Eventually, he slows his touch on my back, then slides his arm around my waist, tugging me back against him.

"Your brain is going a million miles a minute. I can hear it from here."

"I can't help it."

He sighs. "What's on your mind?"

I roll my hips back against his half-thick cock. "Bad things."

"Like what?"

"Oh, so it's okay for me to tell you, but not for you to tell me?"

"Precisely."

"Mmm." But I love to tell Henry things that make him uncomfortable, that makes him blush. That makes him hard.

And most of all, I love to tell him things that loosen his attachment to this ridiculous idea that we won't be perfect together.

"I want you to touch me when I'm half asleep." I have no

shame as I make the confession. There is no part of my mind I won't share with him if he's willing to hear it.

He groans into my hair, his hold on me tightening.

"I think I'll like it real slow. Just your fingers moving inside me, glacial movements. Your thumb on my clit. Then all of your fingers shoved inside me, so I'm full—"

His hand jerks up from holding my waist and covers my mouth.

Behind me, his breath is ragged, uneven. Horny.

"I'm going to sleep on the couch," he mutters.

"Don't." I slide out of his grip and sit on the edge of the bed. Maybe I should have done this weeks ago. I take a deep breath, then tug my tank top over my head. I stand, knowing I'm backlit by the moonlight, knowing he can see what I'm doing, and shove my shorts down my hips. My nudity is highlighted by the light coming through the window.

He grabs me and tumbles us into bed, my body rolling beneath his.

There's a moment of tension, a warring between him and himself, then I see in his eyes when he finally snaps.

We fit together perfectly for all our differences in size. My legs fall open, and I press my hips up, eager to feel him where I'm wet, but he pushes me down, one hand hard on my hip, the other on my shoulder.

I gasp at the arousal that courses through me. "What are you going to do to me?"

"Anything I want," he says lazily, his gaze raking over my body. "You are the sexiest fucking thing. Look at you. Naked in my bed. My hot little secret."

His whole hand covers my breast, making me instantly wet.

"Are you going to fuck me?"

He licks his lips, flicking his gaze up to my face before falling back to my bare tits and then to the dark vee between my legs. "Jesus, Summer. When we get there, let's not call it fucking the first time, okay?"

When. I like the sound of that. "Okay. But we'll call it that the second time, right?"

He chuckles darkly and zeroes in on my lips. "I think we'll start with your mouth. You wanted to learn how to give a blowjob. How does that sound? Should I *fuck* your innocent little mouth?"

14
henry

I BARELY RECOGNIZE the words coming out of my mouth, but the last few weeks have unlocked something dark and wonderful between us. The rules have changed.

And most importantly, Summer wants me to be crude. It fires her up. Me, too.

My whole adult life, I didn't think I had the same kind of intense sexual desires I've heard other people talk about. Turns out, I was waiting for the right little girl to spark my inner monster so I could tell her to open her wet little mouth for Daddy's big, dripping cock.

But even as I hold her down and think about how much I fucking want that, I'm not that guy.

Not before she gets her orgasm. I want her mouth, but I want to give her mine first.

I let go of her and climb off the bed, ignoring her howl of protest. I catch her ankle with my hand—my fingers wrap all the way around her delicate little joint—and haul her to the edge of the mattress, where I kneel down.

"What—" Summer gasps as her legs fall open. "Wait, Henry. . ."

I stop immediately, one hand still on her ankle, the other hovering beside her hip. "What?"

"What are you doing?"

I grin. "I forgot my manners. Ladies first."

"Oh, but—" Even in the dim moonlight, I can see she's blushing furiously. "I didn't shave?"

"So?" I brush her damp curls. "This is fucking sexy, Summer. Don't think for a second it isn't."

"Oh."

"Did you think you should?"

"It seems. . . popular. I was thinking about it."

"Yeah?"

"Would you like it?" She asks it so fucking shyly.

"Like? Sure. Prefer? No." I graze the edge of where her pubic hair starts, loving how sensitive she is. "You can do whatever you want. I think you're the sexiest thing I've ever seen, so I swear it doesn't matter. I mean, my mouth is watering right now. But if you want to shave, I'll be hungry for you then, too."

"Would you help me?" She's panting now, horniness rolling off her in waves.

"If you want me to."

"I want you to do everything."

"Right now, all I want to do is eat this sweet little pussy, exactly as it is."

She moans and squeezes her eyes shut. A trickle of moisture slides out of her, a delicious-looking drop of goodness. I lean in and gently lap it up with my tongue. It's as good as I thought, sweet and precious and earthy. She cries out, and my whole body throbs in response.

"You have to tell me you want me to do this, Summer," I growl out the words. "Tell me to lick your pussy again."

"More." She licks her lips, eyes still squeezed shut. "Henry, lick me again. Please."

I close in, kissing her wet, sticky flesh with a soft, broad tongue. She smells like heaven, a musky goddess scent I never want to wash off my skin. As she trembles beneath my mouth, I use my thumbs to stroke her outer lips, encouraging her to bloom for me. More of that delicious juice floods out of her as her flesh swells in response to my ministrations.

She throbs, too. I can feel it through her clit, through the trembling pulses of her inner lips, connected to that untouched entrance.

Her tiny, tight hole. I lick around it, then test how far she likes my tongue inside her, where she tastes so fucking fresh it hurts my soul a little that I'm doing this.

I'm a dirty old man obsessed with his friend's daughter. Obsessed with his ward, the young woman entrusted to his care. I've jacked off in the shower thinking about her sweet scent on my sheets, and now I'm on my knees, licking up every drop of her innocent arousal.

I'm going to make her come, I realize as she shakes beneath my mouth.

She likes the way I'm devouring her and doesn't that feed the monster inside me. *She'll like it even more when it's your fingers and your cock.*

A million different ways to take her scroll through my mind. I could turn her over and lick her tight asshole. Get my mouth on her tits again and fuck her with my fingers.

Do this, but when she's sleeping.

Do this, but downstairs in the shop.

Do this, but when she's studying—

"Henry, oh, *Henry!*" Her whole body convulses when I latch on to her clit, and it only takes a few steady sucks for her to go off. I soften my hold on her, gently rolling my tongue with the clutching waves rocking through her pussy.

She's shivering and grinning when I lift my head. "Wow."

"Good?"

"Amazing."

I kiss her knee. "Put your clothes back on."

"You promised me a blow job lesson!"

"I'm fine."

"But my mouth is *empty*, Henry, and that is not fine." She rises up on her knees and gives me a stern look that is cute as fuck. "Unless you want to distract me with something else."

No.

I'm clinging to taking this at the slowest possible fucking pace, given that all I want to do is pin her down and breed her. But I'm done pretending we aren't going to eventually do everything. And my balls are so full it hurts.

I stand up, then think better of looming over her. It's better if she's on top for this.

"Move over, then. You'll fit between my legs. . ." I groan as she moves, so fucking eager, and kneels in the perfect position to take my cock in her mouth once I'm stretched out on the bed.

All I need to do is tug down my sweatpants and finally show her the cock that wants to break her in two.

Are you going to fuck me?

I swallow against that overwhelming need and take her hand in mine. Together we grab the waistband of my pants and push it down. My cock bobs into view, and the delighted gasp Summer lets out will be burned into my memory forever.

"Oh," she breathes as she reaches for him, and he twitches at the first agonizing stroke of her soft fingertips against my needy flesh. "You're so big."

"You have little hands." Fuck, just saying that out loud instead of in my darkest fantasies has a thick bead of come pearling at the tip, and Summer's eyes go wide.

"You're. . . Is that. . ."

"It's pre-come. It helps get me all slick, makes it easy to stroke me."

"Can I touch it?"

The wonder in her voice makes my balls pull tight, and

more slick appears. She'll have me coming just from talking about giving me a handy. "Yes, baby. Touch it all you want."

She strokes her fist up to the crown, then lets go, and my cock throbs, waving in the air. She giggles as she realizes it won't stay put for her to touch just the tip, so she gets two hands involved, and I groan at the extra sensation.

And that's before she leans in.

Her hair tumbles down around her shoulders, brushing against my belly, covering her face. She giggles and pushes the tangled strands away from her face.

"This is hard to coordinate," she says.

I smooth the hair off her face, gathering it in a ponytail that I hold behind her head. She makes a pleased sound when she goes to swallow more of me and can't move because of my unexpectedly firm grip.

"Sorry," I mutter.

She shakes her head. "I like it. You've got me trapped here."

My brain stutters over sweet, innocent Summer enjoying a bite of pain. A bit of tight control. It casts the way she gasped when I pinned her to the bed in a whole new light.

There's something so immediately sexual about her. She's been showing me this all summer, that she wants this—that she needs it. She craves it. She is a wholly formed woman with desires as real and complex as my own. That through some sort of miracle might just match my own desires.

Because I want nothing more than to hold her pretty little head still and pump my hips. Fill her mouth.

But not now, not the first time she's doing this.

Her breath is hot against my wet tip as she strokes little exploring circles around the head.

"Lick it," I say hoarsely. "Don't be afraid to make it extra wet. That will help when you take it in your mouth. I'll like it if you get a little sloppy. You can play with it, too. Have fun."

She sticks her tongue out, tasting the pre-come carefully, then swipes it around again, this time leaving a wetter trail than before. I groan at how good the contact feels, how sweet her innocent little mouth is. How pure this exploration feels.

Then she parts her lips wider, her tongue leading the way, and the edges of my vision go dark because I'm in her mouth. She's wet and hot, a little unsure, and fuck fuck fuck, I'm going to blow.

"Pull off, Summer," I groan, but she's going lower, and my cock nudges the top of her mouth, then the back, where the texture is different, and it feels like her pussy. I'm in her body, my hips don't fucking care what hole it is, and I catch her head with both hands, holding her still.

Right on the edge of disaster, I carefully ease her almost all the way off. Her eyes are wide, watching me the whole time as I push her back onto my length.

Her lips are stretched wide, sealed around me, and goddamn it, I'm going to fucking fill her innocent little mouth any second now.

"Swallow." My voice is hoarse as I give her the one-word command.

She gulps around my dick, and that does it. I've wanted the pulse of her tongue against the underside of my cock since the day she walked into my barbershop.

The first spurt takes her by surprise. I can see it in her eyes. There's an edge of panic, but then her mouth works again, and she's lapping it up, every drop I have for her, and I'm thrusting deeper, shooting straight down her throat.

Daddy's come, deep in his baby girl's belly.

I'm shaking when she slides her mouth off, my cock still thick and shiny from her spit and my come. She rests her head on my massive thigh and gives me a happy smile. "Yummy," she murmurs, and fuck if I don't get half-hard again.

I stroke her cheek. "I lost it there. I'm sorry. You were such a good girl, taking it like that. Letting me. . ."

"Fuck my mouth?" She smiles.

I reach down and grab her, lifting her up on top of my body.

"You're a wonder, Summer. God, I don't know what I did to deserve you showing up here and making me so happy. Now go to sleep."

Her soft giggle is followed by a contented sigh, followed shortly after by the smooth, long breaths of unconsciousness.

Daddy's come, deep in his baby girl's belly.

Fuck.

15
summer

THE NEXT DAY I go to campus. I have a meeting with someone in the student services department who helps me pick an elective course, and then I go to the bookstore to pick up some textbooks. I even run into a few classmates I met at the orientation sessions.

Compared to how nervous I was at the start of the summer, it's a fun, easy day. I'm excited about the start of classes now.

I stop at Brewed Awakening, a coffee shop just on the edge of campus—a rival for the best coffee in town compared to Wake Up Call, the shop down the street from Henry's barbershop. I get Henry an iced decaf and a peach iced tea for myself.

As I walk back to Main Street, I think about how pretty Conception Ridge is, with its leafy, tree-lined streets and cozy rows of houses. I can't imagine wanting to leave here and go to Los Angeles, but then again, I didn't grow up here. It's probably just the way life goes—wherever you grow up, there will be some impulse to try another pace of life.

But so far, I really like small-town living. Especially this small town, with its super sexy barber and two delicious coffee shops.

Henry is mid-cut when I get back to the barbershop, so I

check the appointment list. It looks like this is his last customer. A haircut and a shave. I pull out a textbook and start reading as I sip my tea, or at least I try to read.

Mostly I find myself watching how Henry works.

I hop up and offer to sweep when he's all done. Henry gives me a grateful smile that makes me all tingly.

"I got you a coffee," I tell him once we're alone. "Decaf, because it's late."

"Worried I won't get to sleep?" There's something extra warm in his gaze as he looks at me over his coffee and takes a sip.

"I like it when we go to sleep together."

"Me, too." I know he's thinking about last night when he says that. Thinking about us using our mouths on each other and how hot that was.

"Henry?"

"Mmm?"

I climb into the barber chair and hitch one leg over the arm. My skirt crawls up my thigh.

Henry looks at me, his eyes hooded, his gaze hard to read. Am I going to get into trouble for being dirty downstairs?

"Do the blinds close all the way?"

His chest rises and falls twice before he answers. "Yes."

"I want you to shave me the same way you shaved that customer."

He laughs. "It won't be anything like that."

"Hot towel treatment, careful attention to detail. . . I think it will."

"When did you get so bossy?" But he closes the blinds.

Locks the door.

Prepares the hot towels.

Shaving cream.

The brush.

A straight razor and a safety razor, side by side, neatly on a towel.

Everything is laid out just so. Proper. And then there's me, a wanton hussy sprawled in his chair. "I think I've always been bossy?"

"Let's not confuse bratty and bossy." He looks amused, though.

"Do you think I'm a brat?"

"I think for the first time in your life, you've found someone you can manipulate a little, and you're having fun." He catches my chin firmly between his finger and his thumb. "But don't forget that I *let* you do that because you're a very good girl who deserves to have some fun. You're not actually the boss of me."

I shiver. No, I don't think I am. If anything, I want Henry to be in charge. I like it when he lays down the law. "You're the boss," I whisper.

"I'm the. . ." He swallows the next word.

"Daddy?"

"Fucking hell, Summer."

"I like it." When he doesn't say anything, I try to drop it. Try and fail. "Do you like it?"

"Nosy girls don't get their pussies shaved."

"I'll take that as a yes."

He slides his hand around to the back of my neck and squeezes there. "Yes, I like it. But it's complicated."

"Everything is."

He raises his eyebrows, an amused smile tugging at the corners of his mouth. "In fact, yes. Everything is. Now stop with the questions so I can get to work here."

He uses the trimmer first, getting rid of my bush in a few quick zips. All that remains is short stubble, and he smooths his fingers over my mound once I'm basically bare. "Some people like it just like this."

"Do you?"

"Yes." He huffs a laugh and kisses me deeply. "I like it every which way, Summer. I like you, and your pussy is beautiful."

"Thank you, Mr. Body Positivity."

"What do you think of this?"

"It's nice." I spread my legs wider. "But it's not what I want."

"The customer is always right." He gets two hot towels and covers me with them after tucking a dry towel under my butt.

Then he prepares the soap and gets a special bottle I haven't seen before.

"What's that?"

"I'm not putting the usual aftershave balm on your sugar-sweet skin, baby."

"You got me my own aftershave balm?"

He doesn't answer that question.

Which makes me grin. Henry never answers the questions with the dirtiest answers. "What else have you secretly prepared for me, Daddy?"

"Everything," he says gruffly. "I told you. I have all sorts of bad thoughts. Now hold still."

I sigh happily as he crouches in front of me. I don't think it's an angle he's ever shaved someone before in this chair, but he carefully stretches my skin this way and that so he can remove the hair.

His touch is magical, making me hot and needy, quickly getting me as bare as a baby's bottom at the same time.

When he wipes away the last traces of shaving cream, I moan at the sensation. My skin feels so sensitive, and every-thing is heightened.

The Beaver Balm—actually its name—that he applies after feels amazing. Or maybe that's just his fingers moving against my bare little cunt.

"Stop making those sounds," Henry demands.

"What sounds?"

"The *Daddy, please fuck me* sounds."

"Will you fuck me?"

He doesn't say no. Another non-answer that fills me with joy.

"Henry. . ."

He kisses the inside of my thigh.

"There's only a week left before I move to campus."

"I know." His breath is higher now, right against my freshly shaved pussy. "Do you like it?"

"I love it." His lips brush my skin, and I jump. "I'm so sensitive."

"That's the idea." He looks up at me. "Want to come on Daddy's face before dinner?"

16
henry

I **WEAR** the scent of her on my face when we go out for dinner.

I watch her squirm in delight as she sits across from me, still getting used to the way her bare pussy feels against fabric. I wonder how this is my life, how this feels so good and like I'm finally alive.

And I can't want too much of this, because it will end soon. *Too late, I want this forever.*

That is not on the table. At some point, her mother will return from the high seas—so far, we've received a few sporadic email updates. When that happens, Summer cannot be begging me to eat her freshly shaved box.

Not even in secret.

Of course, that doesn't stop me from imagining *what-if* scenarios. What if we fell in love and got married? What if Summer wanted my babies? What if I got to feel this happy forever?

"Something on your mind?" She murmurs the question from across the table, a knowing look on her face.

She thinks my thoughts are still in the filthy deeds we did back at the store.

That's for the best.
This is just sex. This can only be sex.
"You," I tell her. It's the truth, after all.

17
summer

HENRY'S HAND is between my legs. It's the middle of the night, and I wake up because I'm horny—then I realize it's because he's touching me.

I'm soaked, my panties a wet mess, and I desperately want his fingers under the cotton. I push my bum back at him, but he doesn't change his slow, gentle petting.

I don't think he's awake.

My whole body feels like it wants to turn itself inside out. I want him inside me. It's a crystal clear desire. The only thing that will solve this deep need is Henry.

I can't say how I know I need him inside me. I should be scared of the whole idea. I've watched enough porn and spent time stroking him. Looking at him. I find my gaze drawn over and over again to the bulge behind his jeans when he works. His sweat pants when we're alone. Wondering at the heavy shape of him and how it could ever fit inside me.

And there is that frisson of fear. The classic concept of *oh, it could never fit* because I'm so little and he's so big.

But even though I *am* so little and he *is* so big, I also know all about how our bodies change and grow to birth babies. I know that when a woman is this wet and heat is swirling low in her belly, she can take a man inside her, no matter his size.

Mama didn't want me to ever have sex, so she went out of her way to make sure that I knew how uncomfortable that first time would be. How I should want to save it for the right person.

But here in the dark, I know I did that. I know Henry *is* the right person.

He's spooning me, his big arm wrapped around my body and cupping my pussy from the front.

Which means if I just shift my hips back and maybe down, I'll feel it—

His cock.

It's heavy and big against my thighs, now that I've found it. If I could get my panties off and his pants down—okay, that's two complicated steps, but a girl can dream—it would be so easy to rock my hips back and just see if the tip fits inside me.

I hold my breath as I push my panties down my hips. The completely bare skin between my legs feels different—sexier—and very slick. Like nothing is stopping my arousal from spilling out and sliding down my thighs.

Henry murmurs in his sleep as I tug the cotton out from under his touch, then grunts as his hand squeezes and he discovers he's cupping bare pussy.

"Summer," he mumbles. "Baby, you feel so good. I just want to touch you, okay? Just want to make you feel. . ."

My heart hammers in my chest. "Need you," I whisper back. "Want to feel you against me."

He shoves his shorts down, and his cock thumps against me, warm and solid. I spread my legs, lifting my top thigh up to make space for him, and he thrusts his erection against me.

Something tells me he's still asleep, only partially aware of what we're doing.

It's a big, blunt intrusion between my legs. Something not so much for me to push on to, more rub against, but the angle is wrong. He doesn't enter me at all even as I grind; his cock just slips around against my wet pussy. I can't figure out the coordination of it all.

Maybe I'm not meant to. Maybe this is a two-person job.

And then, just when I think I'm going to give up, his other hand snakes around me, wrapping around my waist and pinning me back against him.

His whole body starts, a jolt of awareness.

And then he's groaning, growling my name as he presses his face into the bare skin of my neck.

He changes the angle, and instead of penetrating me how I want it, his cock is now lodged firmly between my thighs. He's pinning me into a specific position, creating a tight space.

Now the pressure is different. The tip of his cock rocks deliberately against my clit. He knows exactly how to rub against that tight, swollen bead, and I forget that I wanted to try and clumsily push myself onto him. *This* is magic.

It's not what my body thought I needed tonight. It's better. It doesn't hurt, and it's beautiful. The way his whole body surrounds mine makes me feel safe. And he takes my arousal from this desperate, subconscious needy ache to a gorgeous heat that swarms my whole body. It fills my limbs with a heaviness that feels delicious.

"Good girl," he murmurs in my hair. "Come for me. Come on my cock. Flood me. I want to feel how wet you get for Daddy."

I shudder. That word is beyond naughty. It takes my breath away how profoundly, deeply I want Henry to be the man who shows me everything.

Henry, who keeps me sane even as I tried to recklessly do everything in my power to seduce him. Henry—*Daddy*—finds all these inventive ways for us to be together without going too fast. Without me doing something he thinks I'll regret.

Think being the operative word, because I will never, ever regret this. I'll never regret coming apart in his arms as he whispers hot, dirty things in my ear. I don't think it can get any better than when I shatter. But it immediately does because Henry loses his absolute shit, gripping me so tight it almost hurts, and his hips jerk against mine.

This is what it might feel like for him to fuck me. Roughly, desperately. His heavy body slamming into mine, both of us sweaty. His words shift from coaxing, arousing sentences to selfish horny individual words. *Mine. Fuck. Little. Pussy. Need.*

Then my name, three times fast as he spills between my legs.

I imagine if we'd already had sex, and if I wasn't a virgin, he might shove me onto my back now. Get hard again, then push it all into me.

So many *ifs* to make that alternate dream a reality. If we had more time. If I wasn't going to school next week. If we met at a different time. If we weren't two different ages. If I wasn't just a teenage girl and he wasn't old enough to be my father. If he wasn't such a good man.

And if I wasn't such a horny little thing who pushed him too far, too fast.

I feel his absence keenly as he silently gets out of bed. When he gets to the doorway, I can see his face in the light from the hallway, and it's tight with worry.

"Sorry," I whisper when he gets back with a washcloth.

He frowns as he wipes between my legs. "For what?"

"That I started that. You were asleep."

He shakes his head. "I was dreaming of you. Pretty sure I did that to myself, shaving this sweet little cunt. It was all I could do to not mark it up before bed."

I suck in a breath. "Really?"

He exhales roughly. "You have no idea what you do to me, do you?"

"I don't know?"

"You turn me inside out, baby. I told you. I want to do bad things to you. That? That was fucking sweet. Nothing bad about that. Never be sorry for wanting to come on my hand, okay? I don't regret anything about tonight."

"Then why is your face all tense?"

He's smiling as he disappears again to dispose of the washcloth. But that's not an answer to my question, and even sleepy and well screwed, I still want an answer.

When he comes back, he makes me put my panties back on.

"Is that it? Are you tense because we could have fucked in our sleep?" A slight fib about my state of consciousness.

"Yeah."

"Would you regret it? If we just once—"

"I don't want to hurt you."

"You won't hurt me. You can't hurt me. It might hurt, but I want that. And I want the other side of hurting. It will be amazing. I just know it will. Come on, Henry, after everything we've done, we can't *not* do it once before I go to school."

He sighs and kisses my forehead. "Maybe I don't want to do it yet, because it means acknowledging that you're leaving soon."

"Oh."

"I'm going to miss you, sweetheart."

"I'll be a few miles away."

"Focusing on your studies."

There's a finality to how he says it, so I don't argue. But before I leave for the dorms, we're going to have to have a real talk about how I'm not giving him up.

18
henry

THREE DAYS PASS.

We can't keep our hands off each other. I don't tell her no, but I keep dodging her question. When will I take her virginity?

Part of me doesn't want to do it. Not before she moves into her dorm. Maybe if she still feels this way later in the fall or over Christmas break. I could book us a cabin in the mountains and make love to her in front of a roaring fireplace.

When she's sure.

When she's ready.

But every day, she shows me over and over that she is both sure and ready now.

It's a pair of sweatpants that does it, in the end. We're doing laundry, so she's wearing a skimpy little tank top and a pair of baggy sweats, everything else in the washer or the dryer. She dances around the apartment, putting away towels and folding my T-shirts in a way she saw on Netflix.

And I'm struck with the fact that I'm a complete and fucking idiot. Too tangled up in our age difference to realize that right in front of me is a person who makes me so fucking happy it hurts. I've been holding myself back. Depriving us both of a deeper connection when time is running out.

My pulse is pounding as I grab a strip of condoms from the box I bought a while ago—just in case—and prowl toward her.

She spins around, a delighted look settling on her face when she realizes I'm coming in for a hug.

"Hello." She makes a pleased sound as I kiss her.

She smells like fresh laundry and tastes like innocence about to be violated. If I ever had a favorite flavor before, it's now been replaced with this.

"What happened to doing laundry?"

"We're taking a break so I can show you how beautiful I think you are." I cup her breasts through the thin tank, playing with her nipples as I kiss her neck.

Mauling her, basically. Fuck, I can't stop now.

"Henry?"

"I'm sorry I made you wait so long."

"Are you— Are we?" She squeals in delight as I strip off her shirt. "You're ready?"

"I think that's supposed to be my question for you." I catch her mouth as she climbs into my arms, naked now, sweatpants on the floor. We kiss like we're on fire, and it feels so right I can't even hold on to the pang of regret I feel. It's there, and then it's gone, replaced by certainty and need.

We're both ready.

I carry her into the bedroom, and she stands on the bed as she helps me out of my shirt, and I lose my pants. I cannot get naked fast enough for my eager minx, and as soon as I am, she sprawls out on her back with an inviting look on her face.

After dropping the condom strip on the bed, I put my hands on her knees, guiding her legs to fold up, then out. Her sexy-as-fuck pussy with its sparse regrowth of soft, dark hair blooms for me. Pink and wet, shiny and swollen.

Ready for my cock, I know that, but I'm still nervous.

Not nervous enough to stop, though. And not nearly as nervous as I am equally confident that this is going to be fucking amazing for her.

I may not have done this a lot in my life because, deep down, I was waiting for her, but the few times I've practiced, I've learned things.

We'll both learn more tonight.

My hands are huge against her thighs, my fingers easily spanning most of her flesh. I love the difference there, how little she is in contrast to my big, brutish size.

It's a reminder that I need to be gentle, no matter how much she thinks she wants what is about to happen.

My cock is dripping at the tip, wet enough to leave a smear against the inside of her thigh as I tease her with my fingers first. She takes the first one with ease and only has a little groan when I give her a second one. But the third makes her pant, and her forehead pinches. And yes, my cock likes that, a bit too much.

I'm only going to take a girl's virginity once in my whole life. I'm going to fucking enjoy it, her ripe, untouched cunt making room for me for the first time.

But despite the way her body reacts to the intrusion of my fingers, Summer knows what she wants. She gets her hand on my erection and tries to pull it toward her pussy.

I pin her down the way she likes and give her a stern growl. "We need a condom."

She pouts and rubs the dripping tip of my cock against her clit. "Are you sure?"

I grunt.

But I still grab the first condom and roll it on. The slick, lubricated protection helps when I notch my cock against her tiny slit. I've dreamed of this moment, worried that it would hurt her too much, or be too hard for me to push into her. . . and it's not.

She's fucking tight, don't get me wrong.

But as big as my fucking cock is and getting bigger by the second as I press into her, the lube and her own arousal ease the way.

She cries out, her eyes going impossibly wide as she takes me for the first time. I don't know if it's *oh* or *ow*, but before I can stop, she's smiling, tossing her head back.

I'm two inches in, then three. My fat dick is bulging at the base, her pussy stretching wide around it, and there's still so much more for her take, but it feels fucking incredible.

Never had anything like it. A first for both of us, and my balls start pulsing. I ease back, knowing I'm going to blow my load in her in a hot fucking second if I don't slow my roll.

"No, no, no, don't stop," she pants.

"Just spreading your sweet juices up my cock, baby."

She turns pink, and now the shoe is on the other foot. Finally, it's Daddy's turn to make her blush, my hedonistic sex baby.

I pump my hips twice, going in further than before on the third thrust. She cries out again but immediately begs me to keep going.

"It hurts so good." Her voice is breathy and full of wonder. "Henry, you're *inside me.*"

I pin her down and do it again. I find a good angle for leverage so I can keep touching her because I can't keep my hands off her. Her thigh, her knee, her calf. Her thin little ankle, flexing in my grip as I thrust my hips, finding all the ways to make her eyes go wide and her mouth fall open in that gorgeous, silent gasp.

There.

That's the spot. That's the secret I've been keeping from her because I knew once we did this, we would never stop.

Now she knows how good Daddy's cock feels buried deep in her little pussy.

And that's all it takes, that filthy thought, and I fall on her, gathering her in my arms.

She clings to me as we move as one, slow and intimate.

"Touch yourself." My voice is a low murmur between us, a private guide. "You might not get there from my cock alone. I want to see your fingers on that pretty clit. Show me what feels nice."

"You feel nice," she pants, but she slides her hand down her body all the same.

"Good girl." I press my forehead against hers and look down between our bodies. I'm so glad we did this in the daylight. I want to remember every expression on her face, every tense flex of her body, every spot she turns pink.

I want to watch her come apart while I ride her like she was made for me, so I can remember what she likes and what she needs.

And her sweet little middle finger, moving in tight circles, is exactly that.

"Daddy," she whispers, the name a prayer on her breath. "I'm going to come."

"I've got you."

"Come with me."

"I'm there. Oh fuck, Summer, I'm there. Come on, baby. You feel so good. So damn tight. I'm going to fill you up, little one."

"Oh my God."

"Call me Daddy." It's a rough demand.

She gasps it out.

"Again."

My balls are churning now.

"Daddy. . ."

"Shhh. . ." Fuck. "Be quiet for Daddy."

She squeaks and clings to me, her nipples hard against my furry chest. Her mouth latches on to my neck, and around my cock, I feel the first trembling clutches of her orgasm.

I crush her to the bed and slam my hips into her, out of control with the need to bury my seed in her belly. "Good girl," I grunt. "So good for Daddy. So perfect. My pretty girl, I love how you feel. Take it. Take it all."

The first spurt feels like it blows the top of my head off, and the rest are fucking glorious. There's a lot, too, like I've unloaded a lifetime of come into her.

"God," I mutter as I lift myself off her.

She stretches out, fully nude. Her smile is incandescent, a shining beacon. "That was wonderful."

That was rough and wild and perfect.

"Are you sore?" I run my fingertips lightly over the tops of her thighs.

"A little." She catches my hand and brings it to her breast. "Not here, though. I just feel good here."

I squeeze her flesh gently, enjoying the way her nipple tightens against my palm. "You're beautiful."

"I think that's what you said to get in my pants before, too." She giggles as I jerk back, and she chases my hand, pulling it back. "Henry. I *want* you to do it again."

"You're sore."

"Only a little. And I know you'll be gentle."

"It'll take me a minute to recharge." I reach for another condom. "If you really want to do it again. . ."

"Yes, again. Always again. Never stop making love to me."

If only it were that simple.

But right now, it feels like it should be.

19
summer

HENRY BUYS me a second suitcase for all of the clothes and books he gave me over the summer.

Now he hovers as I pack, helping me fold clothes, reminding me of the time ticking by.

"You're going to have so much fun." His voice is smooth and confident like he really wants me to leave him. Like he really does want me to go away and have a good time—even if he's sad about it. It makes me grumpy because, in my fantasies, he's possessive in this moment. He pins me to the bed and tells me I can't leave him, I can't go.

But of course, Henry's too good for that. Too nice, too kind.

I have to lean on the suitcase to close it. And once it's zipped up, he hauls it off the bed and takes it through the apartment to the top of the stairs. I stay in the bedroom, listening to him carrying my belongings away from the space he gave me. The space that we've shared for the past few weeks.

The bed where he held me and taught me how to make love.

I'm not ready to go. *I'm* the one who feels possessive.

When he appears in the doorway, I launch myself at him.

He catches me, murmuring my name, telling me it's gonna be okay, but I don't want to hear that. I cover his mouth with mine, refusing his comfort. That's not what I want. I need his hands on my skin. I need his cock in my body. And I will take it if he doesn't give it to me.

I'll stake my claim on him. I'll show him that he can send me to school. He can let me go, but I will *not* fly away.

If you love something, set them free. That's what he's doing. But I can't tell him that I'll be back because I can't bear for him to tell me I shouldn't come back to him. We can't talk at all right now. For all the time we've spent together—all of the intimacies we've discovered together—we haven't figured out how to talk honestly about what we want.

I tangle my fingers in his cropped beard, tugging his mouth open so I can kiss him. There's nothing sweet about it, either. I fuck him with my tongue until his arms start to shake, and I make him release me. I slide down his body and drop to my knees. Unzipping his jeans, I find him ready for me—heavy, slick, shiny. I take him into my mouth and swallow him down until he's grunting my name, over and over again.

Then I push him to the bed. I am a fierce lioness now, and he is my prey. My claws dig into his chest as I climb astride him. I'm not ready, and it hurts. A burn that feels so good. The way he fills me up—too much, too big, too deep—is the perfect kind of ache.

I did that.

"Summer, I'm not—"

I don't want to hear it. I cover his mouth with mine, biting at his lips. I roll my hips, riding him fast and furious. He clutches at my waist, pulling me down on him and then trying to push me off, but I'm there suddenly. I went from zero to sixty, and now I'm crashing, reckless and wild.

It's only after he peels me off him that I realize he's mad. He's swearing under his breath as he zips himself up. "Fuck, fuck, fuck."

"Henry?"

"We shouldn't have done that. That was a mistake." He

groans and stands up, then swears again when he notices that I'm crying. "Summer, no."

"I'm sorry," I sob.

He crawls on top of me and kisses me hard on the mouth, then soft as he licks away the tears slicking down from my face.

"I know you needed that, and I did too. But we didn't use a condom. You can't risk that." He drags in a heavy, shaking breath. "You can't do that, Summer, not with me, and goddamn it, not with anyone else."

"I'm not going to do that with anyone else," I yell at him. Now we're both mad. "I'm not going to do that with anyone else. Ever. You're it for me. Why don't you see that?"

"Because you're just a girl," he growls back. "A girl who doesn't know her own self yet."

The silence that follows is deafening. I stare at him in disbelief. He can think a lot of things about me. He can think that I need to go to college and have that experience, even though I could do that and love him at the same time. But he honestly believes, after all this time, that I don't know myself?

"You don't need to worry about me getting pregnant," I mutter, not looking at him. "It's not a good time for that. I mean, never say never, but I'm going to get my period any day now. I'll let you know when you're in the clear."

"Summer—"

"Shut up," I snap. "You've said enough. And I'm not some little kid you can lecture."

"So the Daddy fantasy is only when I'm indulgent of your every whim?" He grabs me by the shoulders. "I want what's best for you. One day soon, you'll realize I'm on your side, no matter what."

"Don't hold your breath." I push him out of the way. "I'll call an Uber."

"Like fucking hell you will." He follows me into the living room. "I'm taking you to campus and getting you settled in your dorm room. End of story."

I roll my eyes, but my back is to him.

"Don't roll your eyes at me." It's a rebuke and a peace offering rolled into one gruff bark.

I glance back. "How did you know?"

"You move your whole head," he says gruffly. "It's cute."

20
henry

MY HEART IS POUNDING PAINFULLY in my chest. I know I've fucked up here in a bunch of different ways. Letting her take me on the bed like that was a huge mistake. Going in raw and spilling my seed in her perfect teenage cunt—the hottest thing ever.

But also a mistake.

The worst fuck up of all, though, was getting mad about it. What's done is done. And I should have had more patience and understanding around it because it *was* hot. But it was also what she *needed*, and I stomped all over both of those things.

Now she's leaving, and she wants to take a fucking Uber?

No fucking way.

"You're cute," I repeat, closing the gap between us. "When you're mad, and when you're happy. You're cute all the fucking time, and I know this is hard on you. It's hard on me, too. I'm sorry for everything I said in there. I'm a bonehead. Can I try again?"

She nods warily.

"I'm going to miss the hell out of you," I confess. "I need to let you go right now, for *my* reasons. I know you know yourself. I shouldn't have said that. I believe you when you say that I'm what you need. But I'm a grown-ass man who is tangled up in his feelings for a teenager, and that's not something I can just *do*, easily, without giving you a million outs."

"I don't want any outs."

"I know." I gather her in my arms. "Just humor me. Go to college. Have fun. Not condom-free fun, though."

"Don't worry about that," she mumbles into my shirt. "That's just for you."

"Not for me either." I kiss the top of her head. "I'll stock up on condoms for when you want to visit."

She jerks her head up. "Really?"

"How about a standing Sunday dinner date? I hear the cafeterias serve less food on the weekends."

"Saturday and Sunday. With a sleepover."

"Just Sunday, but you can come over early."

"Henry—"

I cut her off, kissing her. Fuck. Yes, I want the sleepover. I want her to unpack right now and never leave.

We cannot slide down the slippery slope.

———

We hold hands on the drive to campus. Her little fingers grip my hand with a fierceness that matches the way she fucked me an hour ago.

The tension in my truck is brutal. This isn't how I want her collegiate career to begin, with her thoughts tangled up in the apartment above a shop across town.

When I park in the designated lot closest to her dorm, I turn the truck off but don't get out.

"Henry, I want—"

"—Listen, Summer, I need. . ."

We both stop and stare at each other.

"Let me go first," I say, lifting her hand to my mouth so I can kiss her fingertips. "God, you're so sweet. And fierce. I see that, and I love it. I'm sorry that today got so messy."

"I'm not."

"I said, let me talk first." I frown at her.

She pouts back.

"I want you to know how important you are to me. I want you to hold that tight and believe it because the last thing you should be doing this week is worrying about how an old man feels about you. I am yours. Team Summer, always and forever. I want you to enjoy the fuck out of your first year at college. All four years. And I'm really fucking happy that I'm just a phone call away if you need me. It doesn't just need to be Sunday dinner."

"I'm going to call. And visit. A *lot*."

"You're going to focus on school, *first and foremost*."

"Now, who's bossy?"

"Me, and that's how it should be." I lean across the console and tuck her hair behind her ear. "Come here. Let me kiss you goodbye properly, here, where nobody can see how hard you make me. And then I'm going to help you get settled in your room."

"I'll kiss you there, too."

"If we're alone."

She squirms in her seat.

I sip at her lips, not in any hurry. This might be the final taste for a while, and I want it to last us both until Sunday dinner. She tastes bright and young, full of potential. Her tongue is so talented now, and she puts it to good use, teasing and licking at me just the way I like.

We've spent the summer so deeply entwined, it's no wonder it's hard to say goodbye. She knows me better than anyone ever has.

I hope she knows how much I value our connection.

My head is buzzing, and my arms feel heavy by the time I let her go. She gives me one final chaste kiss on the cheek before hopping out of the truck.

I take her suitcases and follow her to reception, where she checks in and gets her room key for the first time.

She's lucked out, getting a rare private room. It's small and at the end of a hall, next to the stairs.

I look around the utilitarian space and nod enthusiastically for her benefit. "This is excellent."

"It's okay."

"It's *great*."

"Your best dad impression is duly noted."

That tugs at my gut in a weird and secretly good way. Sometimes I forget I'm supposed to be her temporary guardian, not that she needs one anymore. I'm glad I'm still filling that role a bit while mostly thinking about getting her naked.

"Five days until Sunday pot roast." I'm intent on being upbeat here.

"Five lonely nights." She glances around the room and out into the hallway, then slowly closes the door. Flips the lock shut. "I'm going to miss you so much, Daddy."

I don't stop her when she slides to her knees. I tangle my hand in her hair and lean back against the door. Temporary guardian responsibilities are highly overrated compared to the wet, hot perfection of her mouth.

———

She shows up first thing Sunday morning, coffees in hand, and hangs out while I work a half-day in the shop.

As soon as I flip the closed sign around, she's dragging me upstairs. We fuck on the couch, her riding me. She's on her period, but neither of us cares. I can't get enough of her. After I blow my load inside her the first time, I carry her to the shower, press her up against the wall, and do it again.

Her breasts are sensitive in a good way, tight nipples that

need sucking and a little squeeze to tighten her pussy around me and milk another release from Daddy.

We're insatiable. After breaking for dinner, we sprawl naked in bed until it's dark, and I let her talk me into staying for the night.

I wake up in the middle of the night with her mouth on my cock and haul her up my body. I hold her there, pinned down on top of me, and piston my cock in and out of her cunt.

Dawn is just breaking when I return her to campus. We say goodbye in the truck this time, and there's no tension.

"See you next weekend," she says, all breathless and happy from the nineteen million orgasms over the last twenty-four hours.

"Study hard this week."

"I will." She flashes a brilliant smile, and then she's gone, running across the grass to her dorm.

I head back to Main Street and open the shop.

Maybe, just maybe, this is going to work out.

21
summer

I REALLY MISS Henry's apartment. The dorm is noisy, even after curfew, and it smells bad. Constantly. Like sweat and granola bars and sex. A lot of sex that I'm not having—although I am on Sundays, and that's awesome.

I pour myself into classwork and try not to think about how quiet his apartment is during the day. I make it until the third Friday night in September, when a party breaks out just as I'm crawling into bed. I give up and text Henry.

> **Can I come to your place for the whole weekend? Pretty please? I know you said Sundays only, but there's a party going on, and I want nothing to do with it.**

He replies immediately.

> **Where are you? I can pick you up in ten minutes.**

I tell him I'm at the dorm, and there's no hurry. He shows up nine minutes later, and I run out from the lobby to meet him before he can get out of the car.

"What's wrong?" he asks as soon as I'm in the passenger seat. He has a ferocious look on his face, like he'll kill someone for me.

I like it, but that's truly not necessary. "People were just having a party. There was no way I could study."

"Nobody was pressuring you to do something you didn't want to do?"

I shake my head no and catch his face in my hands, kissing him quickly on the mouth because he's a sweet, lovely man who worries about me.

His face softens as he puts the truck into drive. "And you didn't want to join them? It's a rite of passage."

"Ew, no." I cock my head to the side. "I thought you said I couldn't drink?"

"That was. . ." He shrugs. "I don't know. The summer had different rules. I'm not going to tell you that you can't be an average college kid."

"You don't drink much."

"I had my youthful indiscretions, though. And now I like a pint of beer while I watch a game or a bottle of wine with a nice meal. I just didn't over the summer when you were in my charge."

"They were doing tequila shots when I left."

He laughs. "Those have their place, I suppose."

"Do you have anything to drink at your place?"

"Not tequila."

"What do you have?"

"Beer."

I wrinkle my nose.

He slides his hand over my shoulder and squeezes the back of my neck. "We can stop and pick up some wine if you want to try something. Maybe something bubbly."

"Like champagne?"

"Whatever you want." He squeezes again, his big hand

warm and comforting, and we're happily silent for the three-block drive to the grocery store.

"Have you eaten?" he asks me as we walk through the front doors.

"I had a slice of pizza at dinner. The cafeteria food is taking some getting used to, too."

He stops in his tracks. "You didn't say that before. Okay, let's do this right. First, we need to decide what we'll cook, then we'll pick a nice wine to go with it."

Easy. I want a big salad and fancy pasta. Something we can make together.

We get the produce first, then the rest of the supplies, including muffins for breakfast in the morning, and finish in the wine aisle.

I have no idea what I want, so Henry picks a couple of bottles.

"Nice dinner in tonight?" The cashier is just making idle conversation, but I still slide a sideways glance at Henry to see if he's nervous about the inquiry.

He grins. "Yep."

I didn't know how much I needed to see him be easy about this until now. Something unlocks in my chest, and I brush my hand against his, my pinky finger hooking his for just a second.

Baby steps toward being a real couple.

Baby steps toward me telling him with my whole chest just how much I love him.

———

Back at the apartment, he tells me to get comfortable.

I don't move an inch. "I thought we could cook together."

He raises an eyebrow. "Yeah?"

"It would be. . . romantic."

He slides his hand into my hair, holding me still while he kisses me softly. "I like the sound of that. A lot."

"Good."

The bottle of wine he chooses is sparkling, not champagne but something similar, and he pours me a little glass to sip while we cook.

It's bubbly and not as sweet as I thought it would be, and I really like it. By the time our food is ready, my glass is empty, and I refill it while Henry is setting the table.

Over dinner, I tell him about school, and he updates me on his favorite—and least favorite—customers. He confesses that he's started going to Brewed Awakening for his mid-day coffee instead of Wake Up Call because he likes the proximity to campus. "It feels like I'm a little closer to you."

I beam. "That's because you are." I give him a sly look. "Mid-day, you say? Your usual after lunch caffeine refresh?"

"Don't come looking for me," he says gruffly. But he's grinning.

Running into each other mid-week would be a nice surprise.

Just as he's about to say something else, there's a knock at the door downstairs. It's loud and carries on long enough it feels urgent.

Henry frowns. "Stay here. Sip more wine. I'll be right back."

As his heavy steps fade down the stairs, I think about the warm, fuzzy feeling in my chest. This must be what it feels like to be tipsy, I decide. And I wouldn't like this if I were at the dorms—it wouldn't be warm, but hot and achy and dangerous —but with Henry, it feels good.

I laugh to myself, feeling quite pleased with how the night is going. I'm thinking about having drunk sex with the hot guy who is *very* good with his mouth when I recognize the second voice moving rapidly through the shop downstairs.

"I went to campus looking for her, Henry, and someone said they saw her getting in your truck—*the barber's truck*, they said —and you *kissed* her."

Holy shit. *Mama.* I shove the wine glass away from me, but

there are only two place settings at the table. And Henry lit a candle. Can I get rid of that in time? The wine bottle?

Do I look like I was just imagining Henry's face between my legs, his hands clamped on my thighs, forcing them apart as I plead for him to stop, but never really mean it?

Probably.

I try to stand but then think better of it and do my best to look like I'm innocently eating dinner, a regular, non-romantic dinner.

She bursts into the apartment and shrieks when she sees me.

"Hi, Mom," I say half-heartedly.

"Summer!"

"I thought you were on a cruise ship."

"We have a few days in dock in Seattle, so I decided to come and see you."

I want to snap at her that we've had telephones for, like, at least a hundred years. She could have called or texted or given me a heads up through literally any method, but now is maybe not the time to be sassy.

"And now I see that you're. . . you're. . ."

"Eating dinner?"

"And the wine? Summer Anne Figaro, this is not what you are supposed to be doing with your time here."

"Really? Because I'm pretty sure you sent me here with a broken plan. Did you know that people party every night on campus? *This* is way more civilized than *that*."

"I taught you better than *that*, too. You don't need to party anywhere, here or there. You need to get good grades and graduate college."

Oh, now I can't help but be sassy, even if I know better. "Uh, hello, I know that. And I will. But having a nice dinner on a Friday night with Henry is no big deal."

Her gaze narrows. "I don't like the way you say that. It's too casual. He's your elder, Summer."

Oh, I'm aware. Behind her, he flushes, and I swear, if he gets weird about this, I will tie him to a chair until he shakes that nonsense off. "Henry is—"

He clears his throat.

I glare at him.

My mother pivots and, I imagine, also glaring at him.

He crosses his arms over his chest, fixes a stern look on me, then addresses the intruder. "Jennifer, I know you have strong feelings about protecting Summer from this world. But she is a grown-up who can make her own choices. And as a grown-up, she is my peer. Please don't project your parental expectations of her onto me as well."

"Henry, once upon a time, you wanted to be her *father*."

I gasp out loud. Like, legit screech.

That is a specific tidbit of information he didn't once share with me. Not when he was touching my tits, not when his face was buried between my legs and not any of the times he put his cock in my body and let me call him Daddy.

What. The. Fuck?

They both look at me. Henry looks ashamed, and my mom looks confused. "Summer, why do you think I sent you here?"

I wince. "Because he's a guy you know in the same town where I got into college?"

"I told you. He's the only man I trust."

"Well, news flash, Mama, he's also the only man I thought *I* could trust, too. But he never shared that particular detail with me. So maybe he's not so trustworthy after all."

I'm shaking. It's time to go.

Henry's face is bright red now, but he doesn't try to stop me. When I get to the top of the stairs, I gesture for my mother to follow me. "Come on. Let's go be buzzkills at the dorm party. I hope you like sharing a twin bed."

22
summer

I SPEND the rest of the night refusing to answer my mother's questions about Henry. No, I won't explain why I got upset when she said he once wanted to be my father.

Definitely not ever explaining that out loud.

No, he never hurt me. He was the best host all summer long, and *no*, I don't want to talk about if I maybe have a crush on him.

There's no maybe about it.

But there's a big maybe in another corner of my brain. The private, sad part that worries we went too far, too fast. Not physically, because I'll never regret any of that, but emotionally.

How do I distance myself from him now? When he's the only person who truly knows me?

And as confused and sad and mad as I am, I'm even sadder that he hasn't called. I think he *will*, but maybe not until Mom leaves.

Coward.

After she does two tequila shots with the girls down the hall —and I don't—she gives up on questioning me and passes out on one side of my bed. I curl up next to her and stare at the ceiling.

Once upon a time, we were as close as could be. Now she feels like my fucked-up older sister, and my private life is none of her beeswax.

By one in the morning, I'm seriously concerned I might not sleep at all. And just as I have that thought, my phone lights up.

I slide out of bed and shove my feet into my slippers. The party is still raging in the common room, so I instead go to the stairwell at the far end.

Henry's call has ended, so I dial him back.

"I'm sorry," he says as soon as the call connects. "I should have told you."

I don't say anything.

"Summer?" He sighs. "Thank you for calling me back."

"I couldn't sleep."

"I'm sorry."

"Mom is pretty stressed out at the thought of me having an inappropriate crush on you. Wait until she figures out you like to blow my back out. Me, the baby you once wanted to parent, apparently." I'm whispering the words angrily, and I don't know if that comes across.

"I know you're mad." Okay, so it does.

"It's perilously close to too weird."

"Summer, that was nineteen years ago. I was a twenty-year-old kid, trying to do the right thing by a friend. When you showed up, I wasn't thinking, hey, here's my long-lost, almost adopted daughter. I was thinking, fuck, Jennifer's daughter is a smoke show, and I can't let her get away."

"That is not how I remember it. You didn't want me around. You made me buy new PJs!"

"I didn't want you to know just how much I *wanted* you around. And it's not like I tried fucking hard to get rid of you. From the second you walked in those doors, you were it for me. You, now. You, this beautiful, grown-up creature. And for the record, those pajamas you bought were fucking indecent, and I loved every second of you parading around in them."

"I call you Daddy!"

"I won't deny that I like to take care of you. As a grown-up," he adds. "And there's never been anyone else like that."

"I should fucking hope not."

"Language, Summer."

I roll my eyes. Then I find myself smiling, just a little because he'd like the brattiness if he could see it. "It was weird tonight. Not you. Mom. I feel like I've grown away from her over the summer."

"That happens."

"And now I feel like you're the only person in this whole world who really gets me."

He groans. "I can't be your only person. As much as I want to steal you away from everything and lock you in a tower forever."

"Really?"

"Yeah."

"Forever?" My voice is so soft, so hopeful. I kind of hate how much it reveals.

"Forever and ever." He sounds like he wants to add something else to that, and I want him to. But maybe this is a conversation best had in person.

"I want to see you."

"Your mom will worry if she wakes up and you're gone again."

"She'll know where I am. Who I'm with."

"And that's how you want her to have her suspicions confirmed?"

I screw up my face. "No."

"Do you want me to tell her?"

"God, no." I take a deep breath. "I'll do it in the morning."

"Listen, I want you to do something else, too. For me."

"What?"

"Take a few days away from me."

"No!"

"Summer."

"Ugh, I hate your dad voice."

"No, you don't. You love it. Listen to me, okay? We can do this. I just want you to be happy. But your mom has a right to worry if I am your only friend. That's not healthy. You need to try harder at making friends on campus, too."

I don't respond. We do some of our best communicating through silence.

He sighs. "I'll come and see you tomorrow if you want a hug. But I don't think you should come and stay at my place until your mom heads back to the cruise ship. Take the weekend, spend time with her. Then take the week and make some friends. And when you come over next Friday, you can tell me all about it."

"Ugh, that is so long. And we didn't even have sex this weekend."

He seems unmoved by my plight. "Promise me."

"I promise."

"How about I give you a reward every time you step outside your comfort zone and make a new buddy?"

I giggle. "A *buddy*?"

"You know what I mean."

"Sure. Okay. Can the reward be your cock, buried deep inside my body?"

"Fuck. Don't talk like that."

"Why not?"

"Because it makes me lose control."

"Good."

"I'm not coming to campus in the middle of the night for a booty call in my truck. That's how people get arrested."

"Spoilsport."

"Someone has to be, my little rebel."

———

In the morning, I take Mom to Brewed Awakening. I figure a public setting is either a very good idea or a very bad one, but either way, I want a flat white to go with my confession.

Once we have our takeout cups, I sit down at a table on the patio and give her a serious look. "So last night, you had questions about me and Henry."

"Oh, Summer, that was just silliness. I think I was tired from traveling. Of course, I know you don't have a crush on—"

"I'm in love with him." I'm surprised at how steady my voice is.

She blinks in surprise. "Pardon?"

"Henry. It's not a crush. I fell in love with him this summer. He doesn't know yet. I mean, not exactly. We haven't said those words, but we definitely see each other in that kind of light."

She shakes her head. "He's old enough to be your father."

"But he's not, right?"

She made a face. "Henry? Ew, no. I would never."

"Well, I would. So that's great news."

"Summer!"

"What?"

"Henry?"

"He's lovely. And handsome, and patient, and funny. What's not to like?"

She makes another face, this one more confused than grossed out. "He's always been like a brother to me."

"That must have been weird when he tried to kiss you."

She laughs. "Yes, it was. Did he tell you about that?"

"Yes."

Now her gaze is trained on my face, and the confusion drops away. "You love him."

"Very much so."

"I'm not ready for you to fall in love." She shrugs. "Oh, Summer."

"I was ready. He resisted all summer long if it makes you feel better."

"It does." She sighs. "You know he was only ever my friend, right? There's nothing to be jealous about, honey. It wasn't like that for him, either. Henry just isn't a sexual person, and when I was your age, I was. . . well, I was wild."

I blink at her.

Henry isn't *what*?

And then it slides together. All the little clues.

I stand up. "I need to go."

"Where?"

"To see Henry." I pick up her coffee cup. "Come on. There's another coffee shop just down the block you can go to. See which one you like better."

"I've barely drunk that one."

"Glug glug, Mom. You're getting another coffee in a few minutes."

"You know, when I lived here, there was only one place in town to get coffee, and that was the diner. It was terrible."

"Well, a lot has changed since you lived here, Mama."

Including Henry, apparently. *Isn't sexual.* I'm reeling.

She has a rental car, so we beeline back to campus to pick that up, then I tell her where to park for Wake Up Call.

"Order me a smoothie," I tell her as I hop out of the car. "I won't be long! He'll be working, and I just need to go and see him for a minute."

23
henry

I'M BRUSHING hair off the back of Nash Armstrong's neck when the door flies open and Summer storms in.

Nash is the new chief of staff in the mayor's office, but I wouldn't care if he was the chief of fucking police or the president of the Conception Ridge Purity Club at this moment.

All I care about is whatever put that look on her face, an expression I can't read, and that's not normal for us.

I set the brush down and catch her in my arms. "What's wrong?"

"I need to talk to you." She glances at my customers. Nash in the chair, his best friend Atlas Ross reading a magazine over by the window.

Atlas is a big, brutish construction worker. I give him a nod. "Don't let anyone rob me blind."

"We'll hold down the fort," Nash says, glancing at Summer for a split second before turning back to his friend. "Anything good in that magazine?"

I point Summer in the direction of the stairs to the apartment. She looks like she's going to say something right here, but I give her a stern look. *Not here.*

Whatever it is, it's private.

She scampers up the stairs ahead of me, and once we're in the apartment, she turns around and flings herself at me. I catch her with ease and carry her to the nearest surface, the kitchen counter.

Her legs slide open, and she wriggles against me. "I know you said I had to wait until Mom left, but I needed to see you. Just for a minute."

"Where's your mother?"

"At the coffee shop. Waiting for me." She drags in a deep breath and presses her hands on either side of my face. "Henry, were you a virgin in high school?"

"Of course I was."

"So when you told my mom that you would raise me, you hadn't had sex yet."

"What does that have to do with anything?"

"Everything. It has *everything* to do with *everything*."

"Why?"

"I'm getting to that. And. . . " Her cheeks turn pink, and her eyelashes flutter against her cheeks before she looks back up at me. "After high school, when you were older. . . did you go through a horny period?"

"What?" Fucking hell, I'm not following. And I'm getting turned on. "Jesus, Summer. No. Not really. Why are you asking all these questions?"

"My mom said you weren't interested in sex. She thinks. . . actually, I think she thinks it's okay for me to be in love with you because you're a nice guy. Like, a won't-violate-her-baby kind of nice guy. I dunno. I don't think I'm going to correct her misunderstanding. But I think that maybe you're just this horny for *me?* And if that's the case, then we need to talk about that, because I like it, but then I think it's also more special, and—"

I kiss her.

I need her to stop talking because my heart has stopped, and my brain needs a minute to catch up.

In love with you.

My lips move against hers, demanding and giving at the same time. My grown-up love. My little girl. Mine.

She tastes like coffee and hope.

I didn't sleep a wink last night, worried sick that I couldn't hold her and show her it was going to be okay, and she was blazing a path forward for us?

Goddamn. This woman.

"Henry—"

"I'm not a nice guy."

"I. . ." She laughs and kisses me back. "I mean, you are. But you're also deeply filthy—*with me*—and that's our secret. Isn't it? Nobody else knows."

"Nobody. There's never been anyone else like you for me."

She puts her hands on my shoulders and pushes me back enough to look me right in the eye. "I don't want to stay in the dorm anymore. Not after Mama leaves. I want this all the time. Cooking in your kitchen, studying at your table. I love being here." She catches her lip between her teeth and pauses.

And I'd just gotten my heart to restart. Now it's stopped again, feeling way too damn big for my chest.

"I love you, Henry." Her breath hitches as she gives me a big, wide-eyed gaze. "I never want to leave you again."

"You don't have to." I crush her against me, kissing her mouth, then the corner of her mouth, then down onto her neck. "I love you, too, baby girl. So much. No matter what, this is your home."

"I love knowing you're just downstairs, and you'll come up to me at the end of the day. That we'll get to cook together, and then you'll take me to your bed."

"Our bed."

"Yes." She gasps. "You have customers."

"They'll wait."

"My mom. . ."

"She'll wait." I push up her skirt, grateful for how much she loves her legs being bare, and I tug her panties to the side.

She's soaked for me, wet already, and I fumble in my back pocket.

But I don't have a condom on me. I've been carrying one for weeks and this morning—

"Stay right here."

She doesn't let me go. "It's okay."

"We're using condoms. End of story."

"I just want to feel you inside me."

"You don't think I want that? To feel the hot grip of your cunt around my dick? To be absolutely bare inside you?" I'm panting now as she unzips my jeans. "But you know what comes next. I won't be able to resist the sweet pulse of your pussy, Summer. Once I'm inside you without a condom, I won't be pulling out. I'll bury myself so deep you won't have a choice but to milk me right into your womb."

"Oh." She nibbles on her lower lip, but she doesn't stop her efforts to get my cock out.

"*Oh*, is fucking right."

"I thought you were being. . . You're serious?"

"I will do the right thing by you. Always. But it doesn't mean I want to."

"What do you want to do?"

My chest is tight. "You don't want to know."

"Yes, I do." And she's fucking serious.

She loves me. She knows I love her. We've been dancing around this for far too long.

I thrust two fingers into her, making her cry out. "I want to pin you down and breed you. Fill you with my seed until you overflow, then fuck that back into you, too. I've never been bare inside a woman before. Never wanted to risk it."

She nods, whimpering in need.

I pull my fingers out of her and lick them off, my gaze hot and intent on her face. "But you? It wouldn't be any kind of risk. It would be a promise. To be your man, to give you babies. I would breed the fuck out of you, Summer. Over and over again. So if you rub your sweet little cunt on me one more time and whine about not needing condoms—"

She rocks her hips and notches us together.

My weeping, throbbing cock lodged right at the opening of her tight pussy.

"Breed me, Daddy. Knock me up."

"This isn't funny," I growl.

"I'm not joking." She pants and rolls her hips, sucking me in. An inch. I'm already an inch inside her, hot and perfect. "My mom had me young, and I loved how close we were. I want to have babies with you, Henry. All the babies."

"Come on my cock," I mutter. "Be a good girl for me, and I'll fill you up. You can walk around all day with Daddy's seed dripping out of you under this pretty skirt."

She cries out, and I pin her to me, using her body as a cocksleeve.

"I want to do everything you want. All your dirty little fantasies, all the dark corners of your mind where you think about cocks and fingers and being pinned down. I want to give you all of that and more. I want to shave your little cunt so it's baby soft, then make you sit on my face until you shake."

"Yes!"

"I want to make business calls while my cock is buried in your throat. I want to fuck you on the barber chair downstairs." I'm grunting every fantasy I've ever had at her now. "Want you in my truck. Naked. Wet pussy. Eager mouth."

My name spills out of her mouth, then she tips her head back in a soundless scream, and I follow her into the climax, spurting deep into her as she starts to milk me.

Good. Fucking. Girl.

I kiss her neck, both of us breathing hard. She winds her fingers into my hair, pulling my head up so we can kiss.

"I love you so much," she whispers. "So much. I'm moving back here in a few days. Moving into your bed, and you can't kick me out."

"Never." That gives me a few days to get her a ring. "Summer, you're my everything."

"Same." She kisses me again, sweetly this time, on the corner of my mouth, then she wiggles her hips, and I slide out of her.

"That felt fucking messy," I admit, my face flushing with heat.

She grins. "Good. I hope it takes."

I grip the back of her neck. "So do I."

"I have to go."

"Take a minute to clean up."

"It's fine."

I give her a look. "No, it's not. That's for you and me. Not for anyone else. Go wash your face, you dirty little girl."

She smiles in delight. "Okay, *Dad*."

"We can play that game next weekend," I rumble as she hops off the counter.

Then I dunk my own head under the cold water tap in the kitchen because she's not the only one who has to pull themselves together.

According to the clock above the stove, ten minutes have passed.

But from the way my heart feels changed forever, it was a hell of a lot longer than that.

24
summer

TWO DAYS LATER, my mom leaves. She'll be gone for nine months this time.

I don't tell her there's a chance she might be a grandma when she gets back. One thing at a time. I'll send her a Christmas photo from Henry's apartment.

Our apartment. I can't wait to decorate for Christmas. A tree. Stockings.

But first I need to move back there. As soon as she's gone, I text him, and he's pulling into the parking lot of the dorm a half an hour later.

Middle of the day. He closed the shop for this.

I fly into his arms, and he twirls me around.

"You need to study hard," he lectures me.

I bounce in excitement. "I will. Cross my heart and swear to God."

"No funny stuff during the day."

I wink at him. "Of course not, Henry. Funny stuff is strictly an all-night-long deal. Now take me home."

———

A few days later, I'm in the library after my final class when I recognize a fellow student. Lily, who I met over the summer when she was still pregnant. Now she's searching for a book in the same aisle I'm in. On her chest is a sleeping baby, wrapped tight to her body with long swaths of cotton.

The baby looks brand new.

"Excuse me," I say quietly, almost in a whisper, because I don't want to wake the kid up. "I just want to get past you to those." I point to the shelf she's in front of. "And I thought I'd say hi? It's—"

She blinks at me blankly for a split second, then a bright smile splits across her face. "Summer! Hi." She shifts back. "Sorry. I think I zoned out there a little." She rubs the baby's back through the wrap. "I'm sleep-deprived. Starting my studies this fall was maybe a bit premature."

"I'm impressed. I'm struggling, too, and I don't have a baby." But oh, I want one.

I'm not surprised at the deep pang inside me, the whole-bodied longing for Henry to make a wee little person with me. It's been on my mind all week.

I could bring her to school with me, just like Lily is.

But she just said it's hard.

She did. But she's smiling, too. "How are you finding your classes?"

"Good. I like English Lit and Sociology the most."

"I'm taking those, too."

"I'm surprised I haven't noticed you and this little one."

"So far, I'm still catching up virtually." She pointed to the baby. "Because of him. Not sleeping through the night yet. But my husband is helping, and we're getting there. I should be in class next week."

"I'll save you a seat."

She gives me an earnest smile. "Thank you. I'll be studying in a little bit after my husband picks this one up for a walk. If you want a study buddy?"

Henry would understand if I texted him that I would be late. But he told me he's making a special dinner tonight.

He also told you to make more friends.

"I just need to call my—"

The baby cries, waking up with an angry start. She sighs and shrugs. "Or maybe we can have a rain check? I'll need to nurse him now, and that's easier in my husband's office."

"Does he work here on campus?" I'm way too curious about what that suggests. "Is he a professor?"

"He's in the administration. He got hired after I was accepted as a student, so it's known to the powers that be." She looks like she's choosing her words carefully. "He's older than me, but when it comes to parenting stuff, he has more energy than I do."

"Really?" I lean in. "My boyfriend is almost forty. I just moved in with him, actually. You're the first person I've told about him, other than my mother. Which didn't go that well? It's a long story. I mean, it's fine, but. . . I think babies are in our future."

Her eyes sparkle in delight. "My husband is almost forty-two. I want to hear your story someday."

"I'll buy you coffee, and we can compare notes."

The baby on her chest lets out another cry, and she bounces him up and down. "I think that's my cue to go, but it was so nice bumping into you again."

"Same. See you soon."

———

The shop is closed when I get there, so I use my key and let myself in, then carefully lock up behind me.

It's quiet and dark, so I tiptoe up the stairs.

Henry may have fallen asleep after work. It's been a long week.

But when I step into the kitchen, I see him standing at the counter, looking intently at something in his hands.

"Henry?"

He spins around and moves his arm at the same time, maybe meaning to put the thing he's holding down, but I've startled him, and he's a big man with a lot of power in his muscles when spooked.

The thing goes flying across the island, across the dining room table, and under the couch.

"What was that?" I laugh at the shocked look on his face. "And why are all the lights off? It's kind of gloomy in here."

I cross to the couch and drop to my knees. In the late afternoon light, with no lights on in the apartment, it's hard to see anything, and when I feel around, I touch something fuzzy.

Shrieking, I pull my hand back.

Henry is beside me now, and he's muttering something about letting things go.

That is not my style. Never has been, never will be.

"I'll get it," he barks.

I straighten up. "What is it?"

"Just let me get it." He holds out his hand to help me up.

I roll my eyes and drop to my stomach, so I can eyeball the fuzzy thing under the couch better.

But once I'm there, and I can see it, I freeze.

Henry clears his throat.

I mean, maybe it's not what I think it is.

"I should leave it?" I ask him, not looking up.

"Sweetheart, why do you never leave anything alone?"

A better question is, why is he endlessly tolerant of my persistent curiosity? Even now, when I wouldn't listen to him. He sounds amused, not annoyed.

The ring box is fuzzy velvet on the outside, now slightly dusty on the corners. When I wrap my shaking fingers around it, I take a deep breath, pull my hand back, and scramble to my feet.

By the time I'm standing, Henry is kneeling in front of me. "This isn't how I planned it," he says gently, with a little laugh in his voice. "But it's perfect. I was looking at that when you came home. Thinking about what I would say tonight after we made dinner and had a little wine. I thought about giving it to you over dessert, or maybe in bed. But here works. By the couch where I slept for weeks, fighting against myself because there was no way on God's green earth that an otherworldly creature like you would even want an ordinary man like me. And then when you did want me, when I couldn't deny that anymore, I was convinced surely it was just experimentation. Learning about all the ways two people could be together. And I still grabbed on to it with two hands, Summer. I wanted you however I could have you, even when I thought my love for you would forever be one-sided."

"But I've always—" I cut myself off.

"I know." He takes a deep breath, his whole chest moving with it.

I realize he's wearing a really nice sweater and a buttoned-down shirt.

He dressed up for this, and I lay on the floor and got dusty.

"Henry, I . . ." Tears form, and I can't continue.

"Hey, I'm trying to do something here." He stands up and gathers me into his chest, then picks me up and carries me to his armchair. "Shhh, pretty girl. No tears. I think this is a happy occasion. God, I hope it is."

That just makes me cry harder, and I wrap my arms around his neck. "It is," I whisper between tremulous gasps. "These are happy tears."

He smoothes a hand over my hair, then gently wipes my tears off my cheeks with his thumb. "Nothing makes me happier than holding you in my arms. The first time you were on my lap, and we got carried away. . . that was the happiest I had ever been in my whole damn life. And it just got better from there. You have made me so happy every single day, and I want to make you a promise."

I've stopped breathing. Which means I've stopped crying, too. All I can see is his handsome face as his gaze locks on mine.

"I want to spend the rest of my life making you as happy as you make me. Being your partner in joy, and love, and life." He opens the ring box, and a diamond ring sparkles up at me. "Will you marry me, Summer? Will you be my wife?"

I nod, then I laugh. "Yes. Oh, yes, Henry. Yes, yes, yes." I'm babbling, and I rub my head on his shoulder, sinking into the cuddle.

He lifts the ring out of the box and slides it onto my finger. Then he kisses my fingertips, one by one. When he gets to my pinky, he locks his gaze on mine again.

"It's a promise to always be your lover, too. Your Daddy, whenever you want."

The answer to that is always.

epilogue

One year later

henry

SUMMER STROLLS into the shop sucking on an orange popsicle, and it takes everything in me not to kick my customers out and chase my pregnant wife up the stairs.

"Hello, gentleman," she says politely, but her eyes are locked on my face. "It's a hot one out there today."

Her little tongue swirls around the tip of the icy treat, and goddamn it, she can't do that in front of people. My jeans suddenly feel tighter.

She has a small swell under her sundress this year. Enough that when she smooths the fabric over her round bump and calls me Daddy, nobody blinks.

I never doubted I'd love her even more with a pregnant glow. I didn't realize just how much—or how voracious her appetite for my body would get. Not that she wasn't a hungry little imp before I knocked her up.

But this is a next level need that my wife has now. So she

comes strolling in from a trip to the library, sucking on a popsicle, and I know we're about to have a problem.

"Atlas, I'm going to give you a complementary shave before your haircut," I manage to grunt out.

I already have Nash under hot towels in the other chair. And it's not like these men haven't seen me disappear with Summer before. I don't even bother to explain this time. I just slap the warm towels on their faces and haul Summer halfway up the stairs before need overtakes me. I tangle one hand in her hair and shove the other one up her skirt.

Her mouth tastes like orange popsicle. Her pussy is slick with need. And I have my tongue down her throat almost as fast as I have two thick fingers sliding into her cunt, my thumb on her clit.

She'd be gasping my name if I wasn't swallowing ever sound she tried to make right now.

Orange fucking popsicle.

She's been sucking on them all summer long, and it's a Pavlovian response now. Sticky, sweet, and citrus—one taste and I'm hard as a rock.

Before she was pregnant, I'd have bent her over the stairs and fucked her right here. Or pushed her to her knees and made her swallow every drop of come she teases to a fury in my balls.

But now…now my beautiful wife comes on my hand, in a gasping, glorious orgasm, and I pat her on the bum for the good job.

"What about you?" she asks, her eyes wide, her orange-stained lips swollen from our kisses.

"Later," I promise. "Once the shop is closed."

———

She reappears at the beaded curtain as I flip the lock behind the final customer.

This time it's a bowl of strawberries she's slowly nibbling on. Again, that little pink tongue of hers immediately gets me hard, but this time, there's no reason not to show her just how wild she makes me.

I sprawl in the closest chair, the heavy steel frame more than capable of supporting us for whatever we get up to tonight.

All alone.

In the shop, after hours.

She climbs into my lap, her sundress riding high on her thighs. "Strawberry?"

I let her feed me one from the bowl. It's sweet and juicy, and as soon as I swallow it, her mouth is on mine, chasing the taste of the fruit.

Dropping my foot to the ground, I swivel the chair so we'll be able to see ourselves in the mirror.

After the kiss. After she gets her fill of Daddy's hot mouth, hungry for his little one.

She whimpers and grinds her pussy against the thick ridge in my jeans. I cup her ass, my hands busy under her skirt, guiding her against me. The bowl of berries drops to the ground, and her fingers tangle in my hair.

"Slow down," I grunt. "I want to see you."

She eases back, a sexy little pout on her face, and I tug down the neckline of her dress.

Her breasts are free from a bra today, bare under the white cotton sundress. Her nipples are darker now that she's pregnant, and more sensitive than ever. She gasps as the cool air makes her tips pebble tight, and I cover them with my hands.

I relish how they fill my palms, a nice warm weight and the exact right shape to squeeze.

"I've wanted to fuck you for hours." My gaze is intent, raking over her tits and down to where her skirt barely covers that sweet little pussy I fingered earlier. "Are you still wet for me?"

She squirms and tugs the fabric up, revealing soaked panties.

I drop one hand to brush against the visible wet spot. "Shhh," I caution. "Hold still for me. I just want to take a look."

She swallows another whimper as I tug the cotton aside. She's sticky from earlier, her bare lips coated in clear slick, and as I drift my thumb down the seam of her pussy lips, she flexes her thighs, opening wider.

Eager. Willing. Needy.

"Good girl," I praise her. "You're ready for me, aren't you?"

"Mm-hmm."

"Take your dress off. I want to see all of you."

She wriggles on my lap as I keep stroking her, and the dress goes up and over her head.

Now I can see the baby I put in her belly, the tight swell above her mound, the long curve up to below her breasts. She's only halfway through her pregnancy, still small everywhere except around the waist, and I don't worry about perching her on my lap like this.

Not yet.

In a few months, we'll slow down. And then when the baby comes, there will be a tender period where I'll hold her and love her in other ways.

And down the road, we'll do this all again. All the babies for my baby.

"You're so beautiful," I tell her, because it's the fucking truth. "So goddamn perfect."

She blushes.

I crush her to me, kissing her again. Roughly now. She's not the only one who is needy. I waited a long time to discover this part of myself, this desperate human need to fuck the one I love.

It overtakes me sometimes.

I don't stop kissing her as I unzip and shove my jeans out of the way. As I rip her panties from her cute little ass, tossing them in the direction of the abandoned strawberries.

Then I pivot her around in my lap and sink her onto my dripping cock, my throbbing erection that is all hers, only hers, forever.

Together we watch in the mirror as she trembles, taking me in inch by lurid inch.

It's obscene, the way she's stretched out on top of me, my fat cock forcing its way into her tight little pussy. Her tiny, bare little cunt, all sticky for Daddy.

"Shhh," I whisper in her ear.

A big bearded man holding her against him, her all naked and me fully dressed.

Only my cock is exposed, and I'm guiding that into her naked body.

We both shudder when her pussy lips are stretched wide around the base and I'm fully inside her. I wrap my hand around her waist and drift my fingertips against her swollen clit, her bare pussy lips, then out, to squeeze her inner thigh.

"Look at us," she breathes in wonder.

"You're beautiful," I murmur. "I can't believe you're mine."

"You're so big."

In more ways than one. "You've learned to take me, though."

"I love it." She breathes out carefully. "I want more."

"Ride me, then." I guide her to sit up, and she braces her hands on my knees.

Now I can't see the mirror, but it doesn't matter, because my gaze is locked on the round curve of her ass, and as she pumps her hips, the wet slick of her pussy juice on my cock.

I throb as she pushes back onto me, as I disappear into her little body again.

The tight curl of her asshole makes my mouth water, and I rub my thumb against it.

"Daddy," she whines.

A fun game we play. "Shhh."

"Uh...." She pumps her pussy harder, and the slickness increases.

"Fuck, sweetheart. You like that, don't you?"

"I don't know." She gasps the three words.

I spit on my thumb and press it against her rear entrance again. "I think you do know."

"Daddy!"

"Come on. Fuck me. You've got my cock in your belly like a good girl. So fuck my thumb, too. Take me everywhere."

She cries out, not a word, just a sound, and this time when she sinks down, she rocks back, too, desperately taking the tip of my thumb into her body.

Deep in her belly, my cock pulses out a jet of pre-come.

This is how I knocked her up. Her horny little cunt milking me as I promise to violate her body in new and exciting ways.

"Should I fuck you here, after the baby comes? When you don't want to get pregnant again?" I wrap my other hand around her hip, holding her in place.

She's mine to fuck now. I don't want her to move an inch. I want her to hold fucking still like a good fucking girl.

"I'll always want to get pregnant again," she whispers. "But you can fuck me there now, if you want."

I freeze, my cock thick and primed in her pussy. "Are you sure?"

She twists her head and gives me a shy nod.

I ease her off me, my whole body tense with need. Then I pick her up, carefully stepping over the mess we made on the floor, and I carry her upstairs.

summer

Henry gets naked in a flash, then grabs some lube and climbs on top of me on our bed.

I wrap my arms around his neck, kissing him and trying to rub my pussy on his belly at the same time.

He's fully focused on getting that lube on his fingers, and then—

Oh.

It's different with lube.

Oh.

We've played a lot with his fingers there during sex, but that's all that it's been.

Fingers. On the outside.

Now they're slick and *in me*, just a bit, but like…*inside me.*

"Henry," I squeak. "How many fingers is that?"

He stills. "One."

"Fuck."

"Language," he growls.

I roll my eyes, and that way-too-big finger in my bum slides in deeper, meeting resistance again. "Oh!"

"Shh…"

He's big on that tonight. Good, it makes me wet. Maybe that will distract me from the squirmalicious burning sensation as he takes another virginity of mine. "Daddy, it hurts."

"Do you want me to stop?"

"No." I pout. "Just be gentle."

He kisses the corner of my mouth. "As gentle as I can be. Fuck, you feel good."

And it does, now. Now that I've adjusted to the feeling of that finger, when he starts to move, it feels *very* good. Different from when he's in my pussy. More…intense. More of an intrusion.

More off-limits, in a wonderful way.

I roll my hips, and he grunts. "You like it now? Does that feel good for you, too?"

I nod.

"I need to hear you say it."

"It feels good."

His kiss is deeper this time, his tongue consuming my attention, deep and thick in my mouth.

Almost distracting enough I don't realize he's adding a second finger, but then it's there, and *wow.*

I cry into his mouth and he rolls his tongue against mine. *Take it.*

Fuck.

My eyes roll back in my head, but then I'm fucking against his hand, and I am taking it. I feel hot and ready.

And bless my husband, because he can read my mind.

He rolls me onto my side, away from him, then eases me back.

He's covered himself in so much lube my body couldn't stop him even if I wanted to. I don't. It's perfect.

It's so, so much, too much, and still perfect.

"You're almost too little for this," he whispers in my ear, his arm wrapped around my waist, his hand splayed wide against my belly. "But then you get all turned on and take me into every hole in your body. You're not just a good girl, you're the best girl. You know that?"

I nod, whimpering, shaking.

"Daddy could come just like this. From one thrust into your ass."

I cry out. Me, too.

His hand snakes lower, finding my clit. I sob in relief as he gives me the pressure I need there, and when he eases back, then thrusts into me again, I begin to shatter.

It's in every cell of my body, a wild tremble that won't stop, that turns into a bright light, then a loud shout consumes me.

Henry.

His hand clamps onto my hip, his whole body jerking behind me.

I feel him pulsing inside me. His mouth crushes to the back of my neck, his breath hot and perfect on my skin.

"Almost too little," I whisper back. "But not too little at all."

He kisses my shoulder. "That got out of hand."

"In a good way?"

"In the best way."

"I'm sorry I dropped strawberries downstairs."

He laughs, his belly shaking behind me. "I'll go clean up after I run you a bath."

"I'm okay—"

He cuts me off. "Let me pamper you a little. That was incredible, but you might be sore. And...uh... messy."

I giggle at the way my ever-so-proper husband says that. "Oh yes. I will be."

"Did you like it?"

I close my eyes and hum happily. "I loved it."

santa's baby

a Conception Ridge story

she calls him daddy christmas...

Ford Gamble is my dad's best friend. He's also the reclusive keeper of the Conception Ridge lighthouse. I remember a time when he was around more—the perfect, hotter-than-sin fodder for all my teenage fantasies. And if I'm being honest, for most of my fantasies since then too. . .

Now there's just enough silver in his shock of sexy hair and thick beard that he looks a little like a hot forty-year-old Santa with six-pack abs. And that's what has me heading to the lighthouse on a dark, stormy Christmas Eve when the retirement home where I work needs a fill-in Mr. Claus for their annual celebration.

Except I underestimate the bad weather. The next thing I know, I'm waking up in his bed, and I realize I may have revealed my forbidden fantasies to him in my feverish sleep. Can I convince him to finally let me call him Daddy Christmas? Or will he deny he shares my taboo feelings?

Because I know Ford can't stop looking at me with a wild heat in his gaze. And my desperate Christmas wish is that he's thinking about corrupting his little, not-so-innocent angel.

1
neely

WHEN I CAME to work this morning, the forecast for Christmas Eve was postcard perfect. Just below freezing, a light dusting of snow. . . the perfect backdrop for Santa to zip around the world, bringing presents to children and the young at heart alike.

People like the residents of the retirement community where I work on the outskirts of Conception Ridge. I'm the recreation director's new assistant, and tonight's Christmas party was supposed to be my first big event at Cliffside Village.

But in the eight hours since I left home in a cute little white dress and black ankle boots, the weather turned nasty. *Good thing I have a nice, long coat,* I think to myself as I peer out into the blustery night. My car is parked halfway between the retirement community and the lighthouse where my father's best friend is the keeper, and it's going to be a miserable hike out to it at the end of the night.

"Neely, any sign of our Santa Claus?"

I shake my head.

My boss is about to say something else when her phone rings. "Hello?"

I can tell from the look on her face that it's our St. Nicholas bailing.

"We understand. Stay safe. I'll tell our residents." She ends the call and looks outside again. "Neely, I'll go tell the residents the guest of honor isn't able to make it." She chuckles. "It's a good thing they don't think he's the real deal."

They may all be senior citizens, but some of them still like to remember the innocence of their childhood. And there are a few who. . .

"Wait." I know someone who has a beard and a booming laugh—and he's just down the road.

Also, he's not afraid of storms.

On the other hand, he's a bit of a jerk who hates Christmas, but he's always had a soft spot for me. Would he do it as a favor? A massive, monumental favor for his best friend's kid?

"I can get us a replacement Santa." There's more confidence in my voice than I really feel.

She shakes her head. "Not for tonight. I need you to head home. Our original Santa was caught in the storm while driving down the coast. It's going to get worse here within the hour. Go now."

"For tomorrow, then." I follow her into our office and throw on my long parka. Where are my mittens? I wind my scarf around my neck twice, loop my purse across my body, and shove my hands in my pockets. "Don't tell them Santa can't make it. Just tell them he's going to loop back here after he delivers all the presents to all the kids around the world. Please?"

"You think you can make that happen?"

In my pockets, I cross my fingers. "I will do whatever it takes."

"All right. Good luck on your mission, Christmas elf! Now go home."

Outside, I flinch against the cold, driving snow and make a

beeline for the parking lot. I'm shivering by the time I get to my car, an old beater I inherited from my brother. I unlock it and throw myself behind the steering wheel.

Our original Santa was correct to not even try to make it to the party. I really hope tomorrow is better, weather-wise—but even if it's not, Ford could probably walk over to the retirement home.

A hot, sexy Santa—most likely grumpy, too—strolling over from his lighthouse. *He won't do it.*

He did once upon a time, though.

Part of me has to believe he will again.

I put the key in the ignition to start the car. Nothing happens. I try again, horror mounting. Fuck. My car battery is dead. Why didn't I notice the car light didn't come on?

Because you were thinking about climbing onto Ford's knee and whispering your filthy Christmas wishes in his ear.

With a frustrated cry, I pull out my phone and call home. No answer because they're probably still out caroling. I can imagine my father telling my mother, "McIntoshes go caroling no matter the weather! *Neither snow nor rain nor gloom of night stays these carolers from the swift completion of their appointed rounds!*"

I try my mom's cell next, but there's no answer. She probably left it at home.

Getting out of the car, I glance back at the retirement home, the lights warm and cozy in the distance. But then, my attention is drawn to the lighthouse. I'm equally close to both, and if I go see Ford, I can beg him to be my Santa Claus in person.

I text my mom to let her know my car is dead and where I'm going, then shove my phone back in my purse. My fingers already ache from the cold, so I hurry in the direction of the man I once innocently declared I would marry one day.

He just laughed and ruffled my hair.

He better not try that tonight. I'm all grown up now, and I won't take no for an answer. One way or another, Ford Gamble is going to agree to do this favor for me. And then maybe we can also talk about why he ghosted my family last Christmas and why he was a no-show for my nineteenth birthday party, too.

2
ford

A WICKED STORM is churning up the ocean tonight. I've brewed an extra-large pot of coffee to get me through to dawn because, on nights like this, my lighthouse is the difference between life and death for boats caught out to sea.

In a storm, it's better for them to stay far from the coast, and my job is to make sure they know where that coast is. And where I am, perched high on a cliff above the Oregon coast, on the outskirts of Conception Ridge.

You don't need to stay up. I fucking hate that voice in my head. The one that tells me the lighthouse is automated and alarms would wake me up if the system stopped working.

I could leave, too. Go to the McIntoshes' house for their fucking sweet-as-apple-pie carol singing and board games night like I used to. Dan and his wife always included me, ever since Dan and I returned from our last tour overseas. He got married, and I signed up for this job.

You'll spend your time alone, the posting warned.

Didn't bother me at all. I joined the Army to escape my demons, and the Army just gave me more. I learned I'm not cut out for people. Except for the McIntosh family. We have a bond.

Had a bond. You broke it.

That. Fucking. Voice.

I sigh and get up to pour another cup of coffee. Check the forecast. It's getting worse now.

Back at my computer, I see a text message from none other than Dan's wife, Susan.

I'm so sorry that Neely's crashed your Christmas Eve of Solitude! We were out caroling when she called about the car. I just tried your phones and couldn't get through. The storm is nasty.

Alarm rises as I reach for my phone. Susan's right. The phone lines are having trouble connecting. I try Neely next, with the same amount of luck.

Why would Susan think Neely is here?

Neely, nineteen and a half, and all grown up in so many ways. But she still lives at home, and her parents worry.

I worry, too. From afar.

I grab my flashlight and head down to the ground floor. I'm wearing a heavy wool sweater and a similarly thick hat, but I still grab my parka before ripping the door open, hoping to find the McIntosh girl on my doorstep.

I don't.

Fuck.

I can't text Susan back and tell her I don't know where her daughter is. I pull the parka on and stalk down the path. My lighthouse sits at the top of a hill with a line of trees at the base. On the other side of that. . .

Neely's new job. Of course, I know she's working there. I greedily consume all Neely updates from her parents and her social media accounts.

If her car broke down, she should have gone back to work

and waited there. It's not safe out in the storm—and she's not safe with me, either.

The same moment that dark thought ripples through my mind, I see her stumbling toward me.

I shout her name, and she lifts her bowed head, the hood of her jacket flipping off. Even at this distance, I can see her face is twisted from pain or maybe the cold. And then her foot wobbles beneath her—is she wearing *high heels?*—and she falls, landing on her ass and then going prone on the ground.

Taking off at a run, I get to her side in ten of the longest seconds of my life.

My horror increases as I realize her legs are basically bare beneath her coat. She's wearing tights and heeled boots, and I'm guessing some kind of too-short, inappropriate for the weather dress.

I yank off my parka as I bark her name.

She doesn't respond.

I lift her up like she weighs nothing and wrap her lower body in my jacket. Her hands flop against my chest, and those are bare, too.

"When you wake up, we're going to have a long talk about weather-appropriate clothing, young lady," I mutter to her as I march back up the hill. My pulse is pounding erratically in my chest—and not from the effort of carrying her.

That wasn't hard at all, except for how right it felt to cradle her in my arms.

You sick fuck. She's barely conscious, so I can't disagree with the voice in my head. I am a sick fuck when it comes to Neely. I have no right to the thoughts I've entertained, the desire I indulge in during the darkest hours of the night.

When I arrive at the lighthouse, I have to shift her in my arms so I can open the door, and her jacket bunches up. My hand tightens down on her thigh, practically bare in only a thin pair of tights, and she whines at the contact.

If she's gotten herself frostbite, I will—

Do nothing.

I'm not in charge of her; I'm not her parent. I'm just a guy with opinions about how a girl should dress. Though I'm a social hand grenade, even I know it's not cool for an old man like me to have opinions about how she should dress.

Except for when it's a matter of life and death.

Jesus. I push inside and slam the door behind me.

In my arms, she rouses a little. "Ford?"

"It's me, baby." I think about putting her down on the couch, but I don't have any throw blankets or shit like that.

She needs to warm up.

She needs to be in my bed.

My bedroom is on the ocean side of the lighthouse, a cozy nook of a room with a single window high on the wall. It's dark and warm, only the light from the occasional pass of the turning beacon high above illuminating us. And it has an extra heater that I'll crank up just as soon as I get her under the covers.

"I need you. . ." she murmurs as I unzip her wet coat and discard it.

"You need to get warm," I mutter.

"Be my Santa again." It's a whisper, and her words break as she shivers.

I set her down on the bed, gentle as can be, then pull off her boots. Her tights are wet, and through them, her skin is cold.

I say a prayer to whoever the patron saint of horny old men is and tap her face. "Neely, sweetheart. Can you get undressed? I'll find you a shirt."

No response.

I pull the blankets over her. Fuck. I turn up the heater, take her coat out to the living room, and hang it next to my wood-stove. Taking off my wet clothes, I text Susan to say that Neely is here and already asleep for the night—sort of true—then stalk back to the bedroom.

She's shivering under the blankets.

Fuck it. I strip down to my boxers and climb in with her.

"Let's never talk about this again," I whisper as I tug her dress up to her hips and find the waistband of her tights.

She's so damn little in my hands. My fingers cover a lot of her flesh as I peel them off. I can't help but brush her panties and notice where the soft cotton covers her ass cheeks—and where it doesn't. Not so little anymore, I guess. Her bottom fills my hands as I get the tights down to her thighs, and a flash of forbidden desire crystallizes in my mind.

Neely on top of me. My hands on her hips, guiding her down onto my cock. Those cotton panties ripped away, her wearing nothing at all as I watch my erection disappear inside her perfect little cunt.

Her sexy, untouched virgin pussy.

Daddy's little girl, taking every inch of his massive cock, until he's buried inside her.

I shake it off. It's bad enough I have the fantasies of Neely saving herself for me. It's definitely crossing a line to let them into my mind while I undress her because she needs my body heat.

I leave her dress on because it didn't get wet thanks to her coat, and I tuck her up against me, her chilly hands pressed against my chest, her chilly legs folded in between mine.

It doesn't take long for her to stop shivering and her breath to even out. Once we've built up enough warmth under the blankets, I ease up my grip on her, and she rolls out of my arms and curls up on her other side, her back to me now.

Dark hair spills across my pillow.

I tuck the blankets in around her and climb out of bed, ignoring the way my dick has chubbed up from having her in my arms. Now that she's warm again, I need to put on some clothes. And get her a glass of water and an assortment of medicine.

When I return, I discover she's thrown off the covers.

"Stop that," I growl at her. Because I can, because she's asleep, and she can't hear me being my true, mean self. I tug the blanket back up her now splayed legs. I cover her cotton-covered mound—*white with blue snowflakes; that's going in the spank bank, and I'm going to hell*—and tuck the blanket securely around her torso again.

I go to stroke her damp hair off her forehead, jerking my hand back when I realize she's burning up.

"Neely," I snap. "Wake up."

That does nothing.

"Sweetheart, you need some medicine." I shake two Tylenol into one hand, then gently rub the corner of her mouth with my other thumb, encouraging her to open her lips for me. "Wake up, little one. I know it's hard."

Groaning, she grabs my wrist.

But instead of pushing my hand away, she tugs it closer, pulling my thumb into her mouth.

My cock roars to attention, thick and full, as she pulls on my flesh, her mouth hot and wet.

I groan. It's a feral noise, one of need. My vision darkens at the edges, and I know I could give in to this. Shove down my sweat pants and jerk off as she suckles my thumb.

But I would be the worst kind of monster if I did that.

With another strangled sound, I wrench away from her. The pills can wait.

I'm at the bedroom door when she moans behind me.

"Daddy, don't go." It's a breathy plea that stops me in my tracks.

I turn, and that's my undoing. She's rucked her dress up her torso, the strobing light outside casting a moving spotlight on the curves of her lower body.

"I need you," she whispers. It's coherent enough that I swear she's awake, but her face is still flushed, and her eyes are squeezed shut.

Those perfectly swollen strawberry-pink lips part again.

She's the most beautiful vision I've ever seen in my life, and I don't deserve to have her in my bed. I press myself back against the door to stop myself from going to her—*she needs me* —and squeeze my cock savagely through my sweatpants.

She doesn't need *me*. She's dreaming about something I have no right to intrude on.

The way she sucked on your thumb, though. . . Maybe the voice in my head is a fucking dirtbag, too.

3
neely

I'M DREAMING of one of Ford's hands between my thighs, his other pressed against my mouth. *Shh, be a good girl for—*

And then I'm awake. It's a disorienting shift because the last thing I really remember, I was heading up the path to the lighthouse and thought I heard his voice.

Now I'm lying on my back in a dark room, and it's hot. I've pushed off the blankets— Blankets.

I'm in a bed.

There's a grunt from the shadows, and more comes back to me in flashes. Ford carrying me in here. Ford trying to get me to take medicine. His hand. . . Oh.

I sit up, smooth my dress down over my hips, and whisper his name. "Ford?"

He steps forward as the light pulses across the room again. "You need medicine."

"I'm okay."

"You're burning up."

"Did I faint?" I move to sit on the side of the bed and test my legs out by swinging them. "I do that sometimes. It's not a big deal."

"You have a fever." His voice is strangled now, I realize, and I jerk my head up to look at him better in the dim light.

"You were worried about me."

"Of course I was—" He laughs, sharp and hollow. "Jesus, Neely, you're not dressed appropriately for the weather."

"I thought the lighthouse was closer to the retirement home than it was. It looks closer." I shiver, remembering how cold it got.

Suddenly I'm on my back, and Ford is above me, tucking me back under the heavy blanket. "Hey!"

He scowls. "Medicine first. Then we can talk about how you almost died because of cold exposure."

That's a ridiculous exaggeration.

"Can I go pee first before you lecture me?" I glare up at him.

He cracks a reluctant smile. "Yeah."

As he gets me the painkillers and a bottle of water, I push the blanket off my legs. After taking the medicine, and before I can even wiggle my legs again and test standing, he scoops me into his arms.

"Hey," I protest, but my head swims a little, so my protest is less heated than before.

"I'll bring you to the washroom, and you can have some privacy." He's so gruff. "I'll find you warmer clothes."

"It's plenty warm in here."

He ignores me and carries me across the room and through another door. He's renovated the bathroom since I was here last, but that's been at least five years.

"Nice tile," I say to lighten the mood.

It doesn't work.

"Hold on to the wall when I set you down," he barks.

I roll my eyes. "Yes, Da—"

We both freeze. *Daddy, don't go.* Did I say that out loud as I was waking up? I think I did. I think I can still feel the words in my throat and hear his ragged breathing as I say them, and oh my *God.*

Here I am, giving him lip like a teenager—which is hot for me, but definitely not for him. There isn't a chance in hell Ford will ever see me as anything other than a childish brat if I forget myself.

He exhales roughly. "Let's both be glad I'm not your father."

"Ford, I—"

He brushes his lips against my temple, then sets me down. "I'll be back in a few minutes with clothes for you."

Mortification rolls through me as he leaves, clicking the door shut behind him. I make my way to the toilet and plunk my ass down.

I wasn't lying before. I do sometimes faint. I try to think if he's ever been there when I've done a spontaneous flop. Maybe that time I whacked my thumb with a hammer while my dad and Ford built our deck, but he might have gone home already.

The twisted ankle, thanks to an impromptu soccer game gone awry at a picnic. . . Was he there? He wasn't there when I passed out on the subway because it was too hot and filled with too many people, that's for sure.

After I pee, I wash my face in the sink.

I don't recognize the woman in the mirror. *Get your shit together*, I tell her. *You faint, it's fine. Just tell him that.*

And now he thinks I have a fever.

Have him check me again, but with his lips.

I don't feel sick. I feel like I've already made a fool of myself in front of Ford, so why not go all the way and tell him how I feel?

Stepping back, I adjust my dress. It was up around my waist when I woke up, which means Ford saw my panties. Did he like that? *There's only one way to find out. . .*

The mature thing to do would be to talk about it. Unfortunately, the last thing I want to be around Ford is mature. I wanted all sorts of fantasies that were inappropriate in real life. I want him to touch me in my sleep. I want him to look up my skirt while I pretend to be all innocent.

I want him to lose control around me and want me the same

way I want him. With filthy, dirty, secret desire.

Still unsure of what I'm going to do or say next, I open the bathroom door.

Ford is waiting on the other side with a few folded pieces of clothing. None of them look sexy in the slightest. I swallow my secrets and give him a bland look. "See? I'm still standing."

"Good." He doesn't move. "We should get you back to bed."

"So I don't stay up too late, get into any trouble?" I'm smirking. I can feel it, but I can't stop myself. Ford brings out the absolute worst in me when he puts this stiff distance between us.

"Yes." His eyes flash with a peculiar heat that makes me feel bold.

"I'm fine, by the way. Thank you for coming to find me, but I faint sometimes. It's called a vasovagal response, and it's actually normal. It can be triggered by cold, stress, or pain. It just happens. It's not dangerous."

"Until you freeze to death." He's so bossy and stern. I should be scared, but I'm not. I like the way his voice gets tight, like he's worried about me because I'm Neely, and not just because I'm a dumb kid.

"Ford—"

"No." His face goes thunderous. "If I were your father, you wouldn't be allowed to leave the house in barely there tights on a day like today."

If only that kind of threat actually worked to tame me, instead of making me hot.

"I thought we were both supposed to be glad that you're not my father," I whisper.

He shoves the clothes at me. "Put these on."

"What's wrong with what I'm wearing?" I don't take the bundle.

Now that I think about it, that curious heat in his eyes might mean something promising. The same promise that comes from him peeling off my clothes.

I gesture down to my bare legs. "I guess the outfit was more complete before someone took off those *barely there* tights, of course."

"They were wet," he growls. "And you wouldn't wake up."

I step right against him, lifting my face to glare back at him. "If you want my legs to be covered up again, then I suggest you dress me yourself."

"Don't think I won't."

I wait.

He steps back, sets the clothes on a side table, and picks up a pair of sweat pants that will fall right off me. He kneels in front of me, unaware of the wild heat this position sends racing through my body.

Look at me. See me for the woman that I am.

No such luck, though. He gathers one leg of the sweatpants and shoves it at my foot. "Step into this."

I sigh and do as he commands, one foot and then the other. Somehow he gets them up to my hips without his big, thick fingers touching my legs once, which is truly rude.

He rises as he tugs them up, looming over me again as he roughly pulls them over my ass. My dress lifts with the waistband, and then his hands are under my clothes, fumbling with the drawstring. Now he can't help but touch me, and it feels so good to have his fingers brushing against my stomach, even if it's a purely functional task from his end.

For me, it's magic. He's a little hesitant, like he knows he shouldn't be touching me under my dress, even though it's innocent. Those little moments before he yanks his fingers away from my skin as if touching me has scalded him, but then his touch returns. . . It's the stuff my fantasies are made of.

Of course, in my fantasies, my legs are bare and—

"Neely, stop that."

I jerk my head up, staring at him. "What?"

"Breathing like that." He drags in a rough breath of his own as we exchange a heated look I don't really understand.

How was I breathing? My chest rises between us, then falls as I try to calm myself. Had I given my desire away?

Daddy. . . This is the second or third time I've revealed who I am to Ford. And he's still standing right next to me with that wild, feral burn in his expression.

"Put the shirts on." He points to the other items of clothing.

Shirts. Plural.

My pulse jacks up. "You do it."

His eyes go wide.

I turn around, presenting him with my back. "There's a zipper."

At first, I don't think he's going to do it, but then he steps forward, and his hands are on me again.

Neither of us speaks as he drags the zipper down my back, revealing my bare skin. There's a window in front of me, and I realize I can see our reflection in it.

So can he.

Without saying a word, I lift my arms in the air, and he tugs the dress up and over my head, leaving me topless.

I'm not wearing a bra. I don't need to because the dress has cups built into it, and that's all the support my nineteen-year-old tits need.

Behind me, Ford makes a wounded sound as his gaze catches on the reflection in the window. He drops the dress and sets his hands on my waist.

I press my hands against his, holding his palms to my belly. Behind me, his whole body goes taut.

"I'm all grown up," I whisper, gambling every ounce of pride I have that I read him correctly.

He shudders. "Trust me, I'm painfully aware."

Hope burns inside me. "Do you know why I'm here?"

"Your car broke down."

"Mmm." I drag his hands up my torso, urging him to touch me higher.

His grip on me tightens just beneath my breasts, his fingertips grazing the curve of my aching flesh. "Stop," he growls. "We can't."

I ignore him. "I wanted to ask you to play Santa Claus tomorrow at Cliffside Village."

"Fine." He's breathing hard now, his nostrils flaring.

"That's all you have to say? Not. . . why do I think you'd be a good Santa Claus? Ford Gamble, notorious Grinch?"

He bows his head, pressing his forehead to the back of my head. I feel his hot breath down the bare expanse of my back. His sweatpants ride low on my hips, and I think he can see the top of my little white panties. "Why?"

"Because you dressed up as Santa once for me. Remember? I sat in your lap and told you I wanted a boyfriend for Christmas."

"Fuck, Neely."

"And as I perched in your lap, my legs swinging between your thighs, I'm pretty sure you—"

He roars and rips himself away from me.

The next thing I know, a T-shirt that smells like him is being yanked over my head. "Go to bed. I have work to do."

By the time I get my arms and head through the holes, I only glimpse his feet, quickly storming up the stairs to the second floor.

Upstairs is the workspace for the lighthouse. When I was little, I loved to sit on the swivel chair in Ford's office and pretend I lived here with him as his apprentice lighthouse keeper.

I have wanted to embed myself in every part of his life for as long as I can remember.

It's probably not healthy.

But I don't care.

I give him a minute, then follow him—after I take off his stupid sweatpants that are too big for me, anyway.

Now I'm only wearing his T-shirt and those little panties he's already seen.

Upstairs, the lights are turned off, but I can still see him sprawled in an armchair.

"I told you to go to bed."

"I'd rather talk."

"We're not talking about that."

That. Oh yes, we are. "Are you just going to avoid me for the rest of my life, then? Is that why you disappeared?"

"It isn't right to want you, Neely. I'm messed up. I had to stop coming around. You'll understand when you're older."

"I get it." My voice shakes. He thinks I don't understand? I understand more than he could ever imagine.

"You don't. You *can't*. I helped raise you. I taught you how to ride a bike."

I shake my head. "I miss you, Ford. Yes, you helped raise me, and then you *dropped* me as soon as I . . . what? Grew tits?"

"No."

"Did you figure out that I wanted you, too? Did that send you running scared?"

He groans. "You don't know—"

I walk closer until I'm standing right beside him, my bare thigh brushing against the hand dangling over the arm of the chair. "Do you think *I'm* messed up for wanting *you*?"

"If you think you do, then that's my fault. I led you—"

"You didn't do anything." I press my leg into his hand, emboldened by his confessions.

Maybe I should have seen it sooner, connected the dots.

But I'm still too young, so any sooner would have been even worse. Maybe he'll always be uncomfortable with the fact I'm Dan's daughter, and he watched me grow up.

"You were never inappropriate," I whisper, sliding my thigh back and forth against his knuckles. Pretending he's the one touching me. Wanting him, desperately, to skim his fingers up the inside of my leg. "Not even once I was old enough to want you to be."

4
ford

SHE CAN'T MEAN any of this. She must still be feverish.

Her thigh doesn't feel hot, pressed against my hand. The urge to take the blatant offer and haul her into my lap is almost impossible to resist.

I manage to anyway, and the howling protest of my inner demons is reflected in the scowl on her face as I pull my hand back from her flesh.

Standing, I put my hands on her shoulders and turn her around, pointing her back to the stairs.

"You should go to bed," I murmur in her ear.

"I'm not tired."

"Then I should feed you." I step around her and head for the stairs myself.

"I'm not hungry," she hollers after me.

I ignore her.

In the kitchen, I pull out a bottle of wine, some cheese, and an apple.

Neely stomps past me, grabs the wine, and puts it back in the fridge. "We need to be sober for this."

"For you to go to sleep, wait out the storm, and then go

home to your parents' place unmolested? No, I don't think I need to be sober for that."

She hops up on the counter beside me with the enthusiasm of a nineteen-year-old. Because—

"I'm not hungry or tired. I'm horny." She says it bluntly, like she's all grown up and casual about sex, but her cheeks turn pink.

"I can't help you with that."

She catches my hand and pulls me sideways until I'm standing in front of her—between her legs. She shifts to the edge of the counter, and now she's in my arms. "That's not what I want you to say."

"It's all that I've got." My erection says otherwise, and we both know it.

She grinds her hips against me, my T-shirt riding up so I can see her panties pulled tight against her mound as she rubs on my cock.

"Neely—" The raw fucking need in my voice kills me because it matches the look on her face. "What do you want from me?"

"Everything."

"I'm trying to be a good man here."

"I don't want you to be good." She tosses her hair and pokes me in the chest, her gaze triumphant even as I still feel lost in a storm. "I want you to be free."

How did she know? How *could* she know?

Her fingers climb my torso slowly, like a filthy game of Itsy Bitsy Spider. "I see you, Ford. You've been wound tight my entire life. When do you let go?"

Never. "Letting go is dangerous."

"That's not healthy."

"*I'm* not healthy."

"Says who?"

Society. I don't answer her. She can't know what's in my head. *Daddy wants you to be quiet. . .*

"Tell me," she breathes. It's a command from a little girl who should know better. No, who should be too fucking innocent to realize that I have dark secrets I don't want to share.

Before I can move away, she leans back on her hands and brings her knees up, resting her heels on the counter. "I have fantasies about you. Would you feel better about sharing your sordid thoughts if I shared mine?"

"No."

She grins. "So you do have sordid thoughts."

I laugh out loud. It's harsh and cruel, and she doesn't even blink. "Everyone has sordid thoughts, Neely."

"Not like mine."

"Your sweet little Daddy fantasies?" I crowd against her now, letting her feel the heavy press of my raging cock against her warm cunt. "Those aren't as deviant as you think, sweetheart. Every girl on Tinder wants to call men Daddy."

Her face goes blank. "And do you let them?"

No. Because none of them are her. I haven't had a woman in my arms in. . . I shake my head. I change the subject. "My point is that it doesn't make you dirty."

"It's not just the name." She catches her lower lip, all gentle innocence now. "What if I want someone to be gentle and teach me everything I need to know? Let me be. . . little and tell me to keep it a—"

"But that's not me." I cut her off, even as my pulse pounds. *Our secret, nobody can know.*

"So my first time should be with someone else?" She's breathless now, her eyes big as she stares at me.

Fuck, no. "That's not what I mean."

"It's what you just said."

"Because I'm not thinking straight," I growl. "You're too young for a first time."

Her pink cheeks are back. "Only in role-play, *Daddy.* In reality, I'm well past the age where touching me is legal."

"That's not what your parents would say."

"Then they don't know shit about the laws in Oregon." She slides her legs back down to swing off the edge of the counter and sits up. "But you know what? If you don't want me, that's—"

"I didn't say that." I hook my hand around the back of her neck, my fingers big there, covering her whole nape. I gentle my touch and stroke my thumb up and down the side of her neck. "God, Neely, you have me all tangled up. But don't think for a second I don't see how beautiful you are. If I were any other man, I'd want to do so right by you. Woo you and put a ring on your finger. Convince you to give this old man babies to fill all the rooms upstairs."

"Be that man," she whispers. "Be free. I want that, too."

I shake my head.

She catches my face in her hands, her fingers cool against my skin. It's a sweet, kind touch that makes my cock pulse, a little seed spilling out the tip. She's good, and I'm—

"No," she says firmly. "Whatever shameful place your mind just went, that's not the truth. Whoever told you your dirty thoughts weren't normal, that your very healthy imagination that wants to breed me is wrong—fuck them. They're not here right now. This is you and me, and I know we want the same thing. Are you going to tell me *I'm* broken? That I'm a perverted little girl who wants bad things and is a bad person for wanting them?"

"You're perfect. Don't ever say that about yourself."

"Then show me," she whispers. "Show me I'm perfect. Show me I'm not broken and that there's nothing wrong with wanting you the way I do."

I capture her mouth, her lips soft and innocent and sweet against mine, and I have my first taste of little Neely McIntosh. A kiss I've imagined hundreds of times and none of those fantasies touch the reality of how she trembles and breathes and throbs against me.

My tongue slides against hers, teaching her to kiss Daddy

like a big girl, showing her how good it can feel. But when she gasps, then wriggles closer, that's not a fantasy. That's all Neely, my beautiful girl. The maddening desire that makes my spine itch shifts to something deeper.

She's kissing me back. Eagerly. Hungrily. Her hands tangle in my hair, holding on to me as she gives as good as she gets, her tongue spearing back at me. I groan around her exploration, letting her take over, letting her climb right into my body. Then she's in my arms, and I'm striding to the bed where I thought I was tucking her in for the night not that long ago.

5
neely

MY BACK HITS THE BED, and Ford is on top of me, one hand cradling my head, the other sliding under my shirt, his shirt, and then his palm is brushing my nipple.

"You were right that I noticed when you suddenly had tits," he growls. "Last summer. Red bikini. You climbed out of the pool, and my dick wanted to be inside you so bad it hurt. I came home and beat myself raw, using my own come as lube. You ever done that, Neely? Gotten so slick for me that it's hard to rub out another one, but you can't stop?"

"Yes," I pant. "Every time you come over to play cards with my dad."

"Fuck."

I pull at his shirt, wanting us both naked. "I've wanted this for a long time."

"Shhh. . ." He kisses me again, all tongue and teeth.

He doesn't want to hear about the fantasies I had when he was off-limits.

I get my hands under his clothes and start to slide my fingers into his waistband.

He freezes and grabs my wrist, hauling my arms back to the bed. "Not yet."

"I want to touch you. Feel how big you are."

"Fucking big," he growls. "And if you put your little fingers around it, I'll spill all the seed that I want to pump into your womb all over your hands instead."

Heat rolls through me, making my breasts heavy and my nipples tight. That's the second time he's talked about knocking me up. Am I ready to go from virgin to pregnant on Christmas Eve? "I—"

"Fuck, ignore me." He huffs a laugh and presses his mouth to my neck, kissing me there before he breaks away to peel off the shirt he gave me. His gaze sears me as I stretch out beneath him in nothing but my panties. "Don't worry, baby. Daddy won't fuck you until you're ready. There are a lot of ways I can make you feel real good without putting my dick inside you."

I whine and lift my hips, everything on fire and aching now. "I want that."

"I don't have condoms," he warns. "Are you on the pill?"

I shake my head. "I've never. . ."

His eyes close for a minute, tension warring with desire on his face. Then he rips off his own shirt, and for the first time, I can ogle him half-naked without feeling weird about it.

He's so handsome it hurts. Thick and well-muscled, with dark hair down the middle of his belly, disappearing into his tented sweatpants. The hair crawls higher, too, dusting his broad chest. There's none of the silver hair in his beard on his body. It's all dark and silky-soft looking. I reach for him, loving the way he jerks when I stroke my fingers over his rock-hard abs.

I stop just before the waistband, then keep going over the fabric of his pants. "What's this?" I ask innocently as I trace the rigid length of his cock. "Is this what you want to put inside me?"

He covers my hand with his and presses hard, showing me how rough he wants me to be with him. I squeeze tight, and I feel him pulse as he grunts out loud.

"You've got me spilling already, little girl." He glares at me, and it's almost scary, but there's a glimmer of something else—pleasure, I think—and then he does the most unexpected thing.

He grins. "Fuck, Neely."

I laugh with him. "You keep saying that."

He peels my fingers off his heavy erection and presses me back to the bed again. "Because this is a dream. It can't be real."

"Tell me your dream," I murmur as he leans in to kiss my belly. The brush of his lips sends lightning bolts through me that shoot up to my breasts and down to my sex.

"You, wanting me. That's a dream. Me being able to put my mouth on you. I want to take my time tasting you." He licks a path up from my belly, circling one breast with his tongue before latching on to the nipple.

My back bows, arching up and off the bed. *Oh. Oh, shit.* I had no idea someone else's mouth would feel that good on my skin. Just right and perfect and— "More," I pant. "The other one."

"Excuse me?" He growls and grazes me with his teeth. "Where are your manners?"

I flush with heat, the correction turning me on. "Sorry."

"How do you ask for something you want?"

"Please. . ."

He grunts and moves over immediately. I'll have to remember the power of that little girlish plea. The nipple he was just loving gets cold, sensitive, and wet in the air, but as if he knows what I need, he covers that breast with his hand and pulls the other one into his mouth.

My thighs press together, then flail apart. I grind my hips up, looking for something hard to rub against, because oh, that, oh *wow*, I think I could come like this. "Ford."

He doesn't stop.

I press my hands to his head and cry out his name again, and suddenly his other hand is between my legs, cupping my pussy through my panties. His fingers are perfect, flat and broad and strong against my clit, and I'm flying, coming apart as he pulls my breast deep into his mouth.

6
ford

SUDDENLY NEELY IS COMING in my arms, and if I had any hesitation before about claiming her, it's gone.

Nothing has ever felt this right. Not even close. I'm so fucking glad I didn't try this with anyone else—never shared my darkest fantasies with anyone else— because these whispered words don't feel dark with Neely.

Not here. Not in my bed, not when she's that responsive to my mouth and my hand over her panties.

My perfect, innocent little girl. My grown-up Neely.

Mine.

My woman. I waited for her, even when I didn't know it would be *her*. And now I will be whatever she wants, however she wants, for the rest of her life.

She falls back to the bed, face flushed and eyes bright, then she reaches for me, and we're kissing again.

My girl likes to stroke her tongue against mine and be a little bossy with her mouth. I haul her on top of me and let her play. My cock strains as she nips at my lower lip and licks at the corner of my mouth before sealing us together again, swallowing my groans.

Against my belly, I feel the damp press of her panties. Her

first release has made a mess, and I want to lick it up. Show her how good a mouth can feel on her cunt, and then teach her how to lick Daddy, too.

"Baby, slow down."

She lifts her head, her mouth swollen and pink. "I like it when you call me baby."

"Yeah?" Fuck. Good. I grip her hips and guide her ass against my cock. "I've wanted you to be my little girl for months now."

The tip of her tongue peeks out like she's caught it between her lovely teeth. "Ford?"

"Yeah. . ."

"I want to be naked with you."

"I want you naked, too. I want to give your sweet pussy a kiss next."

She wiggles in my grasp. "I want you to be naked, too. First." She pauses a beat, her eyes sparkling. "Now."

"Bratty demands, huh?" I lift her off me, her little tits wobbling as she flails her arms and laughs. "Sit here and be a good girl for me, then."

She kneels beside me and watches my midsection as I notch my thumbs into my sweats and push them down.

My dick pops into view, thick and veiny and shiny at the top from all the eager dripping it's already done.

"Will you come if I touch it?" Her voice is breathy, her eyes wide, and she smiles when I take her hand and guide her fingers around me.

"Not now. Before, yeah, I thought I might. But Daddy's calmed down a little." I hiss as her fingers circle me and give a tentative stroke. "Sort of calm. Ah, yes. Like that."

"I've never. . ." Her face is soft and dreamy. "I like how you feel."

I prop my arms behind my head. "Then be my guest. Explore away."

"You're really big."

My cock flexes in pride. "Bigger than usual tonight."

"That seems counterintuitive. I'm really little."

Another flex.

She giggles. "Come on, that's not fair."

"Not fair is that you're still wearing clothes."

"Panties," she whispers, and the spark in her eye promises she knows exactly what the breathy word does to me. Another pearl of pre-come appears at the tip of my cock, and she gasps. "Ford, you're. . . that's. . ."

"Keep talking about that little scrap of white cotton protecting your virtue, baby, and there will be more where that drop came from."

She climbs on top of me, straddling my thighs, then takes my dick in hand again, this time rubbing the shiny tip against her belly, at the waistband of those godforsaken panties.

"All right," I growl, tossing her onto her back. "That's enough."

I kiss her again, slow and patient until she's panting hard and her nipples are tight diamonds against my chest. Then I work my way down her body and peel her panties down, just enough to get my first look at her precious little cunt. Wet slick glistens on bare lips, a few days of soft hair growth not hiding an inch of her puffy pussy from my adoring inspection. "You shave this, baby?"

She nods, her cheeks pink as she watches me look at her up close. "Once a week, usually."

"Can Daddy do it next time?"

She whimpers as she nods again.

I kiss her mound, getting closer to the sweet mess I need in my mouth. "Good girl. I want to make sure you don't cut yourself."

"I'm careful," she whispers. "I go real slow."

"Does it feel good? To be nice and bare?" My tongue connects with her sticky slit, and I'm a goner from the first taste. "Oh, honey, you taste so good."

I slide my tongue into the crease of her pussy lips and find her clit, firm and pulsing. As I lick and suck at her bare flesh, my brain cells scatter, and I yank the panties lower, needing them off her so I can see her slit better.

Her pink entrance reveals itself as her thighs fall open, and I taste her there next. Slick spills onto my tongue as I test her tight channel. Tiny. Fuck if I know how my thick, brutish cock will fit into this virgin girl, but damn if that isn't a fucking turn-on.

I'll be forced to take my time with her.

It's for the best, anyway.

I replace my tongue with a single finger and gently circle where she'll eventually take me with ease before I move my mouth back to her pussy lips and eager clit. Every few licks, I look up at her, making sure she's still with me. Still pink-cheeked and swollen-lipped, her lust-drunk gaze locked on where I'm ravenous for the scent and taste of her sex.

"You taste perfect," I tell her, my voice rough.

"I want to kiss you again."

"You'll taste yourself."

Her eyes light up. "Is that a warning?"

I prowl up her body, one hand still teasing between her legs. "It's a promise."

7
neely

I'VE TOUCHED myself before and licked my fingers off, but that's nothing compared to the scent and taste of me all over Ford's face.

And he loves it. He can't stop telling me that, even as I lick the corner of his mouth and wipe off his cheek. He catches my fingers and licks them, not letting any go untasted.

"I want you to come on my face," he rumbles.

But I already have my hand on his thick erection again, trying to rub it against my pussy. His hand is in the way, but the sound he makes when his hard meets my wet is amazing.

A gasp, a growl, and a grunt all rolled into one.

"I want to come on your cock," I whisper back.

"It's not that easy your first time." He presses his forehead against mine. "Better if you come first."

"I already did once," I point out.

"That was just the start." He sucks in a breath as I wedge the pre-come-covered crown of his cock in beside his finger, where he's just inside my body a little.

Even this much feels overwhelming. Full and too much and not enough at the same time.

"Ford."

"Neely, this isn't up for negotiation." He swears under his breath, then flips me over, slapping my ass lightly. "Who am I?"

"My big sexy crush."

Another slap, then he hauls my hips into the air, his fingers back between my thighs as soon as I'm in the position he wants. Face down, ass up. "Who am I?"

"My father's best friend."

That makes him roar, and one of those fingers slides deeper into me than before. "Neely McIntosh, who the fuck am I?"

"You're my Daddy," I moan, grinning into his sheet.

"So you need to do what I say."

I shiver. "Is that so?"

"Yes, that's fucking so. You need to dress warmly and come on my face."

"That's it? Two rules?"

Behind me, he squeezes my ass cheeks with both hands, then presses them apart, showing him. . . all of me. Every naughty inch.

"There will be more rules," he murmurs, his breath hot against my crease. "Once we get to know each other better in this new relationship. But those two are nonnegotiable. Understand?"

"Yes, Daddy. I—" The rest of what I might say is lost at the deliriously good first swipe of his tongue against pussy. How is it even better from behind? I thought it felt amazing before, but I'd also been able to stop him and ask for a kiss.

Like this, I'm not stopping him. I grind back against him shamelessly, rubbing against his face as he gets comfortable. My whole body goes limber and warm as he eats me out, and this time when he eases a finger into me, my body is slick and ready. His thick knuckle stretches my entrance in a good way, and then he adds a second finger, and I take that, too.

He's fucking me. Finger fucking, and it feels good. I'm full, and a climax is building. *Ford is fucking me.* Working his fingers in and out of my body, his mouth on my clit. I'm a sloppy mess for him, and it's everything I thought it could be and more.

Especially when his other hand grips one ass cheek and his thumb slides over my back hole. I jerk in surprise, and he murmurs something I can't catch because when he does it again, it lights me up. Less surprise, more *oh wow, yes, Daddy*.

I lose it, a climax ripping through me, and he rolls me over as I cry out in pleasure.

He crawls on top of me, a big man, all warm and furry and hard and soft. Perfect. I'm so, so ready by the time he notches his cock against my slick, swollen pussy.

"I—" He's breathing hard as he pauses. "Tell me this is okay."

I nod slowly, smiling from ear to ear. "I want this."

He presses into me.

Ready may have been a premature assessment of the situation, though.

He's big. Bigger than I thought. Bigger than I ever could have imagined. And the mind-searing pleasure that comes with the initial entrance of his heavy cock into my body quickly gives way to something else. A brain cell scattering sensation that's almost like pain, but not.

He won't fit, I think. It's stupid; of course, he will. But he *can't* right now because I feel like he's stopped, and then I have a second horrible thought.

He's changed his mind.

Fuck.

"Breathe, Neely." His voice is so deep, so warm, and it grounds me.

I blink my eyes open.

"Let Daddy in." His low, private words light a fire inside me. His ardent gaze searches my face as he starts to move again. "You feel so good, baby. Your sweet little cunt was made for me. You'll see. Let me in so I can show you how good you can feel."

"I don't know how," I whisper back. "Show me."

He shifts his weight, one big hand grazing down my torso, lighting a path of goosebumps and funny feelings from my breast to my belly to my hip. "Picture me inside you. Daddy's cock, all the way in your little belly. It's okay that I'm big. It's *good* that I'm big. I'm going to fill your sweet hole all the way up. That's what you secretly want, so think about it."

"How do you know?" I ask in wonder.

"The same way you knew what I wanted." He shudders as I make a tentative rock of my hips. "Yes, baby. Fuck, you're getting wetter thinking about it, aren't you?"

"Is this what you dreamed of? Being too big for me?" As I say it, I feel what he feels, a slickness from inside me, making it impossible to resist the hard press of his erection.

His hand squeezes my hip. "Yes." And then he takes the filthy fantasy a step further. "Close your eyes, Neely. Pretend you're alone in bed at your house. All turned on and horny because Uncle Ford is staying over, and you want him to sneak into your little girl bedroom and touch you."

I gasp, my body lit up with electricity now, tight and taut and wonderful. Between my legs, a whole new level of heat blooms. How did he know? "Would you have?"

Before. When I was too young.

He swears under his breath. "No."

I smile and blink my eyes open at him, my hips moving now, my slit slippery and smooth as I rock beneath him. His heavy cock pushes deeper into me. "I think you would have."

He thrusts, making me gasp, then jerks his hips back. "We can play that game sometime. But this is where I wanted you for the first time. My bed. Alone. Little Neely all grown up. A woman for me to claim."

I want that, too. I want it all. "Then claim me."

He locks his gaze on mine as he presses into me again, this time not stopping until he's all the way inside, fully seated and taking up so much space it's hard to breathe. Or maybe it's hard to breathe because his gaze is so dark, so intense, that nothing exists outside the two of us in this moment, me beneath him —finally.

When he moves again, it's different.

This time, when his heavy length drags out of me, I'm instantly hollow. I need him back, so I move, too, chasing him, clinging to him.

Needing him.

He wraps me in his arms, his body heavy and protective as we slip into a perfect rhythm. He knows just how to cradle me so his cock rubs against the right spots, lighting me up inside. He knows how long to hold himself inside me until that overwhelming feeling subsides and gives way to the deepest, most unimaginable pleasure.

I thought I knew what it would be like.

I thought I knew what I wanted.

Those girlish fantasies pale compared to being Ford's lover. I couldn't have guessed at the wild edge to it, this desperate flutter inside. The *if he doesn't fuck me harder, I might die of need* kind of edge.

"More," I plead.

He gives me more.

"Harder," I beg, and he gives me that, too.

Everything I vocalize between panting, gasping sounds, he gives me—and more.

"You feel incredible," he whispers against my mouth before kissing me and fucking my mouth with his tongue like his cock fucks my pussy. He rides me like I'm exactly the dirty girl I want to be for him.

He sees me and wants me, just as I am.

I wrap my arms and legs around him, clinging to him as I climb closer to release. "Who am I?"

He huffs a laugh as he plants one hand beside my head and scoops his other arm around my waist, locking us together. I'm a rag doll to him, little and pliant. "You're mine."

"Your what?"

Inside, I feel his cock swelling, getting bigger. Stretching me from the inside out. "My little one."

"Your little one," I breathe back, starting to float. I feel tight inside, on the cusp. "Your. . ."

"My baby." He groans, his next thrust rough. "God, I want to fill you up."

A fresh wave of heat slams into me, imagining his come deep inside me, then spilling out. I cry out, clenching around him, and he fucks me through it, pounding me into the bed now, rough and wild.

As soon as I collapse, he pulls out with a grunt and slides his erection against my wetness. The head bumps against my clit and pushes through my folds as he spurts his release on top of my mound and up my belly.

I reach for it, sliding my fingers through the warm evidence that I undid him completely. "I thought you were going to finish inside me."

He's breathing hard as he kisses me. "Almost did."

"Would I have felt it? There's so much. . ."

He makes a wounded sound. "Yeah, baby. You'd have felt it."

"Will you do that soon?"

He bites my lip instead of answering, then climbs off the bed. "Don't move."

"Where would I go?" I call after him as he disappears into the hallway. "I'm covered in your come."

He laughs and reappears in the doorway with a towel. "I'm very aware."

"You didn't answer my question," I tell him as he wipes off my skin.

He's careful and thorough, his gaze lingering on the swollen and sore flesh between my legs. "What question was that? I got distracted by how pretty you are."

I blush. "You like looking at me there?"

"I sure do." His fingers replace the towel. "I wasn't too rough, was I? You still look so little and soft."

"I'm fine." I catch his hand and rock against it. "Think about how messy I would be right now if all of that was inside me."

He grunts. "It'd be sliding out now."

I shiver. "When will we do that?"

"Ah. That was the question. When am I going to finish inside you?" He exhales roughly and stretches out beside me. "Come here."

I roll into his side, and he arranges me so I'm plastered against him. Touching as much as possible, his arm tight around my body.

"One thing at a time," he finally says. "You might wake up tomorrow and want nothing more to do with me."

8
ford

"NO," Neely says hotly. "I'm not going to—"

"Settle down." I kiss the top of her head. "I just don't want to rush you."

She traces her hand down my torso. Her little fingers against the thick broadness of my chest, then lower, tangling in the dark hair at the base of my cock. . . the sight of it makes me want to mount her again.

It makes the words out of my mouth a lie, too, but it's a lie for her own good. That's what Daddies do, I figure. I don't know. I've never done this before. But it's what I want for her—freedom and choice.

Only part of me wants that for her.

I can't deny that. There's another part of me that wants to bar the door and never let her leave. Keep her here until she's round with my child. God, I would fuck her three times a day at least. Her little legs spread wide, my cock disappearing into that pink slit I'd have to shave for her because she wouldn't be able to reach.

Or maybe she'd grow a cute little bush for me to bury my face in, celebrate that she's all grown—

"Why do you hate Christmas?"

I grunt at the subject change and at the feel of her fingers around my cock. "I don't hate it."

I hate myself. It's not the same thing.

"You used to come to our house."

And I would dress up as Santa. The last time I did that was when she crawled into my lap and wished for a boyfriend.

She gives me a shy smile, like she isn't jerking me off, ready to ride me again. "We like having you around. So why don't you come over for the holidays?"

Because I'm a wicked man who doesn't deserve gilt wrapping paper and fucking Christmas carols. "Don't worry about it."

"I'm in your bed. Naked. I'm going to worry about it. I want you to come with me tomorrow."

I laugh out loud. "Fuck, Neely. No."

"Why not?"

"Because Dan will take one look at your rosy little cheeks and know I bounced you on my dick as you called me Daddy, that's why."

"So?" She waves her hands. "I mean, obviously, I don't want to talk to him about it. Ew. But it's *not* ew, not between us. It's private and wonderful and *ours*, and he will be polite about it."

"No, he won't."

"Ford." She stops stroking my cock.

"Neely." I reach for her, and she slides out of my grasp.

She gives me a dark, wild look.

"What?"

"You. . . you said. . ." Two bright red spots appear high on her cheeks. Her eyes are dangerously bright now. Fuck me. Fucking hell. "Ford, you told me you wanted me to have. . . And now you're saying you aren't mine to bring home for Christmas? That was all just talk?"

I scramble off the bed, but she's already racing out of the room. By the time I reach her, she's pulling on one of my sweaters.

Armor, I guess, against the bad man who broke her heart.

I catch her around the waist and spin her around. "Stop. No. Of course you're mine. I'm sorry." Fuck. I kiss her tear-stained cheeks. "I just don't want to rush you."

"Really?" She pushes against my chest. "I thought you wanted to claim me."

"That's the bad man part of me, baby."

"I thought we talked about this. You don't have to hide that from me." She gives me a defiant look.

"I don't want to scare you."

"I want to be scared. Show me everything."

"And then take you to your family Christmas? Dress up as Santa for you?"

"Yes!" She throws her hands in the air. "Are you kidding me? Yes, that's how it works. Be my freak here and my bae out there."

"Your. . ." I swallow hard around the knot in my throat. "And your. . ."

She climbs up my body, wrapping her arms around my neck and her legs around my waist. "Or be my Daddy at home and my boyfriend around town?"

"I want more," I growl, everything clicking into place. I've been an idiot. A fucking idiot of epic proportions, locking myself up in this lighthouse for years, refusing to live because of an ephemeral fantasy.

But I was waiting for her.

I don't have to lock myself up any longer.

I palm her ass, my fingers questing between her legs because her pussy is mine. "I'm not boyfriend material, baby. I'm too possessive, too needy. Too demanding."

She shivers in my arms. "Then demand away. What do you want of me?"

"I want your curiosity. All the time. Baby wants to see Daddy's dick? Crawl on me and ask. I want your sweetness. You've had a bad day? I want you to curl up in my lap and tell me about it. I want your promise, too. I want to hear forever dripping off your lips as I claim you."

I want to wife her up, too, but I gotta do it right.

"Forever?" She wriggles against me, and fuck, I missed an opportunity to fill her with seed before.

I'll rectify that immediately. "You sore, baby?"

"No," she whines as I circle the slick center of her body.

"You sure?"

"I want you."

"That's not the same thing." I haul her to the oversized couch and lie down, moving her around until her sweet little pussy is in front of my face. It's swollen and red, like a big brute bashed his way into her, and I can't fuck her again.

I need to.

I lick her instead as she writhes on top of me. I'm buck ass naked, but she's still wearing my hoodie, so I can't feel her tits on my belly as she flattens out, grinding her pussy back against me.

And then her mouth is on my cock, just the tip, suckling it, and the world tilts on its axis.

Fuck no, the first time she takes my cock down her throat will not be in a sixty-nine while I'm blissed out on the scent of her cunt. I'll fucking hurt her by accident.

"Baby," I growl. "Stop that."

"You don't like it?"

"I fucking love it. But Daddy said stop."

She stops.

Fuck, I love that.

"Turn around," I order, and we rearrange ourselves so she's perched on my lap. My cock stands between us, an obscene reminder of how big I am against her little body. She took all of that inside her.

Take her again.

I haul her in for a kiss instead, burying my hands under my sweatshirt, holding her close.

She rubs her slit against my dick, and the plan to show her how to suck Daddy properly, carefully, goes out the window.

"I need you again."

"Take me."

"I should have come in you before." It bursts out of me, a rough confession.

She shivers as she rises on her knees, fitting us together. "You gotta mean it, Ford."

"I mean it." In this moment, the Daddy slides away, and I'm just a man confessing his feelings.

Neely gets really close, her mouth brushing mine in an almost kiss as she works her arousal around the head of my cock.

"I want some of you inside me tomorrow when you take me home." She eases me deeper, her face tensing at the intrusion. "And when you put on the Santa costume. . ."

"We haven't talked about that yet." I'll do it. I'll do anything she wants.

"We had more important things to discuss." She's got half of me in her now, and I need to see it.

I angle her back so I can see her pussy stretched around the veiny length of my dick. Pink flesh, slick and wet, clinging to me as I work her body, making her take it.

Tell her.

Because I can't pretend I don't want everything with her.

I say it as soon as she's got all of me inside her. I hold her there, her legs spread wide across my lap, her clit rubbing against the lowest part of my abs. I drag my gaze up from the prettiest sight I've ever seen to the most beautiful sight I ever could have dreamed of—Neely staring back at me in complete lust.

Her sweet face is flushed, her lips parted, and her eyes hooded with need.

"I love you," I say hoarsely. "I'm going to love you forever.

I'll be everything you need, anytime and anywhere. You're it for me, Neely. I'm yours."

She cries out, a little strangled sound, and I haul her close again.

"I love you, too," she whispers as I kiss her. She says it again once I peel off the sweatshirt and a few more times while I take her tits in my mouth.

It's a prayer, a chant. We say it back and forth, joyfully and reverently, and then hungrily as she gets closer. She shakes in my arms, her thighs trembling as I fuck her from below.

"Come for me," I growl. "Show me how much you need this, too. I'm going to love you forever. That starts right now. Nothing between us, ever. No limits. Whatever you need."

"I need you." She cries out again. Ah. Oh. God. "Daddy. . ."

"No limits," I repeat. "We'll do it all."

"Love. . ." She freezes with me deep inside her, then I feel her go, a ripple that pulls my release out of me in long, milking squeezes.

And she gasps again.

Yeah, she can feel it. Heavy spurts.

Dangerously good, that feeling. Fuck.

"Ford?" She's panting as she slides off me.

"Yeah, baby?"

"I think I am a little hungry now."

9
neely

WE STAY up until two in the morning. Ford finally gets a chance to feed me, and we pepper each other with curious questions as Christmas Eve slides into Christmas Day.

"What happens if you go on vacation?" I ask him as he makes me a grilled cheese sandwich in the kitchen that is probably twice as old as I am.

"The weather service would find a temporary replacement."

"Would? Have you ever taken a holiday?"

He shrugs. "No point."

"We're going to change that."

"Are we?"

I give him a wicked smile. "Think of the teeny tiny bikini I might wear on the Mexican Riviera."

"On a private beach? Because I don't want anyone else to see that," he growls.

"But what if I want people to see the wolfish way Daddy looks at me?"

He grunts. "If you want it. . ."

But I'll save the most scandalous bathing suits for a private swim.

"Do you like your job?" he asks me after I feed him the last bite of my sandwich.

"I do. It's. . . the residents are a lot of fun. And I was happy I didn't have to leave town to find work. I thought about it, though."

He frowns. "Where would you have gone?"

It's my turn to shrug. "I don't know. I didn't get far in that thinking. It was more about if the grass might be greener." I chew on the corner of my lip. "Or if it might be easier to not work literally next door to where you were locked up, all brooding and hot and off-limits."

He gives me a crooked smile. "If you keep working there, it's a pretty short commute from here—although I'll need to walk you there and come get you in bad weather."

I roll my eyes. "Okay, whatever, on that point."

"Don't think I've forgotten how you *passed out*."

"Maybe it was all an elaborate ruse to get in your bed," I say, laughing as he hauls me into his lap and lazily spanks my ass three times.

———

I'm the first one to wake up in the morning. Ford is sprawled out on his back, an arm thrown over his face, and he's breathing deeply, evenly.

It's my first chance to really look at him without him growling or distracting me with orgasms. Not that I'm complaining.

But this is a wonderful Christmas gift. I rake my gaze over his heavy torso, seeing a few scars here and there I'd never noticed before.

Careful not to wake him, I gently fold the blankets back, revealing his heavy cock lying against his thigh.

"Having fun?"

I jerk my hand back just before touching him. "You're awake."

"I'm a light sleeper." His voice is rough and warm.

"Good to know." I scramble up his body and press a kiss on his mouth. "Merry Christmas."

"It sure is." He carries me into the bathroom, cranks the shower on, and then washes my hair and body. Once I'm squeaky clean, he lets me play with his cock as he gently rubs me to a quick and very satisfying morning orgasm.

"Can you show me how you. . ."

His eyes light up. "You want to watch me jerk off?"

"Mm-hmm."

He's rough with himself, more than I thought, and efficient. His eyes flutter shut as his cock grows, then open again, locking on my face as he mutters my name and comes in a long, arcing spurt.

"You think of me?"

One corner of his mouth quirks up. "Yeah, baby."

"Any specifics you want to share? You know, for inspiration. . ."

"You're the fucking inspiration." He licks his lips as he rinses off, then kisses me roughly, backing me up against the tile wall. "You want to know?"

"Always."

"I think of you as Daddy's little girl." His eyes glitter as he rubs his thumb at the corner of my mouth. Then he pushes against my lips, and I open for him, pulling the digit in and against my mouth. "You did that last night. In your sleep. That's what I remembered just now. It's better than any fantasy I'd had in the past."

"That's so hot." I kiss the end of his thumb, then give him what I hope is a seductive look. "Speaking of so hot. How do I get you into a Santa suit this morning for a visit over to the retirement home?"

He laughs. "I've already said yes."

"Just trying to nail down the specifics," I say brightly as he turns off the shower.

He gets out and grabs two towels, wrapping one around me before using his to dry off his hair and beard.

Which reminds me. . . I tug on the dark brown curls closely cropped to his jaw. "We'll need to do something about this. It's shorter than I remember."

"Santa felt like a trim."

"I have some white hair dye at home. It's a temporary spray."

He laughs out loud. "Oh, sweetheart. No."

"Ford, please—"

"You wanted Santa, Neely. I can play Santa. But a young Santa. Nobody wants jovial bullshit from me, anyway."

"Do you have a suit?" I'm trying to remember if my parents dressed him up when he played Santa for us.

"I have a hat and a red Henley. Add some black suspenders and red work pants, and it's a good approximation."

"That's really hot." I tug my towel around me to keep warm and gesture out of the bathroom. "What a perfect way to start Christmas morning. Yes, let's get you into that."

He wraps his towel around his hips and steps into the main room—and promptly stops.

I push him from behind.

He doesn't move.

"Ford."

"Neely." He clears his throat. "Your parents are here."

10
neely

I PEER AROUND HIM.

Sure enough, my parents are pressed against the wall of glass windows around the door to Ford's residence. And they don't look pleased to see us coming out of the bathroom in nothing but matching towels.

"It could be worse," I whisper. "We could be naked."

Ford grunts. "Let's get dressed."

If we disappear into the bedroom together, my father might just break through the windows. "You go get dressed," I say smoothly, with a confidence I am one hundred percent faking. "And I'll let them in."

"If you're going to open that door, I'll be right beside you."

"That's very sweet, but my dad might drag you outside, and it's a bit cold for a towel only." I pause for a second. "Please don't kick his ass, okay?"

"He's my oldest friend, Neely. Honor code demands I let him kick mine, anyway."

"Nope, I don't like that." I shove him toward the bedroom.

"I'll be ninety seconds, baby."

I turn so my back is to my parents, just in case they can read lips. "Love you, Daddy."

He grins.

Okay. We're going to be okay.

Taking a deep breath, I unlock the door. "Merry Christmas!"

"Neely Anne McIntosh, what the hell are you doing?" my father barks.

My mom gives me a pained look. "Same question without the curse word, darling."

"Come on in." I step aside. "Ford is just—"

"We saw enough to guess what Ford is *just*—"

The subject of conversation steps into the room dressed exactly like the hot young Santa he promised me. "Neely, why don't you get dressed."

I scurry past him and lock myself in the bedroom.

Then I press myself against the door, trying to listen for violence.

I hear nothing. No murmurs, no breaking of furniture, nothing in between.

I'm not really sure what Ford thinks I'm going to wear today. But then I see he's hung up my dress, and when I take it off the hanger, I realize my tights are carefully folded there, too.

Will the residents notice I'm wearing the same outfit as last night? Maybe not if they're dazzled enough by my hot, older boyfriend.

I wriggle into the tights, smooth on the white dress, and dig my booties out from under the bed. I don't think Ford owns a hairdryer, so air-dried finger waves will have to do.

I take a deep breath and open the bedroom door.

Ford is nowhere in sight.

Neither is my dad.

My mom is standing by the window, looking out at the ocean.

"Hi," I breathe.

"This is quite the surprise." She glances back at me. "They went outside to talk."

"Ford said he'd have to let Dad kick his ass." I wince.

"Is he?"

"Your father wouldn't do that."

"Mom—"

"How long, Neely?"

Is twelve hours the wrong answer here? Probably. There's no right answer to that question.

"Last night was the first time. It just happened."

"Did he—"

I need her to not ask that, even though I know she's my mom, and she probably has to ask. "I came on to him."

"And is it—" This time, she's the one who cuts herself off. "I don't know what to ask here. You've never dated anyone. I thought you weren't interested in that yet, which I realize is ridiculous. You're older than I was when I married your dad. And I suppose now that I think about it, all the signs of a crush were there. But Ford? I never thought he would. . ."

"He wouldn't. If I hadn't come on to him, he never would have."

She presses her hand to her forehead. "Dare I ask what the Hot Santa get-up is about?"

The front door opens, and my dad steps inside.

Ford isn't with him.

"What did you do?" I demand to know, whirling around.

"Calm down, Neely. He's getting something from his truck." My dad looks slightly uncomfortable but less angry than before. "And I thought we could have a minute to talk alone before he comes back."

"I asked her if he forced her," my mom says.

I glare at her. "And he didn't."

"It's our job to ask."

"Also your job to remember that I am an adult. And Ford is a very good man." I could wind up for a long defense of my love, but I don't need to.

My dad holds up his hands. "All right. He, uh, insists he has the best of intentions towards you." The way he says it, I can see that it pains him to be this understanding. But what he says next is softer. "And he says that he will do whatever it takes to make you happy, including stepping aside if that's what you want."

Oh, no.

"That is *not* what I want." I grab my mom's hand and drag her over to where my dad is standing. Out the window, I see Ford standing just outside.

Watching, waiting. Letting me handle my parents and trusting me to get them on our side. I wish we'd had more time to talk about this, how we would break this to them.

"Look at him," I say to them both. "He's dressed up as Sexy Santa for a bunch of Conception Ridge's finest senior citizens. That's not something Ford Gamble would do if not for love, right?"

My mom laughs. "It's a good point. Although he only has that outfit because he agreed to play the role for you when you were little."

"Father fucking Christmas," my dad mutters. "You have him wrapped around your finger."

"He's a hip, young Father Christmas. More of a Daddy Christmas," I say, knowing I'm toeing the line of what's appropriate. But there's a chance they may hear me slip and say that. Better if it's a ha-ha Christmas joke than something. . . darker.

My parents choose not to react.

I choose to move on.

"He refused to let me spray his hair white. So he's still *Ford*, you know?"

Mom is the one who cracks first. She nods. "I think we can be pretty understanding, given the right circumstances."

"And what circumstances are those?"

Mom grins gleefully. "Ford joins us tonight for round two of carol singing."

My dad shrugs. "I can't argue with that."

I give him a hug, then squeeze my mom. "Thanks."

She squeezes me back. "Love you. Now go get your man. He has some senior citizens waiting for him who want to sit on his knee."

Oh. Shit. I hadn't thought that through.

She giggles and pokes at me. "The look on your face. So possessive of him already?"

"Susan," my dad barks.

Ford opens the front door and steps inside.

All three of us laugh, and he looks between us in confusion. "All right?"

I nod as he moves to stand beside me. He doesn't hesitate before tucking me against his body and wrapping his arm around me.

"We'll get out of your hair," Mom says. "And we'll deal with your car later."

"I'll help her with it," Ford says, his voice rumbling with confidence.

My dad sizes him up. "Dinner's at five tonight. Don't be late."

I'm dying to know what their conversation outside was like.

And the second my parents are gone, heading back down the path, I turn on my brand-new boyfriend. "Well?"

"Well, what?"

"How did you? What did you?"

"He told me he didn't enjoy seeing his daughter come out of my bathroom in a towel. I told him it was none of his business, but for what it's worth, I like it so fucking much it hurts because you're the ray of sunshine I've been waiting my whole adult life for."

My jaw drops.

My heart explodes.

It takes me two tries to find my voice again. "And what did he say to that?"

"He said he wanted to punch me. I said I understood. He told me not to hurt you, and I promised I wouldn't."

"That's it."

"Yeah."

"Wow."

"It'll take some time for him to trust this, but. . . he's known me a long time, Neely. He can see that I'm changed because of you. You did that."

I throw myself at him, and he spins me around. "I love you," I whisper as I kiss him. "Also, I'm probably going to be jealous of some of the ladies at the retirement home. So just be warned about that."

"I'll keep them all at arm's length because I'm a taken Santa."

"By me," I say in a little girl voice.

"That's right. You're Santa's baby girl. Nobody else gets inside these suspenders."

I giggle.

He kisses my nose. "Glad we got that cleared up. You looked so worried when I came inside."

"Oh, that. . ." I wave my hand. "Parents and stuff."

"And irrational jealousy," he adds.

I roll my eyes. "Damn it, I thought I hid that better."

"You have an expressive face." The corner of his mouth quirks up. "Never change, Neely. Always be too innocent for this world."

"I'm not—"

He cuts me off with a kiss. "I like the innocence," he murmurs.

Oh.

I smile shyly. "Okay."

"Shall we go?" He grabs my coat and scarf from by the fireplace and helps me get dressed for outside. He loans me a pair of gloves and brings a blanket to cover my legs in his truck.

"We're going less than a mile," I point out.

"You. Collapsed."

"All right, blanket it is." I snag my purse.

11
ford

WE DRIVE OVER, my truck tires crunching over the heavy amount of snow that accumulated overnight.

Inside, the residents are gathered for breakfast, so we have a few minutes before I'll make an appearance. She leads me to her office, which is really just a desk outside of her boss's office, but she's proud, and I'm thrilled for her. My office is just a desk upstairs from my bedroom, after all. And when I was her age, my office was one-eighth of a tent on an Army base halfway around the world.

"You like working here?"

She pulls out an elf hat from her bottom desk drawer. "I do. Even more than usual today."

"You gonna be Santa's little helper today?"

"I'll be right beside you the whole time," she whispers back. "Daddy's little helper."

My balls pull tight. "Keep that up, and they're going to ask me to leave before we even get started because I've bent the elf over her desk."

She giggles.

I'm only partly joking. I won't fuck this up for her because I know this is important to her. Not many people would care this much about having Santa show up to talk to a group of people who haven't believed in the magic of Christmas for sixty-odd years.

Except when Neely wants something and makes it happen like a force of nature, maybe that is the real Christmas magic. It didn't take much for her to knock down my carefully constructed walls. And I'm damn glad she did.

I catch her face in my hands. "Can I kiss you here?"

Her eyes twinkle. "Are you kidding me? I'd be grumpy if you didn't."

I catch her lips in mine, soft and sweet, then lick against the seam of her mouth. She parts her lips, letting me in, and I take a last thorough taste of her before we need to be on our best behavior for a few hours.

She presses her hands against mine, holding on tight as I deepen the embrace. Fuck, I love this woman.

And I really love the dazed look she gives me when I finally let her go. "Ready?"

"Mmm." She sways on the spot. "Daddy Christmas indeed."

I raise one eyebrow.

She straightens up. "Come on, Santa. Let's do this."

She gives me a hefty bag of wrapped gifts, explaining that they're books and puzzles and that the residents may swap them after they open them, so it doesn't matter what order I hand them out. She tucks a bunch of candy canes into my pocket. "I'll replenish these as needed."

"Any excuse to put your hand in Daddy's front pocket?"

She squirms. "Maybe."

I laugh out loud.

An older woman pops her head in the door. "Oh, Neely! Is this our Santa? I heard a hearty ho, ho, ho."

I hope that's all she heard. Or maybe I don't give a fuck who knows I'm head over heels in lust and love with a very grown-up little girl.

"Diane, this is Ford." Neely slides a glance my way. A private, *you're mine* kind of glance that makes my chest puff.

I hold out my hand. "Nice to meet you."

"Thanks for joining us," the woman says as she shakes my hand.

"Of course."

I follow them both to the dining hall, where I make the rounds, shaking hands with everyone. Then I sit near the fireplace, on a nice wide bench, to listen to every secret Christmas wish the residents might want to share.

The first few people come up, get a present, tell me how much fun Neely is—I'm not surprised—and move back to their tables.

But then a tiny scrap of a thing, who introduces herself as Bertie, sits down next to me, in a real settling in kind of way, and explains she's ninety-one years old and she won't be rushed.

Neely smothers a grin. "I think that's my cue to go get more presents from the office. Take your time."

"And what do you do when you aren't playing Santa?" Bertie asks, her eyes sharp and curious.

"I run the lighthouse just up the road."

She winks. "I once dated a lighthouse keeper. Silent fellow. Patient. Had the stamina of an ox."

I choke on what I was going to say next.

"Are you lonely over there?"

I think she's teasing me. Pretty sure she's joking.

I lower my voice so she's the only one who can hear me. "Not anymore. I have a special someone now."

"A Mrs. Claus?"

"We haven't had that conversation yet."

"What's your hold up?"

"She's younger than me."

A sly smile spreads across her face. "How much younger? Is it our Neely?"

We haven't talked about taking our relationship public, but I can't hide how I feel about her. "Bertie, you're going to get me in trouble here."

"She looks happier today than she ever has in all the time she's worked here." Bertie stands up. I hand her a book, and she presses it back at me. "No, thank you. That little tidbit is all the gift I need this morning. I adore a secret love story."

Neely arrives back, her arms full of presents, as Bertie strolls away whistling. "What did I miss?"

I straighten my suspenders. "She thinks you look happy this morning."

"And did she correctly guess that you put this smile on my face?" Neely giggles. "I forgot to warn you that some of them are quite naughty."

Another older lady sidles up beside my little elf. "That we are, Neely. That we are."

"Darla, have a seat next to Santa."

"Hello, Santa," she purrs.

I grin. "Hello, Darla. Have you been a good girl this year?"

12
neely

BY THE TIME we get back to the lighthouse, I'm aching to be back in Ford's arms. It's so hard to be on my best behavior when all I want to do is climb him like a Christmas tree.

He takes off my coat, then goes to shrug off his suspenders.

"Hang on," I say. "I haven't sat on Santa's knee yet."

He points to the couch. "There?"

I shake my head. "Upstairs. That armchair you were in last night."

He gestures for me to lead the way.

I feel his attention burning into my back as I sway my hips up the stairs.

He sits in the chair and pats his knee. "And how about you, little one? What would you like for Christmas?"

I perch on his thigh, my skirt riding high, my legs swinging between his. His hand is warm and sure in the small of my back, and he's smiling at me indulgently. It occurs to me that I already have everything I want for Christmas.

"It can be anything you want," he prompts. "Maybe something sparkly?"

He's clearly leading me to a more grown-up variation on my boyfriend wish from years ago. Deep down, Ford is very sweet.

I, on the other hand, am focused on being a pervert. "Actually, Santa, I was hoping you might teach me how to give a proper blow job."

He groans. "Yes, baby. I'll show you anything you want."

I slide to my knees, kneeling in front of him. He unzips his pants.

His cock is thick already and growing in front of my eyes.

"Put your hands on me." His voice is low and private, even though we're all alone. "Start stroking as you think about what you want to taste first."

I wiggle closer, doing as he says, and then I lean in and lick the slit at the tip, where I sucked him for a moment the night before. For as hard as he is—solid, heavy, and long—his erection has a velvety softness to it, too, and up close, it's really beautiful. I lick again, my tongue flat and broad, getting used to the unique taste of him. It fills my senses, a delicate earthy note that makes my thighs flex and my pussy warm.

"Is this okay?" I ask as I swirl my tongue around to the base of his crown.

"Oh baby, you're doing just fine. A little too fine, maybe. Playing with fire." He gathers my hair in one hand, holding it behind my head—gently but firmly holding me still. "I like the little licks. You can do that as long as you want. But when you're ready, I want you to open up and see how much of me you can take in that pretty little mouth."

"Yeah?"

He nods. "Let me teach you how I like it."

I open for him, and he feeds me his cock, sliding it over my tongue, making my lips stretch around him.

He's bigger like this, somehow, and it's hard to breathe around the girth of him, but there's a thrill of success when I figure it out. Breathe, suck, breathe, suck—and then I taste him, a burst of an incredible flavor, and I know he's dripping for me. His hands tighten in my hair, his thighs clench, and his abs are twisting in my peripheral vision.

This may be my first blow job, but I am rapidly bringing this giant of a man to pieces.

It's a heady thrill.

"Santa likes to fuck your mouth, too. Can I try that, baby? Can you hold still for me?"

I nod, and his hands shift, holding my face as he pumps in and out of me.

"Oh, Neely, your sweet mouth feels so good. Fuck, I'm going to come." He tries to pull out, and I stop him, sucking him back into my mouth as he shouts out that I'm a good girl, a bad girl, his girl, oh *fuck*.

My pulse races as he unloads on my tongue, thrilled at the secret naughtiness of it, and then it's a lot, suddenly.

"Push your tongue against my cock and swallow," he urges. "Then you won't taste it as much."

I gulp it down, then pull off him, gasping for air.

He pulls me into his lap, wiping the corners of my mouth and kissing me as he heaps praise on me again. "That was so fucking hot. You wanted to learn, and then you were a natural."

He turns me around so I'm splayed in his lap, my back to his front, and he tugs up my dress roughly. "It was so hard to watch you parade around in this little white dress all day, knowing the sweet cunt that was just out of view." A groan rips out of him as he slides his hand into my tights and discovers I wasn't wearing panties all day, either. "Neely."

"Yes, Daddy?"

"You're a very naughty elf."

"I don't have any other clothes to wear," I confess.

He strokes my outer lips, then delves deeper, spreading my slick arousal up to my clit. "I'll help you pack a bag tonight. After dinner."

"Are you going to bring me back here with you?"

"I never want to sleep apart, ever again." He scrapes his teeth against my neck, his breath hot on my ear. "Daddy has so much to teach you."

I spread my legs wider, eager for another lesson. He strokes me slowly, unhurried, our breaths the only sound high up in the lighthouse at the edge of town. I come on his fingers, and he holds me through the aftershocks, then licks his fingers clean.

13
neely

Christmas Eve, one year later

WE ARRIVE for breakfast and stay all day, and much to my parents' delight, we bring overnight bags. I live with Ford, of course. I have since that night a year ago, but my mother wants her whole family together on Christmas morning.

We even have matching pajamas to wear.

I have another reason for agreeing to her saccharine plan—a chance to play out a fantasy I've been whispering in my boyfriend's ear for a year now.

After the last puzzle piece is put in its rightful place and a final mug of hot cocoa is downed, I yawn and tell everyone I'm ready for bed. I kiss my mom's cheek, give my dad a hug, ruffle my little brother's hair, and then wrap my arms around Ford's neck, interrupting his game of cards with my father.

"Don't stay up too late," I tell him.

He gives me a sweet kiss on the temple. "Do you want me to come up with you?"

I shake my head. "I'm zonked."

And I yawn again for better effect.

Below the table, I can see his cock twitch against the flannel

"

pajama pants, heavy and full already. He couldn't get up and follow me right now, even if he wanted to.

My mom beams at me, so pleased with the unexpectedly sweet way my relationship with Ford has played out.

Sorry, Mom, you have no idea what I'm going to get him to do later tonight.

The door creaks open. I hold my breath and pretend to be asleep.

Ford whispers my name. Then he quietly closes the door. I can hear my parents laughing downstairs.

He stops at the side of my childhood bed. Silence fills the room. No more floor creaking, no more attempts to get me to wake up. He's just staring at me, curled up on my side.

In the silence, my senses heighten. I hear him breathing, a little unsteady. I keep pretending, and soon his exhales return to normal.

Heavy, thinking breaths.

How he's going to do this, how I'll react.

Then I hear a quiet shove of fabric, and skin meets skin. He's stroking himself.

That makes me hot. I ache for him to peel back the blanket and discover that I'm naked, but he takes his time.

"Fucking sexy little thing," he mutters, the first sound to pierce the silence in a few minutes. "Matching pajamas and hot cocoa, like I don't know you're a horny minx."

The slap of his hand on his cock speeds up for a moment, then he stops. "Need to see you."

I hold still as he tugs the sheet away.

He swears under his breath and pulls back. My whole back is bare to him, down to my thighs, and I picture him looking at my ass. Wanting to lick me there, touch me. Push inside me and make me cry.

His clothes hit the floor next with hurried sounds. He climbs into bed with me, and the warm press of his body against mine —the hard naked length of him, the overwhelming size as he squeezes against me in my too-small room—breaks me of my pretense. I murmur and shift, pretending to wake up.

"Ford?"

"Do you always sleep naked, Neely?"

I do at home with him. But he means here, in the bed where I once dreamed of him taking my virginity under the cover of darkness. "No. . ."

"Why are you naked tonight?"

"I fell asleep by accident. I was. . ."

"Were you touching yourself?" His hand lands on my hip then strokes from my belly down to my bare mound. He shaved me himself this morning.

"Shhh. We don't want anyone to hear us, baby." He covers my mouth with his other hand as his fingers slip through my slick cunt. "Daddy needs your pussy tonight, though. Can you be a good little girl for Daddy? Be quiet while I fill you up?"

I nod, panting, and he eases his hand away from my mouth.

I love it when he says stuff like that. Most of the time, he doesn't actually fill me up. We both want it, but I'm still young, and he wants to wait a bit longer before we have babies.

If some of his seed took, though, we'd both be over the moon.

Maybe that's what I'll whisper to him in the morning as he opens presents. That I'm ready to try for real.

I'm wet, but I'm not quite ready for him. "You're too tight," he groans.

"I want it," I whisper back.

He pulls out and spits on his hand. I close my eyes, my face burning in delicious humiliation. *Use me.*

"Need you," he whispers. And then he's in me again, a thick intrusion, a relentless push this time. It takes my breath away, how good he feels in my belly. I'm pulled taut, stretched and filled to the limit, and he plays me like a precious instrument. One hand mauling my breasts, the other grinding against my clit.

Daddy's intent on me getting there fast, and I do, I soar. As I climax, he rolls me so my mouth is muffled by my pillow. Then he pumps his hips faster, erratically, chasing the release himself. My bed squeaks under his heavy weight, and he tells me they'll hear, but he can't stop himself. There's no turning back now, and he needs to breed me.

I float.

It's a buzzy, wonderful feeling—a heavy, dreamy fog, and I stay there as he cleans me up and tucks in again behind me.

So I almost don't hear it.

"Marry me." It's a rough, raw plea whispered against the back of my neck.

"Ford?"

He turns me around, both of us still shaking from the best sex of our lives. He's holding a diamond solitaire ring, glinting in the moonlight coming through the gap in the curtains. "I couldn't wait until morning. I know you're happy living with me, and I wanted us to date for a while to give people the sense that we're not going too fast. But I'm ready for the world to know what we already know. That you're mine. Forever."

I nod. "Yes."

"I want to fill you with babies, Neely McIntosh. We've been playing with fire this past year. And I need you to be Mrs. Gamble by the time the first one bursts out of you."

"Okay."

"And there's no denying that we're perfect together—"

I grab his face in my hands and kiss his mouth to shut him up. "Yes, yes, a thousand times yes!"

He stills. "Yeah?"

"We can do it next week if you want."

"I want to do it right."

I kiss him happily.

He grins against my mouth. "Was it the fucking in your little girl bedroom that finally did it?"

I giggle. "Maybe. You should probably molest me some more just to really cement the warm fuzzy feelings."

"Jesus Christ, Neely, the filth you come up with." But he's laughing, too, and then I'm on top of him, and he's hard.

Again.

Already.

I rock my hips, my pussy slick against his belly.

He catches my hand and slides the ring on my finger. I brace myself on his chest as I lift just enough to find his cock and sink onto his length. He was firm already, but he grows inside me, making me whine in pleasure.

This time it's just us. No dirty talk, no pet names. Me and my fiancé quietly making love.

And it's perfect.

epilogue

five years later

ford

I'M on the phone with one of my colleagues at the national park service when I see them walking up the hill. "I have to go," I say briskly. "My wife and kid are home."

Neely is wearing a long winter coat, and underneath that, warm layers I personally inspected before she headed out the door to work this morning.

Our baby—preschooler, but I'm having trouble admitting the passage of time is a thing—is wearing a one-piece snowsuit, and the best mittens money can buy.

They're adorable.

I race down the stairs and meet them on the wide step outside the lighthouse.

Neely gives me an amused look. "Miss us?"

"Every damn day."

"Language," she murmurs. "Little ears."

"Every damn day," our daughter replies. "Damn. Day."

I snort, and my wife thumps me in the chest with her mittens. They're the best money can buy, too.

"I made stew," I offer.

"Nice change of subject."

"Damn stew," Bella Bean mutters.

Now it's Neely's turn to choke on a laugh. "Bella, honey, that's not a nice thing to say."

"Hmm?" She looks up at her mama. "What?"

"Pardon." Neely gestures for Bella to repeat after her. "We say pardon, not what."

"Okay." Bella toddles off towards the wood stove, where she carefully sets her mittens in their spot to dry next to the heat source.

Then she flops on the floor, like an exhausted, well-padded starfish.

I stroll over to her and glance down when I'm directly above her. "Can Daddy help you out of your snowsuit?"

"No." Bella sighs again. "No *thank* you."

I pivot my head towards Neely, who shrugs. She gestures for me to come back. "Daddy can help me out of my snowsuit," she says with a wink.

And now she has my full attention.

I prowl back to my wife, who fists the front of my sweater and pulls me in for a kiss as I tug the zipper on her coat.

"This feels like a trap," I rumble against her mouth. "Not that I'm complaining."

She nips at my lower lip. "I missed you, too."

"How long has Little Miss Grumpy been in a mood?"

"Since I picked her up at daycare. She didn't want to come home because she was busy building something with blocks."

"Ah." I press my forehead against hers and wind my arms around her waist, inside her coat. She feels good against my body, her breasts lush and plump, permanently bigger now that she's had Bella. Her hips are wider, too.

Not my little girl anymore. Now my big girl, all grown up in every way, and sexier than ever.

I give her a rueful smile. "And here I was going to do my best tonight to convince you it was time for a second baby."

She laughs gently. "I mean, I want you to try to convince me…"

"Early bedtime for everyone it is." I squeeze her ass playfully, then take her coat and mittens. "If you want to take some time to yourself, I'll get Bella sorted out. She can help me finish dinner prep."

"Me? Helper?" Bella pops up off the floor and tries to unzip her snowsuit, crankiness forgotten.

Neely gives me a thumbs up and points upstairs, mouthing that she's going to get out of my way, something about the magic Daddy touch.

I'll give her the magic Daddy touch later.

For now, I'm Dad. Totally different thing. Equally awesome, though. I scoop Bella up and ask her about the blocks, and her day at preschool, and what she wants to have with stew.

"Buttered bread," she says very carefully.

And the accompaniment to the stew is sorted, thanks to my sous chef.

———

When I knocked Neely up, I expected some push back from her parents—didn't happen—and an adjustment in our relationship —which also didn't really happen.

What did happen was I became a certified expert in three things: noise absorbing wall coverings, blackout curtains, and baby monitors.

Neely calls me Spy Daddy, which amuses me greatly. I have bedtime down to a fucking science, and once Bella is out, she's down for the count. Which means from eight until eleven— three glorious hours—I get Neely all to myself.

Sometimes I share her with a book that she's really into. Sometimes we just watch TV.

But most of the time, I take her to bed.

Six years into loving this woman, and I still want to spend every night giving her big girl kisses until she's wet and slippery for me, then burying myself in her pussy. And thanks to the renovations I did, what happens in Daddy's bed is a special secret between Daddy and Neely.

And when Bella gets a bit older, and we have another baby, we'll have to move.

Which is something I need to talk to my wife about before she sinks fully into being my little girl for the evening.

"Babe," I say, catching her hand as she moves around our bedroom putting laundry away.

"Mmm?"

I don't have her attention. I catch her around the waist and haul her bodily into my lap.

"Oh," she says, giggling. Fully focused on me now. "Yes?"

"I had a couple of calls today about work." I take a deep breath. "They're going to put up the posting for this lighthouse next week."

She frowns. "What happened?"

"Nothing happened."

"Then why do you have to re-apply for your job?"

"It won't be my job anymore. It's time for us to move on."

"No!" She twists around, her legs wrapping around my waist, her arms tight against my neck. "Ford, I love it here. This is our home. This bed is where we made love for the first time."

"We can't stay here forever."

"Why not?"

"Because at some point, Bella's going to outgrow that little room we have her in, and I want to have more kids. And soon, because I'm an old man now."

"You're not." She gives me a sorrowful look. "You're perfect."

"You're biased." I kiss the tip of her nose. "Do you not want to have more babies?"

"I want all your babies," she whispers.

"Then we need to live in a house that has room for them." I squeeze her tight. "My supervisor is going on sabbatical for a year. I'm going to try that out, see how I like being the person people report to."

Her eyes light up. "Are you going to wear a suit?"

I laugh. "Not often." I pause. "I could probably get a park ranger uniform, though."

"Oooh, I like that." She wriggles in my lap. "So this is why another baby is on your mind."

"Knocking you up is *always* on my mind." The familiar rush of heat gathers deep inside me and my grip on her tightens. "Can I tuck you in?"

"Will you give me a goodnight kiss?"

"A quick one." That's a lie. "Did you brush your teeth?"

Her eyes twinkle. "Yes, Daddy."

"Good girl."

I kiss her mouth softly.

She shakes her head. "Not like that."

"No?"

"I need to be in the bed."

I brace her ass in my hands and stand up, holding her with ease. I may be getting older, but I can still carry Neely around, and we both get a charge out of her being a little limpet on me. She clings to my neck until I pull the blanket back, then she scampers into the middle of the bed.

I crawl on top of her, treating her with the utmost care as she stretches out. The soft, yearning look she gives me is equal parts pure innocence and secret filthy fantasy.

"I love you so much," I murmur as I brace my arms on either side of her little body. "Do you know that?"

"Yep."

"Good." My cock thickens in my sweatpants, stretching up

toward my belly. If she looks down between our bodies, she'll see it tenting the fabric. In a second, she'll feel it, too, as I settle on top of her. Pinning her down. "My little Neely."

"Kisses," she prompts.

"Eager?"

"Always."

"You know the rules."

"Our kisses are secret," she whispers. "I remember."

I bring my mouth down on hers, feeling a surge of love and lust for my wife, my naughty little girl, who gives me every fantasy I've ever dared to imagine—and some I haven't—and makes them so much better.

We do this effortless roleplaying now, the words as much a part of the foreplay as the kissing itself. But even without the erotic setup, Neely's wet mouth parting for me would be enough for me to want to fuck her into the mattress.

Put two babies in her this time, that's how hard she makes me.

As I give her my tongue, showing her how good it can feel to have Daddy slide into her body, she wriggles out from under the blanket. The weight of my lower body has her almost pinned, but she's nimble, and suddenly her tank top is pushed up, her panties are riding low on her hips, and she's rubbing her belly against mine.

"Mmm, Daddy," she breathes. "You feel nice and warm. I love your furry tummy."

"Neely..." I love how fucking stern I sound. A sharp tone I would never in a million years use on Bella, but here, with my grown up girl, I get to be sharp.

She freezes. "Yes?"

"You aren't going to sleep."

"Your kisses got me all excited."

"You need your sleep."

"Why?" She lets go of me and sweeps her hands down her

body, then back up again to cup her breasts, just for a second, before she drops her arms in mock frustration.

"What is it, sweetheart?" I ghost my palm over one of her breasts. "Do you ache here?"

"Yes. I need…"

I know what she needs. "Shhh, it's okay."

"Touch me." She clasps my hand to her chest, then moans and arches into my firm grasp. "More, Daddy."

"More touching?"

"More kisses." She tugs her tank top all the way up, revealing tight nipples and pebbled skin. "Here?"

I'm lost to it. I dip my head and suck her sweet peak into my mouth, swallowing as much of her flesh as I can. She whines and grinds against me, and my free hand rips her panties away.

I need her bare for me, so I can give her a proper good night kiss. The kind that fixes every horny ache she has, every powerful need to seduce me, so she can finally go to sleep, sated and happy.

Moving my mouth to her other breast, I drag my fingers through her slick folds, thinking about how good it'll feel to fuck her. My cock is drooling now, and I'm not going to be able to hold out much longer.

I move down her body and plant my hands under her ass, lifting her hips up.

"Daddy?" She pants the nickname, an incomplete question I still understand.

"Yes, baby. I'm going to kiss you here. Just the way you like."

"I need it."

"I do, too." I duck my head and lick a long, slow path from below her tight hole to around her clit, and back down again. She tastes incredible, like endless pleasure and forbidden secrets.

Sometimes when we play this game, I make her come on my face, and then I actually do make her go to sleep. We did that a lot when she was pregnant, and really did need more sleep than I do. And some nights, when it's storming, I like to stay up all night to make sure the lighthouse remains working, and the coast guard doesn't need any data from me.

But not tonight.

Tonight I'm not actually going to kiss my little girl goodnight. Tonight, this is foreplay, because what I really want is to breed my wife.

When her thighs pull up and wrap around my head, I give her my mouth again, redoubling my effort, and bring her to the brink, but as soon as I feel that first trembling shake, I pull up and rise above her.

I must look like an absolute menace, her big, furry man with her juices all over my face and an angry cock pushing its way out of my sweatpants.

But Neely only moans and lies back, eager for whatever I want to do next.

"I need you, baby girl." I groan as I shove my pants down, freeing my cock. I stroke it once, slicking the precome at the tip around the whole head.

Daddy's seed is already eager to get into her little pussy.

"Ford," she breathes, her eyes sharpening as she watches me jack myself between her legs. "Are you going to come inside me?"

"I have to."

"I'm not on birth control," she breathes.

A new game.

One that makes my cock throb in anticipation. "That's how it should be, sweetheart."

"You could get me pregnant."

"I fucking hope I do." I palm her belly with one hand as I use the other to drag the tip of my cock through her wet cunt. "You'll look so good swollen with my child."

She whines and circles her hips, trying to corkscrew her way onto my cock.

"Is that what you want?"

She nods.

"You gotta say it. Tell me that you want this, too."

She stretches her arms up over her head, making her tits jiggle. "I want Daddy to knock me up. I want to be your pregnant secret, trapped here in your lighthouse. I'll get big and round, and you can fuck me every day, morning and night."

The sound I make as I spear into her is unholy. She's swollen and wet for me, but still tight, always tight around my cock—because my cock is always massive for her, thick with need.

My guttural grunt is matched only by her breathy, innocence-lost cry.

My balls slap against her ass with the first thrust, then again as I find a blistering rhythm.

Thank Christ for good insulation.

"Daddy's inside you," I grunt, desperate now. "Nothing between us, Neely. You're mine. I'm going to breed the little cunt tonight."

"Yes…"

"Fill you up three times, just to make sure it takes."

"Daddy…"

"You'll have to call in sick tomorrow. You'll be too sore to move." My balls pull tight, already eager to paint her insides white.

"You'll take care of me…" She whispers.

"I'll fuck you again. All day long."

That makes her smile, even as her eyelids flutter shut, her face twisting because she's getting close. "I…"

"I can't resist you, Neely. I should let you go. But I can't. I just want to drag you back to my bed, every damn day. Fill you with come until it's dripping out of you."

She whines, her neck flushing.

I bow my head and get my mouth on her tits again. I suck, hard, as I piston my hips between her legs. She rides my cock like the horny slut she is, just for me, and when she comes apart, I follow her, stroking my cock in and out of her in shallow little pumps that get my come flowing, then I thrust deep again, depositing that seed right at the mouth of her womb.

Neely wraps all her limbs around me, holding me tight, and as I shudder above her, she eases me down. Wanting my weight on her, my heavy warmth.

Deep inside, the rippling aftershocks of her climax grip my now-sensitive cock, threatening to get me hard and milk me all over again. Fuck.

I pulse my hips, and she wiggles, trying to make me hold still. "Shhh. That's enough breeding for one night."

"Never," I growl, but when she lays a gentle kiss on my cheek, I chuckle and settle down. I find her mouth and kiss her softly, lingering on her lips until my heart rate returns to normal.

Then I ease out of her and roll her onto her tummy, her preferred position to keep my jizz inside her.

We're old pros at this now. I go to the washroom to quickly clean up, then come back with a glass of water and a warm, wet washcloth for my lovely wife.

She is still on her tummy when I return, her legs tightly locked.

"So, another baby," she murmurs as I clean up the inside of her thighs, now sticky with my come.

I lay a line of kisses up her spine. "Yeah."

"I'm looking forward the bedtime kisses when I'm big and round and going to bed early..." She twists around and gives me an eyebrow waggle.

I grin. "I was thinking about how much I like those, too."

She rolls onto her back and casts about for her discarded panties. I find them and slide them up her legs. "Thank you," she whispers as I carefully smooth them over her sweet mound. I kiss the cotton-covered secret and breathe in the scent of us on her.

My girl, marked with my come, finally tucked in for the night.

She holds out her arms. "Are you coming to bed with me?"

"Yep." I turn off the lights and crawl under the blankets with her.

She snuggles in against me, her fingers tangling in the hair on my chest. "I love you, Ford."

I squeeze her tight against me. So fucking lucky. "I love you, too, Neely."

She makes a happy sound.

Then she sucks in a breath. "I just remembered…"

"What?"

"I was going to ask you this earlier, and got distracted."

"By dick?"

She giggles. "Yes."

"What is it?"

"Apparently the other retirement home, on the other side of town, has heard how popular you are as our Santa…"

"Neely."

Even though it's dark, I can feel her smile against my skin.

"You cannot whore me out as a sexy Santa to every group of older ladies around town."

"I don't see why not?"

I groan. "Because…"

I can't think of a reason. None that match how happy it makes my wife to see me in those God damn suspenders. Six years and counting… I guess it's official, I'm Conception Ridge's hot Santa for life now.

As long as they're all fine with me knocking up my favorite elf on a regular basis, that's fine by me.

Thank you so much for reading Above the Shop! If you want to stay in touch while I write future books set in Conception Ridge, please join my Secret Chloe Maine Book Daddy Appreciation Club on Facebook: facebook.com/groups/chloemainebooks

And here's another sweet look at the Gambles!

about the author

Chloe Maine has written other books before, but none of them as purely id-driven as Before He Was Her Headmaster. She delights in the fantasy of bending big men to the wicked desires of supposedly innocent women. When she's not writing, she's probably reading. She lives in Canada with her own big man, raising the babies they made together.

facebook.com/chloemainebooks
twitter.com/chloemainebooks
instagram.com/chloemainebooks
tiktok.com/@chloemainebooks